# LOCKHART
## A NOVEL

BY
JT HINE

*Copyright © 2020 by JT Hine*

All rights reserved. No part of this book may be used or reproduced in any manner without written permission from the author, except for brief quotations in critical articles or reviews. For information, contact: jt@jthine.com

https://jthine.com

ISBN: 978-1-7331755-4-8 (paper)
ISBN: 978-1-7331755-5-5 (eBook)

Book cover design: ebooklaunch.com

Editor: Kerry Genova, writersresourceinc.com.

First edition: April 2020

# Dedication

*AL POPOLO ROMANO.*

*To the people of Rome,*
*To those there born*
*And those who came,*
*Who call the Eternal City*
*Home.*

# Acknowledgments

First, I am grateful to those who took time to read the first draft, three working titles ago: Anne Carley, Jackson Duckworth, Amy Taylor, Joan Sax, Ronnie Lamkin, Daniel Hine, Virginia Ritchie, and Maureen Young.

Beth Molmen edited that draft, and Kerry Genova edited this book. Kim Olson proofread the final version.

I have been pleased with the cover design and interior formatting by Dane and Adrian at ebookslaunch.com.

None of these wonderful people had anything to do with any errors you may notice. Those are all mine. I would not mind knowing about them: jt@jthine.com.

# 1. Bomb

JOE LOCKHART FELT and heard a thump ahead as he coasted downhill. A mass of hot September air rolled over him like a gust of wind. He sped past the traffic that choked downtown Rome during the lunch hour, even on the weekend. On his left stood the American embassy, still called Palazzo Margherita by the locals. Wondering about the noise, he decided not to stop at the embassy annex to his right, where he had been going.

As he negotiated his way across the oncoming and left-turn traffic in front of the embassy, the smooth asphalt of the Via Veneto turned into the bone-jarring cobblestones of the Via Bissolati. Then he recognized the smell of burning oil.

He expected to see a stalled car with smoke pouring from its engine. But the traffic still moved past the international airline offices that lined both sides of the street. The sun reflected off the walls and windows of the tall buildings, aggravating the heat and the oppressive, oily feel of the smoke.

Traffic began to back up. The wail of sirens came up behind him. Pulling his bicycle over, he put a foot on the curb to watch two police cars and a fire truck go by. Beyond the bend, and he could hear them stop.

Joe dismounted and pushed his bike onto the sidewalk. Ahead, the firemen hauled hoses across the street while the police funneled the bumper-to-bumper traffic into Via San Basilio and Via Carducci, on either end of the scene.

Black smoke billowed from a burning car and flames licked the front of the Pan American Airlines ticket office. The ground-floor windows gaped like monstrous mouths. Glass and debris lay everywhere. And two bodies.

Joe had never seen a dead person before. A young woman leaned up against the building. Her body made an unnatural right-angle bend from the pavement up the wall, and her hand still clutched the shopping bag flattened against the wall. Joe's stomach quivered. The blackened corpse had no face.

The other body was only legs, sticking out of the window of the ticket office. The rest of him was inside. Fresh blood ran onto the sidewalk. Joe froze. He felt alone, looking from outside himself.

The firemen moved quickly to spray water and foam on the flames. Ambulances and more police cars arrived.

"*Dietro, ragazzo!*" Back, boy! A rough hand on his arm snapped Joe back to reality. A cordon of police shoved him and the gathering crowd back up the Via Bissolati. Mounting his bike, he pedaled into the stalled traffic, back toward the American embassy.

His stomach gave him just enough warning to pull into the side street that went behind the embassy. He jumped off his bicycle and ducked behind the overhang of the large fountain on the corner. There, he threw up and held on to the wall until the shivering stopped. The mess ran through a grate into the sewer below. Joe cleaned himself at the fountain and rinsed his mouth. After a long drink of cold water, he waited for his pulse to settle. Even on the hottest days, the greenery hanging over the wall of the embassy created a cool corner next to the fountain. The spring blooms had long since fallen, but the sweet fragrance of the plants soothed him.

Joe needed to return some books to the US Information Service library in the embassy annex and look for a book about Admiral Farragut for a history report. He rode back up the Via Veneto.

The annex occupied a seventeenth-century palazzo between two luxury hotels. The entrance hall had a Stars & Stripes newsstand and mini bookstore on the left, with the USIS library on the right. Directly ahead, a pair of swinging doors led into the lobby, with the Army Post Office service counter. Most of the offices inside were manned by armed forces personnel and civilians working for the Military Advisory Assistance Group, which oversaw the Marshall Plan. Though Italy had recovered from World War II, the massive organization that had rebuilt Western Europe in less than fifteen years was still winding down. Government agencies that normally did not operate overseas maintained liaison offices in the annex, such as the FBI, the Department of Agriculture, and the Coast Guard.

The cool air inside the doorway reminded him sharply how hot it was outside. As he was about to turn right, he noticed a young woman with her arms filled with newspapers and books trying to open the door from the Stars & Stripes shop. He turned and held the door for her.

"Thanks," she said, with a smile that reached her blue eyes. "I should remember to do this in different trips." Obviously American, with her blond hair in the bouffant style, she wore a light blue cotton blouse and a beige skirt. Joe walked over to the heavy, swinging doors to the lobby and held one for her.

"No problem. Have a nice day."

"You too." She smiled again, then smoothly moved through the door toward the grand staircase on the left. *I've held countless doors for women*, he thought, *so why am I holding my breath?* With a silent sigh, he stepped down into the library.

The place was probably the size of a small-town library in the US. He wasn't sure about that, never having lived in a small town. Dark wooden shelves lined the circular room. Smaller, free-standing bookcases shared the floor with couches and reading desks. Daylight from the street came from long windows at ground level, which covered the upper half of one wall. Library patrons could see the waists and legs of the pedestrians on the broad sidewalk outside. The card catalog and the librarian's station formed a circular fortress of wood and marble in the center of the room.

He found what he was looking for and sat at one of the tables. The images and the smells of the car bombing made concentration impossible. He decided to check out the book and go home. Soon he was riding down the smooth, open roads that crossed the Villa Borghese gardens and coasting to the Piazzale Flaminio. What used to be the assembly point for triumphal marches by the Roman legions was now a vehicular madhouse. Buses from several different lines met the trolleys, and passengers ran between them. Romans hoped to have a subway station there someday. Joe took back streets to the Lungotevere delle Navi, then upstream to the Risorgimento Bridge over the Tiber River. A quick ride among the trees along the Viale Mazzini brought him to the foot of the Monte Mario overlooking the city, and the sweaty climb home.

છાભાભ

"It would have been so much worse on a weekday," said Nancy Lockhart, reading about the bombing in the newspaper that evening. Sitting in a comfortable armchair in the living room, she wore a plaid skirt and a white cotton blouse. Only on Saturdays could she skip the business suit, hose, and heels. "The ticket offices were closed for lunch, too, so the usual crowds of airline travelers weren't there."

Joe looked up from the couch, where he was taking notes with a copy of *Damn the Torpedoes, Full Speed Ahead: The Story of Admiral David Farragut* on his lap. "Who did it?" he asked.

"They still don't know, but a neofascist group threatened something like this yesterday. Did you see this picture?" She turned the paper around to show him a photo on the front page. It was the woman with the shopping bag.

Joe nodded and turned back to his book. His mother did not need to know just how close he had gotten to the blast.

"Some of the people in the office are convinced that the right wing is planning a coup, but almost as many believe that it would be impossible." Nancy folded the newspaper. "Did you finish that history report?"

"Almost."

"You won't have time tomorrow if we want to go to Tivoli after church."

"Okay, Mom. I know. When do you want to eat?"

"Let's walk down to the piazza for supper. We both have too much work to do for cooking and dishes."

Their housekeeper-cook, Angela Ceccarelli, had stocked the small refrigerator for the weekend. Joe's mother was a good cook, but she and Joe also enjoyed these walks to the tree-lined Piazzale delle Medaglie D'Oro at the top of the Monte Mario. Sometimes they would walk to the Parco della Vittoria near the *piazzale*, with its stunning view of the Eternal City. Nancy Lockhart was tall for a woman, with the grace and form of the champion tennis player that she had been. She had rich, auburn hair, while his was sandy colored like his father's. Joe was taller than she. With bright hazel eyes, long lashes, and a similar nose and mouth, people often mistook them for siblings, rather than mother and son.

It was dark by the time they reached their favorite *rosticceria*. Pointing to the food under the display window, Nancy picked the roast chicken with roast potatoes; Joe asked for sliced *porchetta*, the traditional Roman roast pork with rosemary and other herbs, also with potatoes. They took their trays to one of the Formica-topped tables in the brightly lit room. Back home less than an hour later, Nancy went into her study to work. Joe sat at the dining room table, finishing up the history report.

༺༺༺

That night, Joe dreamed about the bomb, but the body in his dream was that of his father. Screaming penetrated his sleep. The smoke from the burning car cleared. He found himself looking up at his mother's terrified face. She was shaking him.

"My God, Joe!" She let go when she saw he was awake. "What was it? You haven't screamed like that since you were nine."

At first, he could not answer. Sweat had soaked his bed linens and pajamas, and he began shivering. Nancy hugged her son, dampening her own nightgown. The only light came from the street. Brakes squealed; someone was making the turn to go down the hill.

"It was Dad." He stopped shaking. As he swung out of bed, she pulled the covers off. "Already I can't remember the surroundings much, but he had no face." He went to the dresser for some fresh pajamas. "I think I'll be okay now, Mom."

Nancy went to the linen closet for some sheets. "Are you sure? I will never forget the nightmares when you were little. They went on for two years after your father died."

"This feels different," Joe said. "This scene was like the picture of the bomb in the paper."

They remade the bed together in silence.

"Want some hot chocolate?" she asked when they had put the wet sheets in the laundry hamper.

"That would be good." Joe slipped into dry pajamas, then followed his mother to the kitchen. She had put a kettle of water on. When she turned around, he saw the tears running down her face.

"Mom, what's wrong?" He crossed the room and hugged her.

"Nothing really, except the feeling." She let herself sob against her son's shoulder. "Doctor Lambert told us that these dreams would come back every so often. I wasn't ready. It's been almost ten years. All the pain of watching you scream came back to me. God, it was terrible. You were so helpless."

Joe fought back the lump in his throat.

"Wasn't he the one who gave me Tootsie Rolls?"

"Yes, and you always left the sticky things in the car." She laughed despite the tears.

"He never figured out that I didn't like them." He chuckled, grateful for the distraction.

The kettle whistled. Joe went to the stove with the cocoa while Nancy got out the cups. She found some cookies and set them out.

They sat across from each other at the kitchen table. The hot chocolate felt good.

"Mom, did Doctor Lambert say how long this would last?"

"He said that we would carry your father's death with us for the rest of our lives. Most of my colleagues said he was wrong to let you into the hospital so much near the end. But I had a hunch he was right."

"I don't like remembering Dad that way, but I wouldn't have wanted to stay home. I know he wanted me there." He tried to picture his father as the strong, handsome man he had been, not the shriveled skeleton he became, wasting away in Saint Mary's hospital in Richmond, Virginia.

"Nights like this, I'm not so sure," she said.

"I'll be okay, Mom. I'm not nine anymore. The details are fuzzy, but it didn't feel like the old dreams. It was something else."

She reached across and squeezed his hand.

"Look at this. You wake up screaming, and I'm the one getting help."

"It's your line: 'we're a team now.'"

Back in bed, Joe realized that his mother had not looked for her cigarettes the whole time they were up.

☙☙☙

Six thousand miles away, Siegfried Kanter stubbed out his cigarette in the marble ashtray on the table. His company's security people had swept the suite in the Waldorf-Astoria, or he would not be having this conversation.

"Does anyone have a better idea?" His expression was severe, but then, it usually was.

"Not me, Sig." This from the Texan with his booted feet stretched beneath the coffee table. His sunburned face set off his white hair dramatically. The tallest man in the room, his lanky frame and the bolo tie betrayed his origins in the oilfields.

Beside him, the smartly dressed Italian shrugged. "I think it will work, gentlemen. As long as our pigeon does not wise up." He held himself erect, as befitted a recently retired general of the Italian Carabinieri Corps. "Do you think this channel will be secure, Sandro?"

A slightly plump man, Sandro was the only one of the four whose hair was thinning. Like them, he wore a custom-tailored suit and shoes. "It should work just fine, Ettore. The people in my office here have worked with him for years. He understands no Italian, so he won't understand anything not in English in the files he forwards to New York." He played with the Montblanc pen that his wife had given him.

"Our contacts in the Smithson Italia offices in Milano and Torino are ready to insert the codes into the company correspondence for New York before it goes to Rome," said the general. "Only the New York copies will have the coded information, so the others in Rome won't be suspicious."

Silence reigned as Siegfried looked around again. "Manfredo?"

"Nothing to say, really," said the fifth man in a British public-school accent. "I can't think of a better way to do this, in spite of my misgivings."

"Are we all agreed, then?" The other men nodded. "By next week, our companies will buy a minimum number of shares of Smithson Pharmaceuticals on the New York Stock Exchange to qualify for 'major investor' status. Any problems with that?"

"Are the carabinieri buying stock, too?" said the Texan with a grin. The others smiled. They knew that Ettore Arcibaldo was the only one likely to be exposed if the operation failed. The general's smile did not extend to his eyes.

Sandro raised his hand. "One thought. We should not all buy at once. I must move money from the home office in Zurich anyway. It would be less conspicuous if we made our purchases over two weeks."

"Makes sense," said the Texan. "Let me go first, then Sig early next week. Manny's a major investor, so if Sandro picks up his shares, say, one week after Sig, no one should notice."

"It will raise Smithson's share price," said Sandro, "but not enough to attract the attention of the financial press."

"Hey, we might cover our costs with this!" The Texan laughed at his own joke.

"That settles it, then." Siegfried turned to Arcibaldo. "Good luck, General."

They rose and shook hands. By prior agreement, they left the suite two minutes apart and did not gather for dinner. On Monday morning, each was back in his office, having gone to New York for a "shopping trip over the weekend." The general was in a public meeting in Rome with his political supporters.

          ☙☙☙

That same evening, Officer O'Toole stopped at the corner outside the United Nations building and turned back. The black Ford Fairlane with diplomatic plates had been parked in that spot all day yesterday. He shone his flashlight inside, but the car was empty and clean. He keyed his radio.

"3255 here. There's a car parked in front of the UN in the no-parking zone since yesterday. Diplomatic plates, but at roll call, we were briefed to be extra careful."

"No one at the UN works those hours," said the dispatcher. "Secret Service should know. Hang around, 3255."

"Ten-four."

O'Toole paced next to the car. The heat from the day was radiating back from the asphalt and concrete, making him sweat. He hoped that he could clock off on time tonight.

Ten minutes later, a black sedan pulled up behind the Ford. A tall man in a business suit got out and approached O'Toole, holding out his credentials. US Secret Service.

"Ashford, Diplomatic Protection Detail. What's with this car?"

"Been here since yesterday morning. Normally we'd ignore it because of the plates, but, you know, with tomorrow's show."

Ashford nodded as he returned to his car. He pulled out the microphone to his radio and called in the plate number to his office. In less than two minutes, he had his answer and waved to O'Toole.

"Stolen plates. Have the precinct get a tow truck here ASAP. And keep civilians away."

ଔଔଔ

Manny Romero drove his tow truck into the NYPD impound lot with a wave to the guard at the gate. With the smooth confidence of years of practice, he turned into the last place at the end of a row, lining the Ford Fairlane up with the other cars. He lowered the sedan and unhitched it. After parking his truck in the garage, he walked home.

Special Agent Ashford reported the suspicious car to the FBI and sent a request to ATF (Alcohol, Tobacco, and Firearms Division of the IRS) to have the car checked as soon as possible. Then he closed his office and went home to try to get some sleep before meeting the Italian delegation coming from Rome.

At ten a.m. the next morning, the president of Italy arrived at the United Nations with an escorted motorcade, the third of a dozen European leaders who would arrive that day.

Also, at ten a.m., the New York Fire Department responded to a call from the NYPD impound lot. The explosion at the end of a row of cars destroyed five vehicles and blew a hole in the fence. Flying pieces of fencing injured three bystanders outside. The newspapers carried the story on page six the next day. Their front pages carried pictures of heads of state arriving for the General Assembly of the United Nations.

# 2. THE JOB

"OH, *SCHEISS!*" NANCY SHOUTED and slammed her fist down. "They're making a secretary out of me again."

From his room, Joe heard the commotion and went to his mother's study, the best-furnished room in the apartment. In addition to a large oak desk, there was a couch, a coffee table, and two telephones. An antique engraved print of the Roman Forum by Piranesi hung above the couch. Every horizontal surface was covered with papers. Smoke swirled around the desk lamp.

"What's wrong, Mom? I know that much German." He crossed the room and opened the window.

"I'm sorry, Joe." Nancy stubbed out the half-finished cigarette and cradled her head in both hands, elbows on the desk. "Sometimes the work gets me down. There's so much, and some of it is so damned infuriating."

"Can I help?" Almost immediately, he thought his reflex sounded stupid.

"No, I – wait a minute." She handed him a single sheet of paper. "Can you read this?"

Joe looked at the letter, typewritten on fine paper, with the letterhead of the del Piave Group. He recognized the stuffy Italian of textbooks, government documents, and posters.

"Sure."

"Read it in English."

"Dear Sirs: Referring to your letter of the fifteenth – "

"Why did you say 'Dear Sirs'?"

"Because 'egregious gentlemen' sounds stupid in English, and you always start your business letters, 'Dear sirs.'"

His mother's face brightened. "Maybe you could help with this stuff. Here I am, the vice president for operations, spending too much time translating correspondence about this project. Maria Grazia may be the best secretary I ever had, but she's not up to this. And this project is too sensitive to hire an outside translator."

"Why do they need translation at all? Doesn't everyone in the office understand Italian?"

"Yes – well, almost. But we forward these to New York and Richmond along with other files. The decision whether to go with del Piave or one of his competitors will depend on how well they sell their projects to Smithson in the States. The rules allow for submissions in Italian or English. The others write their proposals in English, so we only need to translate del Piave's."

"Why don't I write them out for Maria Grazia to type? You fix them a little like your other letters."

"This is not playground stuff."

"Mom, I'm eighteen. I don't go to playgrounds. Besides, my friends wouldn't be interested in this."

"Okay, then. If it doesn't interfere with your homework, you're hired."

"Hired? Like, a job?"

"Of course. If this weren't so sensitive, we'd pay a freelancer. Let's see if you can handle another two of them, then I'll have the company pay you."

"How much?" Looking at the red rising on his neck, Nancy arched an eyebrow.

"Let's talk details after you try a couple more. I can't let you carry that kind of cash, but we could open a savings account for you."

"I've never had a savings account. That would be great." He sat at the coffee table with a pad and a pencil and started to write.

Sleeping was tough that night. Joe tossed and dreamed of pacing in a big office like his mother's, dictating to a stenographer. Businessmen from all over Italy would ask him to translate their letters so they could make deals in America.

The next day, Nancy was humming an aria from *Così Fan Tutte* when Joe dragged into the kitchen. She choked off Mozart halfway through the measure.

"You don't look so hot."

"I'm okay, just kind of excited about the translation work."

She put the Moka coffee maker on the stove, while he cut some hard-crusted *pane casareccio* bread and set it out with some jam. Normally, they ate an Italian breakfast, bread or pastry and caffé latte, coffee with milk. An American breakfast would take too long and require too much cleanup.

"Remember, if this leaks to your classmates or anyone else, it's off."

"Yes, ma'am." *She's really into a corner on this*, he thought.

By eight o'clock, they were leaving together. Joe pushed his bike to the stop where his mother would catch the number 96 bus downtown. After returning the greetings of the neighbors there, he rode slowly to the corner until he was out of sight of the waiting commuters. Then he turned left onto the Viale Medaglie d'Oro, a relatively new street, with smooth asphalt, and stately Mediterranean pines on either side.

He hunched down on the handlebars and let the Monte Mario push him a mile through the cool morning air. Traffic was light, and these streets were too steep for trolley tracks. Plenty of those lurked at the bottom, waiting to grab his thin tires and throw him over the front wheel. In less than two minutes, he cleared the yellow light at Piazzale degli Eroi and turned right for the long, gentle climb to his high school at the edge of the Eternal City. Most days, that downhill rush made riding four miles to school each way worth it.

ೞೞೞ

"*Buon giorno, dottoressa.*" Good morning, Doctor. The secretary rose and held the door to Nancy's office at the corporate offices of Smithson Italia. She was as tall as Nancy, which was unusual for an Italian, with the strawberry-blond hair and blue eyes found among northerners. Only the cadence of her flawless Italian let on that she was Roman, born and raised. Nancy loved to hear her contralto voice, especially after a day of conferences or phone calls with plant managers from Milan, Cologne, Paris, or Manchester. The secretary wore a simple silk dress, and she looked like a fashion poster.

"Buon giorno, Maria Grazia. I have yesterday's proposal from the *cavaliere* del Piave if we don't have a fresh crisis this morning."

"No crisis, signora." She glanced quickly at the door to the hall. "The boys haven't come in yet."

Nancy chuckled. Her secretary could be referring to the other clerical staff or the management, but it did not matter. They were the only women on the entire floor, or maybe the whole building.

She had surprised everyone when she arrived by hiring Maria Grazia and by not bringing a personal assistant with her. The secretaries at Smithson Italia were all handsome men; she did not need any more gossip than she was already causing as a female executive. Rather than resenting Maria Grazia, the other secretaries admired and respected her.

Opening her briefcase on Maria Grazia's desk, Nancy gave her the letter that Joe had written out.

"This is not your handwriting, signora."

"Joe translated it. What do you think?"

"Very easy to read – as easy as yours. Why Joe?"

"Read the way he writes. I only corrected the financial terms."

"You know that I am willing to do these for you."

"Don't worry about your job. We hired you as a secretary, not a translator. Around here, at least you and I know the difference.

"Read. Then tell me what you think." Nancy waited while Maria Grazia read.

"He writes well. His prose captures the cavaliere's point precisely. I would not have thought of the English metaphors to match his."

"I thought so too. But we can't go outside with this material."

"Your son is more a part of this company than any of us. He has grown up with Smithson."

"Would you type that up this morning, please? I want to run it past someone who doesn't know him, another native English speaker."

"*Sì*, signora."

In her office, Nancy unpacked her papers and checked her calendar. Mercifully, she did not have any meetings in the morning. She looked at the wall clock: too early for the phone calls from the United States or England. The people from Richmond were probably circling the new Fiumicino International Airport. They would not be here for at least two hours.

She walked downstairs to the Bar La Bella for an espresso. Through the window of the café, she noticed Luke Arland, the new vice president from New York, and Sandro Moretti, the president, crossing the street together. After chatting with the comptroller at the counter of the bar, she went back up to her office.

Maria Grazia had left the typed-up letter on her desk. Nancy read it again on her way down the hall. She turned at the door marked "Strategy and Investment" and walked in.

"Buon giorno, dottoressa." The man at the desk rose and smiled. Slender and fit, he had teeth that were brilliant and perfectly straight, thanks more to the mineral content of Roman water than any dental intervention. His jet-black hair tended to curliness, so he kept it groomed back.

"Hello, Giacomo. Is Doctor Arland in?"

"Of course, dottoressa, and he is alone."

"Thank you."

Giacomo knocked once and opened the door for her.

Luke Arland was looking out the window. Turning around, he beamed. The suit brought out the green in his hazel eyes.

"Nancy! What a great way to start the day, with you to bring sunshine into my dark hovel." His tendency to self-effacement contrasted with his athletic good looks. The sandy-blond hair, which had been crew cut when he arrived in August, was growing out, but it would take another month or more before anyone could do anything except put a hat on it. At least he had a new wardrobe of tailored suits, so he did not look like an extra in a movie about the FBI. Nancy had ribbed him early on about New York fashion – or the lack thereof.

"Hi, Luke. Easy on the charm." She smiled and walked to his desk before he could come around, putting the furniture between them.

"What can I do for you, fair lady?"

She handed him the letter. "Tell me what you think of this."

He read it.

"Is this what del Piave sent us yesterday?"

"Yes. If you were in New York and had never heard of us here, what would you think of it?"

"If I got this as a proposal, I'd buy into it."

"That's what I thought. I think this is exactly what he is trying to achieve."

"Why ask me, Nancy? I'm not surprised that you can write like this."

"I didn't."

He gasped lightly. "Who else has seen this?"

"Would you believe Joe?"

"Your son?"

"The same. I had him do this last night, just to see what he could do. Now I realize what all those As in Advanced English Composition mean."

"He certainly knows how to express himself. And express the cavaliere, too, I think."

"I'm thinking of giving him a couple more letters as they come in to see how he does." She looked out the window as if in thought. "Should I be concerned because he's my son?"

Luke gave her the letter back. "I think we have a new in-house translator we can trust, and you can stop being a secretary for the rest of the board, just because we can't use an outsider."

She reached over the desk and gave him a light tap on the cheek. "Thanks, Luke." With that, she whirled gracefully around and slid out the door. The tap left them both wondering why she did that.

Nancy swung by the president's office on the way back to her own. Sandro Moretti's reaction was enthusiastic. He had not wanted her translating the correspondence on the Aprilia plant project, but she had insisted on not using Italian staff for this material. She decided that she did not need to test Joe any further.

"The gentlemen from Richmond will be here at eleven, signora," Maria Grazia said as Nancy walked in. Nancy stopped in her tracks.

"Who scheduled that? It's almost lunchtime." Lunch was the main meal of the day, and most employees went home to their families for the meal.

"They insisted. I warned the others."

Nancy sighed. "Let's have La Bella send up some brioches and *tramezzini* sandwiches."

"Already ordered."

Nancy smiled. "Thank you." She gave Maria Grazia the letter from del Piave.

"You can make copies for the management meeting tomorrow. And would you please contact Mr. Sacchi in Personnel to hire Joe as a translator? Technically he can work for anyone in the company, but the Aprilia project has priority, and I'll be his supervisor."

"Of course, signora. What salary?"

Nancy knew that her secretary had a child in school too. "Whatever we pay the freelancers, but let me know first. I can't have it going to his head."

They shared a laugh, then Nancy went into her office.

ෙෙෙෙ

When Nancy came home that night, Joe was assembling a salad. Angela had fixed a lasagna before going home. The table in the kitchen was set. When by themselves, they preferred to eat there because it made cleaning up easier. Angela often reminded them that she could do the dishes in the mornings, but neither Joe nor Nancy liked having a mess in the sink.

"How much homework do you have?" she called from her study. Joe heard the briefcase hit the coffee table. He dried his hands and came out.

"None," he said. Nancy opened her mouth and lifted an eyebrow. "I had a study hall today. Got it all done."

"Good, here's a pair of letters for you." She gave him the two pages and picked up the pack of cigarettes on her desk. Seeing Joe scowl, she put them in the drawer.

Joe sat at the coffee table to look over the letters. Nancy unloaded the other papers from her briefcase and organized them on her desk.

"I'm starved," she said. "A team from Richmond came to the office today and held a conference during the lunch hour."

"That's uncivilized!" Joe grinned.

"Damn right." They went to the kitchen. Over supper, Joe answered questions about his day, and Nancy complained with good humor about the bigwigs from Richmond, Virginia, where the Smithson Group had its world headquarters.

After washing the dishes and putting away the leftover lasagna, they returned to Nancy's study. Joe sat at the coffee table again and began writing. Nancy worked at her desk. Twice, she opened the desk for her cigarettes, tossed the pack back, and closed the drawer.

After the niceties, Joe ran into ordinary words used in strange ways, so he got the heavy Zanichelli Italian-English dictionary from his room. The words were all there, but something was not right.

"This sounds weird, Mom. What are 'actives and passives on a scale'?" He held up the letter so she could see.

"Technical terms, Joe. *Attivi* are assets, *passivi* are liabilities, and *bilancio* is the financial statement."

"My dictionary didn't have that."

"I'll get you a financial glossary from the office. Meanwhile, this is still fine because I know what he meant." She took a blue pencil from the caddy on her desk, corrected the three words, and gave him the paper back. "After a few of these, you'll understand all these words. And you saved me writing it out myself."

"Do I get paid?"

"I think so. We'll have Payroll open an account for you."

"Neat."

ೞೞೞ

The next day, Brother Mark came down from the school office during lunch with a message for Joe from his mother. "Be home by four p.m. Must go to bank together." After thanking the monk, he went to find Mr. Santoro, the English teacher, to tell him he would miss the yearbook meeting. With some hard riding, he locked his bike below the apartment building at three fifty-five. Nancy was waiting in the lobby.

"Hi, Mom, what's the hurry?" Under his suit, his shirt and undershirt were soaked. He took off his jacket to start drying off.

"Let's walk to the Cavalieri Hilton. We need to open the account together, or you can't put money in and take it out. I figure the most convenient place to do that is the Banca Nazionale del Lavoro branch in the hotel, which closes at four thirty. Is that okay with you?" An imposing structure of glass and brick overlooking the city from the Monte Mario, the new Hilton was Rome's first American luxury hotel. It was also right across the street from the Lockharts' building.

"Sure!" Joe's body tingled. *My own bank account. Real money.* "Do you have to make deposits and withdrawals for me?"

"No, you can do that yourself. It has to be a joint account with me because you're under twenty-one. I can check whenever I want, so don't take money out unless you've told me."

"What about other money, like the Goldoni?" Joe almost always spent all the money he made selling snacks at the concession stand at the Goldoni Theater. With a savings account, he could keep the money out of his pocket.

"Deposit anything you want. I only want to know before you make a withdrawal."

While they waited for the next teller, Nancy gave him a sheaf of papers from her briefcase. "Sign these. One is your contract with the company; the other two are a nondisclosure agreement and a noncompetition agreement. We're making you a freelancer because you get benefits coverage as my dependent."

Joe read the long, printed paper used for legal documents. The contract emphasized that Joe was not an employee of Smithson Italia SpA and that the occasional assignments did not obligate the company to provide employment benefits, including insurance payments, contributions to the *Cassa Integrazione* for unemployment, etc. As a *libero professionista,* Joe could work for other clients unless otherwise provided in written agreements between the parties.

The noncompetition agreement was one such agreement. Joe was not to accept assignments from other clients in the pharmaceutical sector for two years after his last assignment for Smithson Italia. The nondisclosure agreement referenced severe penalties for violating the confidentiality of the relationship. Joe would not let anyone know of his work for Smithson Italia and would report any suspected leaks to his supervisor, Dr. Nancy Lockhart.

"Pretty serious," he said as he took out the fountain pen from his shirt. It had leaked again, ruining two garments as his sweat carried the ink from the pocket to his undershirt. "But it only repeats what you told me."

Nancy nodded. The teller waved them over.

Twenty minutes later, Joe had a passbook with his name and more money in his account than he had made in two years at the Goldoni Theater.

A month later, translating the letters from del Piave had become routine. Nancy would bring one or two home each week, which was not so much as to interfere with his schoolwork or extracurricular activities. At the end of each month, Smithson Italia would send Joe a check for a thousand lire, or $1.60, per page.

# 3. Mario

ONE MONDAY IN OCTOBER, Joe smelled something burning as he opened their apartment. He dropped his book bag.

"Angela?" he called. The odor came from the kitchen.

Angela sat at the kitchen table, sobbing heavily. Reaching behind her, he turned off the heat under the pan of dried-out pasta sauce.

"Angela, *che succede?*" What happened? He sat next to her.

"Oh, *Signorino* Joe, didn't you hear the news on the radio?"

"No, I just came home."

"It's terrible, terrible." She bent down and sobbed some more, alternating wringing her hands and pulling on her hair. Usually, she kept it tied back, but now it was loose like a black sack over her head. Though only in her late thirties, tonight her strong frame seemed worn and ten years older.

Joe felt confused and frustrated. He turned up the volume on the radio, but some politician was droning about state investment plans.

"Can I help? Please, tell me what happened."

She looked at him; he had never seen a face so red and distorted. The tears streamed, and her cheeks and eyes were puffy. "They killed Mario."

"Your brother in Milano? The doorman at the Quinsana Hotel?"

She nodded and took a deep breath. She gripped the kitchen table with one hand, and Joe's arm with the other.

"Something exploded outside the hotel. It killed him and three others. One was young Giulio, who just started working there. The others were hotel guests."

"But who? Why Mario?"

Angela shook her head. "The radio said something about a bomb in a parked car, but I don't understand these things."

"A car bomb? Terrorists use car bombs. Listen, here comes another bulletin." Joe stood and poured her a glass of water while the radio broadcast the update. The bomb was a new type, more powerful than any seen before. An obscure left-wing radical group claimed responsibility in telephone calls to the *Corriere della Sera* newspaper and the American consulate. The caller threatened more bombings until the Yankee imperialists left the country.

Angela began sobbing again. Joe put his arm around her shoulders.

"Let me call my mother. Maybe she can take you home." The Ceccarellis had neither a car nor a telephone.

He went to the study and dialed his mother's direct line.

"Mom, did you hear about the car bomb in Milan?"

"Yes, but I'm in a meeting – "

"Angela's brother Mario was killed. He was the doorman at the Quinsana Hotel."

"Oh my God. Where's Angela?"

"Here. She's too upset to take the bus home."

"I'll be there as soon as I can." For something like this, she would check out a company car, he knew.

Twenty minutes later, Nancy Lockhart came through the door. While she helped Angela straighten herself out, Joe collected Angela's shopping bags, and Angela repeated the story. Angela leaned on Nancy as they made their way downstairs to the garage. Soon, they were heading toward the Tuscolana area on the other side of the city.

Angela got confused trying to explain where she lived because she had never gone home any way except by bus. After circling the Piazza dei Re di Roma twice, they ended up on the Via Appia. Joe suggested that they follow the bus route, which she knew. Ten minutes later, they parked below Angela's apartment building, one of the many tall, monotonous public housing projects recently built under the Marshall Plan.

Joe supported Angela as they climbed four floors to the apartment. The walls showed signs of wear, but the halls were swept, and the lights worked. Her husband answered the door. He immediately embraced his wife and led her in. He was not much taller than Angela, in his late forties. Joe remembered that he worked for the City Public Works Department. From his calloused hands, Joe could see that it was not a white-collar job. He motioned Nancy and Joe to come in.

"Please excuse the house. We are all very shaken, I hope you understand." He introduced Sonia and Giuseppe, Angela's sister and brother-in-law, who had both found jobs in Rome. Sonia took Angela to the bathroom. Mr. Ceccarelli offered coffee.

"Thank you, Signor Ceccarelli," said Nancy. "We really must go. We want Angela to be with her family now."

"You are too kind, signora," he said. "I don't know how to thank you for bringing her home."

"It's nothing, sir." Nancy paused. "Is there a telephone number where we can leave messages? At a time like this, it would be helpful."

"The café downstairs," said Giuseppe. He gave Nancy the number.

Nancy gave Angela's husband her card. "Angela does not need to come in tomorrow. If she wants time off to go to the funeral, please call me at work. Even if I am out, my secretary can take the message for me."

"Signora, you are too generous."

"Thank you, signore, but it's not enough. Only time will heal this wound."

After shaking hands all around, Joe and Nancy left the grieving family.

"Too late to start supper now," Nancy said as they drove away. "Let's eat at the Scoglio di Frisio on the way home."

"Okay with me." It was a quiet meal.

༂༂༂

"Done," said Joe, shoving the sheaf of notebook paper across the dining room table at his friend. "There's the piece about Cavour and Bismarck. What do you think?" He slammed the history book and the encyclopedia shut and piled them up.

Benny Liu frowned. "Joe, I can't read this. Here, mine's written more neatly." He shoved his notes across to Joe.

"No fair. This is Chinese!"

"Of course, it is, but I can read it. Your handwriting is atrocious. At least my characters are all recognizable."

"Yeah, but your penmanship in English isn't any better than mine."

"Let's type it."

"You have a typewriter?"

"Dad got me one for my birthday. I've been working on it every day." Benny reached under the table, pulled up an Olivetti portable, and took the cover off. After slipping a sheet of carbon paper between two pieces of paper, he rolled the pages into the carriage. "We each need a copy."

"Cool. So, you can type all this tonight?"

"I know that I can do my part about Garibaldi's *Mille* and the Prussian Army because I know what it says."

"What about my part? I can't type."

"Dictate it to me. Let's see how that works."

Joe picked up his part of the paper and began reading steadily and slowly. Benny's machine erupted in a rhythmic din. Every time the bell would ring at the end of a line, Benny pushed the carriage return lever to the right without breaking the rhythm of his fingers. The lever advanced the paper one line and stopped at the left margin.

"Hold it," he said. "Gotta put in the next page."

"Amazing! You learned to type like that in two months?"

"Not hardly. Dad let me work in the office last summer and started me in the typing pool. They taught me the ten-finger touch method there." He lined up the next piece of paper in the carriage. "There. Let's go."

Joe's part of the report was typed in less than fifteen minutes. Joe watched in awe while his friend added his contribution from his Chinese notes.

"Can you teach me how to do that?"

"Maybe. The hardest thing is not using your index fingers. Ten-finger typing is fast because your hands don't move much, just your fingers. And they only move over certain keys. Here sit down."

Benny showed Joe where to hold his hands and which keys to hit with each finger. Joe pecked out a couple of uneven lines.

"This looks messy, compared to yours."

"Well, how even was your gear shifting when you tried Hans's moped?"

"I gotta have a typewriter. I'll never get points off my papers for penmanship again."

Benny's mother came to the door of the dining room.

"Benjamin, have you finished your homework yet?"

"Yes, Mother." He put the cover on the typewriter and began collecting his books. Joe checked his watch.

"I'm sorry, Mrs. Liu. Benny was showing me his typewriter. I forgot the time."

"That's all right, Joe, but Grandmother will be starting her evening prayers soon." The Liu family was Catholic. Benny and his brothers had been baptized, but the parents remained unbaptized neophytes out of respect for Mr. Liu's mother.

Joe packed his book bag. It was a canvas backpack, roomy but conveniently sized. He wrapped the contents in plastic on rainy days.

The strange tones of Chinese sacred opera on the record player and the pungent smell of incense came from the living room as he slipped silently out the front door.

Soon he was riding through a light drizzle along the winding Via della Camilluccia. Dark with trees and poorly lit, the country road climbed steeply away from the Via Cassia, up the back side of the Monte Mario. He hated busting his gut up this lonely road, almost as much as he loved the downhill flight in the other direction. People were beginning to build out here, but the villas and small apartment buildings were set back and hidden by trees.

Nancy was in her study working when he got back. The air was thick with smoke. She had left the door open, so the whole apartment stank. Before he could say anything, she looked up with a scowl.

"Were you at Benny's all this time?"

Joe bristled. "Of course. I told you that on the phone."

"Don't give me that tone, young man."

Joe almost burst, grinding his teeth. "Yes, ma'am."

"What were you doing that took so long?"

Joe had told her that, too, but he refrained from reminding her. "We had some pictures to develop for Photography Club, and we had to finish the big history report for Brother Mark by tomorrow." He coughed and closed the door behind him. This was not the night to pick a fight about his mother's smoking. He hated that he could not get away from the stench in his own home. The Liu house was the only place he knew where nobody smoked. He wished his home smelled as pleasant.

But, then, he had told his mother that too.

༄༄༄

Autumn in Rome brought the rains, which would not let up until April. Sometimes it would pour for three weeks straight. It got cold too.

Pedaling his bike on the Via Aurelia, Joe felt the water dripping off his nose. He could not stay dry. Either the rain leaked down his collar, or he sweated up his clothes under his raincoat. He had two cheap suits he wore in the winter for this problem, one blue and one tan. They looked terrible: always crumpled, with mud splattered on the legs. Although he kept fresh socks in his school locker, the winters ruined his shoes. More than once, one of the brothers had told him that he was pushing the coat-and-tie rule with the condition of his suits, but no one had called his mother yet.

Still, there was the gang, and that made it worth it. Joe wheeled into the Alfa Romeo car dealership near the school and leaned his bike against the window of the coffee bar. The other guys were there, and the Beatles were singing "Twist and Shout" on the jukebox. Joe ordered a cappuccino and a *ciambella* doughnut. Matt Fisher was the only one at school with a driver's license. He got it in Florida last summer. In Italy, you had to be eighteen before you got even a learner's permit and twenty-one to own a car. Matt's uncle let him drive a black Fiat 1500 sedan, which carried Benny, Greg, and Doug from Vigna Clara every morning. Aldo had a moped, as did Hans. Seven students who did not live at school or take the bus. Joe would ride his bicycle through a blizzard for these morning meetings with the Beatles and the gang.

"Hey, Joe, when you get a Vespa or something?" asked Hans. He had arrived this year, and his English was still rough.

"Why should I? I can lose you anywhere in Rome, and you know it."

"*Ja*, if traffic there is."

"So? There's always traffic."

"Race today you want?"

"No way. Brother Bob almost banned us from school grounds for that last year."

"You should have seen it," Greg said to Hans. "Aldo lost it on the gravel in the parking lot and went through the glass doors into the cafeteria."

"*Basta*, Greg," Aldo growled. Enough. The others chuckled.

"Five minutes to bell, guys," said Matt, slapping Aldo on the shoulder. "Easy, Aldo. We're friends here."

They always left together, and they always arrived together, motors revving, Joe doing his tailspin dismount at the bike rack and Matt tooting his horn. The teachers hated it, the boarders envied it, and they loved it.

❧❧❧❧

"Mom, I think I want a Vespa."

"Are you finally interested in a learner's permit?" Nancy broke some bread and dabbed it in the marsala sauce near her scaloppine.

"Vespa just came out with a new 50-cc model. I saw it at the showroom on the way home from school. You don't need a license for 50 cc and below."

"I thought you didn't like the 50-cc bikes."

"This isn't one of those bicycles with a motor. It's a real scooter. Enclosed mudguards, lights, gears, everything. Even has a storage compartment that would keep my books out of the rain." A nasty squall beat loudly on the kitchen windows.

"Do you have enough for it yet?"

"I will with a couple more letters, and I can shop around for a better deal. They want 150,000 lire at the dealer I saw."

"I don't know. I worry about it."

"Mom, c'mon. I can already drive. Aldo and Hans let me drive their mopeds. And it's miserable in the winter on my bike."

"You're the one who won't take the school bus." An old family argument.

"Do you think I could stay for track and yearbook, fix supper on Angela's day off, or run errands on the way home if I took the bus? Or have my homework done when you come home with a del Piave letter?"

Nancy put down her fork. "Don't con me with the homework bit, Joe, but you made your point. It would be nice if you could keep a suit and a pair of shoes long enough to outgrow them."

"Mom – " Joe cut himself off when what she said hit him. "You mean you don't mind?"

"Well, I'm not thrilled, but we've beaten the subject of your getting to school to death for years now. I'm still worried. But I must admit you pull your weight around here, so why not?"

"Thanks, Mom." Nothing else seemed to fit.

"You're welcome."

The next morning as they left, she brought up the Vespa again.

"Don't buy anything without checking with me. I want to put the word out around the office. Someone may have a line on a good deal."

"Okay. I don't have enough for the Vespa and road tax tags yet anyway."

# 4. Luke

UNLIKE MANY COMPANIES, Smithson Italia did not work on Saturday. After sleeping in late, Joe walked to the Cavalieri Hilton Hotel to deposit his money in the night depository slot of the bank branch. Nancy went with him to buy a new umbrella. Having a large luxury hotel across the street was convenient. The shops were expensive, but they were open late and on weekends.

As they came out, the rain stopped. The sun blinded them, reflecting off the puddles and wet cars in the parking lot. As they stepped into the driveway, a red Jaguar XKE came to a sudden halt in front of them. Nancy jumped back, and Joe froze.

"Going my way?" said the driver. Joe thought he might be a movie actor: sandy blond hair, chiseled features, broad shoulders. The back of Joe's neck tightened: he had seen enough handsome men try to pick up his mother. Around the Hilton, they were often rich too.

"Oh, hello, Luke. You startled me."

"You know him?" Joe mumbled to his mother.

"Luke Arland, this is my son Joe."

The man leaped from the car, leaving it idling and crossed around to shake Joe's hand. "I've heard the world about you, Joe. It's a pleasure to meet you finally." He turned to Nancy. "Not just a lift. I must take you somewhere. Have you had lunch?"

"Well, no, but – "

"No buts, let me treat you."

Nancy looked at Joe. Her son shrugged.

"I'll take that for a 'yes.' Let's go to Frascati to that place where we had my welcome-aboard luncheon."

"Do you think you can find it?" Nancy got into the car. Joe had to squeeze sideways on a deck behind them. The XKE was a real sports car with only two seats.

"Sure," said Luke. "And the view should be stupendous today." He closed the door behind Nancy, ran around and jumped in. In no time, they were flying out the Via Aurelia to the Grande Raccordo Anulare, the brand-new ring road that connected about half the roads leading into Rome. That someday it might be a true beltway all the way around was a running joke among political skeptics.

Luke drove with confidence, but also a certain care. After his initial reaction, Joe found himself warming to the new vice president of Smithson Italia. From what Nancy had said, Luke had arrived from the States in late August but had impressed the board. "So naïve he makes us think sometimes," she had said.

They took the Via Tuscolana, heading southeast away from the city. Like many Roman highways, the Tuscolana was lined with tall Mediterranean pines. It ran straight to the base of the Castelli Romani hills before starting its winding climb.

"You seem to have found your way around pretty quickly," Nancy said.

"Not hard when you're single with a car and nowhere to go." He hazarded a look and flashed a smile.

"Where do you play tennis?" Joe asked, shifting the bag at the end of the shelf with his feet.

"Mostly the courts at the Cavalieri Hilton, and I play near Elio's restaurant in the Hills. That's how I've learned the roads around Frascati and Lake Albano."

They climbed the Alban Hills and walked from the car across the park in front of the Villa Torlonia with the white marble fountains of its Water Theater carved into the hillside.

They ate at a restaurant that overlooked the *Agro Pontino,* the Pontine Plain. The air was exceptionally clear right after a rain. Rome shimmered in the slight haze from its own heat to their right. To their left, Joe saw the silver expanse of the Tyrrhenian Sea. The coastline looked like a white stripe across the scene. Without it, he could not tell where the flat, wet farmland ended and the sea began.

His mother seemed to relax as they talked about sports. Luke quizzed Joe about the Italian *campionato*, the professional soccer series, and the *Giro d'Italia,* the premiere bicycle race. Joe grilled him about the World Series.

"It catches me off-guard to see such a typical-looking American kid not know much about baseball," Luke said at one point.

Joe shrugged. "We don't have a baseball team at school. Or football. Too much equipment, and the travel's too complicated. There's no one else to play but American military schools. The closest one is Naples, so any game is at least a two-day trip."

"But that doesn't stop your basketball team. I've read about the Roman Eagles. You guys are the NBA of the Mediterranean."

"Yes, sir, we do that well, but fielding a basketball team is easier. We can pack everything we need in the team's personal luggage. Uniforms and basketballs are all there is to buy."

"The school's only ten years old," said Nancy. "Brother Roger, the headmaster, wants to build a pool for a swim team, but that will take a few more years of fundraising."

"So, what do you play, Joe?"

"Nothing, really. I'm always the last kid chosen in pickup games. Kind of klutzy, I guess."

"Now come on, Joe," said his mother. "You ran track last year."

"Oh, yeah. I run the 440 and 440 hurdles. Two meets in the spring season."

"Ever play tennis?"

"No, but I wouldn't mind learning."

"When are you going to do that?" Nancy chuckled.

"There are lights at the Hilton courts." Joe grinned. "I could play from eleven thirty to midnight after the Goldoni Theater closes, right?"

"Only if your homework is done."

"You're one busy guy, Joe," said Luke. "What's at the Goldoni Theater?"

"I run the concession stand in the lobby. Mrs. Simonetti, the manager, hired me during a school play that we were doing there. She knew I ran the snack bar at school for Brother Andreas."

"And Scouts. And church. And Photography Club – I saw the pictures in your mother's office. Anything else?"

"Anything you say may appear in my column in the school newspaper!"

Luke laughed and signaled for the waiter. "Coffee, Nancy?"

"Let's take a walk and get a coffee on the way. Joe?" Joe nodded in agreement.

Luke wrote in the air with an imaginary pencil. The server, still crossing the room, stopped, bowed, and turned to go get their bill. "You drink coffee, Joe?"

"Sure, don't you?"

"Yes, but when I was in high school, no one did."

"I started three years ago during the coffee hour in the church courtyard one Sunday. The Coca-Cola had frozen in the bottles, and I nearly did too."

Nancy reached into her purse for her cigarettes. Luke reached over and touched her hand. "Please," he said. She put the pack back and set the purse down.

After Luke paid the bill, they rose and walked toward town.

"Joe, you're eighteen, aren't you?" Joe nodded. "I'm an Eagle Scout, too, but I had to leave Scouting at eighteen."

"I'm an assistant scoutmaster now. Green tie and all that. I stand around with the other Scouters and pretend to ignore the boys instead of showing them what to do."

"I remember." Luke smiled. "Though sometimes I wonder how we ever figured it all out. Best leadership training I ever had."

They stopped at a bar for espresso. Nancy purchased a bag of red wine biscuits to take home.

"Frascati is famous for these things, Luke. Try one."

He agreed and bought another bag of the hard cookies.

Soon they were speeding back to the Eternal City. Luke left them outside their apartment building. Saying he had to meet some friends downtown, he declined an invitation to come in.

ଔଔଔ

The Beatles had started singing "Twist and Shout" on the jukebox when Joe arrived at the Alfa Romeo dealership bar. A deep voice surprised him from behind.

"Hi, Joe."

He turned sharply. "Hello, Mr. Arland. What are you doing here?" Joe asked the barista for a cappuccino and waved at his friends, then joined Luke at the counter. "I meet my friends here on our way to school."

"Sorry about crashing your huddle, but I need your help."

"Me?"

"Yes, I need a confidential translator, but I can't ask your mother. She already has too much to do." He glanced at the gang. "Is there someplace we could meet for a few minutes later?"

Joe thought for a minute.

"The lobby of the Hilton after school?"

"Great. See you about four?"

"Yes, sir, but I need to be home by four-fifteen."

"I'll be there." And he was gone. Joe shrugged and took his cappuccino to the jukebox.

"Who was that?" asked Matt.

"A guy who works with my mom."

"Looks worried," said Aldo. "What's he want with you?"

"He's got a job for me, I think."

"Wants a date with her, I say," said Doug. They laughed while Joe's ears and cheeks burned. He glared at Doug and clenched his fists.

"Easy, man," said Matt. "You got a good-looking mom, and you know it. Doug's joking." Joe took a deep breath and relaxed.

Doug took his hand and elbow. "Sorry, Joe. No offense meant."

Aldo nodded at the wall clock.

"Five minutes to the bell, guys. Let's roll!"

ଦଃଦଃଦଃ

When Joe walked in at exactly four o'clock, Luke Arland was sitting in an armchair in the lobby of the hotel. He rose as Joe approached, and they shook hands. In his tailored blue suit, Luke could have graced the cover of *Gentlemen's Quarterly*. Joe normally did not care what his clothes looked like, but now he was conscious of the stains and wrinkles of his tan suit and the mud drying on his left pant leg.

"Thanks for coming. Here's what I need." He picked up a fat file with letters, brochures, and some long documents stapled together. Joe backed up.

"I can't do that in one night, sir."

"Oh, I'm sorry, I didn't expect you to." Luke seemed distressed by his own failure to anticipate Joe's shock. "I thought you might take only as much as you could handle, a little at a time."

Joe regained his composure. "Why can't you use anyone at the office?"

Luke motioned to a sofa, and they sat. Luke opened the file on the coffee table in front of them.

"It's a personal problem. You know I'm new here. I can handle enough Italian for dinner at a restaurant and the gist of some of the shorter meetings. But I can't read the background material in here. The others, including your mother, have read this stuff."

He signaled to a waiter and pointed at Joe, who shook his head and tapped his wristwatch: no time for a drink. The server nodded and turned to a table close by.

"I can't ask them to translate something that no one needs but me."

"So, you won't be typing it or giving it to anyone?"

"No, reading it myself. Then I'll file it. Of course, if we need an English version, we'll have your translation, and we can type it then."

"Why didn't you ask my mother to bring it home?"

"Two reasons. One, she doesn't work for me, and two, she's the busiest person in the company. It wouldn't be fair to add something else just because I can't read Italian as fast as I need to yet." He paused. "Will you take the job?"

"How much?"

"Whatever the company's paying you now. And you do the stuff your mother brings home first. Always. It's more important."

"A thousand lire a page then. Will you give my mother the money, or have Mr. Sacchi mail me a check?"

"Cash, and I'll give it to you myself when I pick up the translations."

"Mom could bring them to you, couldn't she? I'll ask her."

Luke put his hand on Joe's shoulder.

"I'd rather you didn't." He lowered his hand and leaned over. "Did you know that you are the only outsider authorized to see this material?"

Joe shook his head. "I thought that was only for Mom's stuff."

"Well, you are, so I can't go to anyone else. I'd be very embarrassed if your mother and the others knew I was having you do this. But I need help, and I'm willing to pay."

"Okay. Let me try something small at first."

"Thanks." Luke selected two one-page letters. "There was a lot of discussion about these two, so I probably need them first. I'll take them when you can finish them. Here's my card: call me when they're ready, and I'll meet you."

After Joe put the papers in his backpack, they stood, shook hands, and left. As he pushed his bicycle toward his apartment building, Joe saw Luke walking briskly to his XKE in the parking lot.

CRCRCR

The letters were easy, and Nancy did not bring any work for him that night. He called Luke the next day from a payphone at school. They met at a café that Joe passed every day on the way home. Luke gave him two thousand lire and some more items from the folder.

"I'll collect these as you finish each one. It will save me bringing the whole collection."

The work for Luke put Joe over the top for a new Vespa by the middle of November. But his mother had not brought home anything for him, so he could not ask her about it.

# 5. Vespa

TWO DAYS LATER, Nancy came home with a break.

"I may have found a lead on a Vespa 50 for ninety thousand lire. Is that good?"

"That's great, Mom! I haven't beaten one-fifty anywhere, and most places are raising prices."

"I think you only have a choice of light blue or yellow."

"Those are the only colors. I wanted the blue."

"Oh." She took a pair of letters out of her briefcase. "Can you afford it yet?" Obviously, she was not checking on Joe's account.

"At that price, sure," he said. "How soon can we set this up?"

"I'll ask tomorrow. It involves buying one of the scooters in a lot being made for Sears Roebuck and shipped to Livorno. The shipping company combined an order of their own with the Sears buyer, and you can buy one of those."

"How do we get it?"

"I'll find out. Let's have supper. You've got two letters if your homework is finished."

૱૱૱

Riding in the rain seemed especially chilly for the rest of the week, but Joe didn't mind. He was bursting to tell the gang, but he wanted to surprise them after he bought the Vespa. Mr. Peterson knocked five points off his class participation in math on Friday for daydreaming, but nothing could spoil his mood.

Monday, Nancy had the details. The next day after school, they drove to a warehouse on the edge of Trastevere, the neighborhood across the Tiber River from central Rome. The rain stopped as they turned off the Viale Trastevere and began looking at house numbers.

"Why didn't you tell me it was the Mayflower line?" Joe recognized the marquee on the building. "Giosué is in my class."

"I only had the address, and I didn't work with his dad on this deal."

She parked the car. Joe leaped out and went to ring the doorbell. The *portiere* pointed them to an office at the opening of the courtyard inside. An Italian businessman met them at the door to the office. His gray suit had been tailored from expensive fabrics, and his longish, salt-and-pepper hair was stylishly cut.

"Signor Barbera," Nancy said in Italian, "a pleasure to see you again." The businessman took her hand to his lips with a brief bow, then turned to Joe.

"I've heard much about you, young man," he said, with a firm handshake. He led them to a large room with dozens of cardboard boxes stacked three high on pallets and one down on the ground.

"*Eccola*," Mr. Barbera said. Here she is. "Check it out first." With a grin, he handed Joe a rigger's knife. Joe felt his hands shaking as he carefully cut the edge of the box on three sides. The side fell open like a drawbridge.

Inside was the most beautiful machine Joe had ever seen. The ones in showrooms had been in the air and rain or test-driven. This one smelled of preservative. The flawless finish gleamed. It would not last, he knew, but he relished the perfection of the moment.

"Enough, Joe," his mother said, snapping the spell. She smiled. "You have to buy it first."

"Let's put some petrol in the tank, and make it start at least," said Mr. Barbera. He motioned to a warehouseman, who took a can of gasoline from the shelf and a small bottle of motor oil. "You know how to make the *miscela*, young man?"

"Yes, sir, the Vespa 50 takes two percent, which you set at the gas pump. Or add a half bottle of oil to a full tank of gas at home. I read the owner's book at the dealership."

"We have a love-struck boy here, Signora Lockhart. See why we call the Vespa a *she*?" Nancy nodded.

Joe and the warehouseman rolled the Vespa out of the box. They mixed some gas and oil in the tank. Joe checked it over, put the hand shift in neutral, set the choke, and stepped on the foot crank twice to move fuel to the dry engine. Then he gave the crank a good push while twisting the throttle handgrip. The scooter roared to life. White smoke filled the courtyard as the preservative burned off the engine and exhaust system. Joe put the choke in and let the engine idle for a minute before turning the key to "off."

"*Va bene,*" he said. Okay. "How do I buy it?"

They went to the office while the warehouseman checked the tire pressure, broke down the box, and put the owner's literature in the storage compartment of the Vespa. The warehouse supervisor had the papers ready: title, road tax forms, registration forms, and a little booklet that looked like a driver's license, but only proved that the road tax was paid.

Joe counted out the ninety-thousand lire and ten thousand more for the taxes and legal forms. The three of them signed several forms. Joe folded his title and receipts into his coat pocket. The road tax book fit in his wallet.

"I'm going to be a nervous wreck all the way home now," said his mother. "I'll follow you."

"Mom – "

"I'll meet you there. Just call if you have any trouble at all."

"I'll be there first, but only by a little. It *is* a Vespa."

Nancy Lockhart sighed and patted his shoulder. Mr. Barbera smiled as they watched her go to the car. Joe could tell by the way she looked away as she drove off that she was crying. The businessman put his hand on Joe's shoulder.

"It is tough on the mothers when their *giovanotti* – their boys – become men. From what I gather from your mother, you have been the man in the house for a long time. Still, these special times come only once." He stepped back. "Are you sure you can drive this?"

"Yes, sir, but maybe I should practice a little in the alley here. You don't need to stay now."

"But I want to, Joe. I remember my first scooter, and I would not trade this for anything."

"Okay, then, here goes." Joe kick-started the scooter, squeezed the clutch, and twisted the handgrip to first gear. The power surprised him. The first time the scooter almost ran away from him; the second time he stalled. Barbera laughed as Joe got the flooded engine going again.

"More guts than a moped, eh?"

"Yes, sir, but I'll get the hang of it."

Joe did some tight turns, practiced a few emergency stops, some downshifting and tail spinning.

"I think you got it," said the man. "Now you should go home."

"I agree. Thank you, Signor Barbera."

"*Niente*. Nothing. Just be careful. Don't go faster than you normally do on your bicycle for at least a week. That way, you'll always be able to stop or get out of the way."

"Thanks. Arrivederci." Mr. Barbera waved as Joe drove off in a cloud of white smoke. His heart was pounding as he eased into the traffic on Viale Trastevere. He avoided passing any cars at first and pulled into the first gas station. With a full tank of the correct mixture, the warm engine stopped smoking after about a block.

The only tricky part was the balance between clutch and throttle as he worked the gears up and down. Otherwise, the scooter handled like his bicycle with a heavy load. He knew where every slippery trolley track lay in the street, and how to recognize leaves or debris by their reflections on the cobblestones. He was grateful that it was not also pouring down rain.

By the time he crossed the bridge and headed upstream along the Tiber River, he felt more confident.

The one-way traffic moved more quickly, and soon he was negotiating for space with everyone else. But he kept his speed down and only passed cars that were not moving at all. Even so, his mother was just getting out of her car in the garage when Joe arrived. They walked upstairs together.

Nancy Lockhart was silent most of the evening.

"Does this bother you, Mom?"

"Yes and no, Son. Every once in a while, your growing up hits me, and this is one of those times. It happens to parents, and we can't help it. It's not a bad thing."

"Okay." Joe pulled a book from his bag and turned to his homework.

ଔଔଔଔ

Wednesday morning broke sunny and clear, though the weather forecast called for rain later in the week. The streets were dry, but Joe felt more like parading than speeding.

As he drove into the Alfa Romeo dealership, Joe's heart was beating faster than when he raced his bicycle there. He did a little gunning in neutral as he spun to a stop behind Matt's car. Cheering loudly, the guys spilled out of the bar to admire the new wheels. Everyone wanted to ride, but he only let Hans and Aldo try it in the parking lot.

"Neat," was Aldo's judgment after a spin around the driveway. "More power than my moped."

Joe glowed in the attention he got at school from the boarders and bus riders that day. It died off by the weekend. Matching the clutch and gears in his left hand with the brakes in his right hand and under his foot became second nature. His legs stayed dry behind the protective shields of the scooter. Riding out in the traffic lane, he no longer got drenched by passing cars going through puddles. Still, he quivered every time he crossed trolley tracks or the broad white-painted stripes of a crosswalk. The rails may not grab his fat wheels now, but he still had only two of them. He was not taking anything for granted.

# 6. SANDRA

ON THURSDAY, the seventh of December, Joe got home early. With the Feast of the Immaculate Conception on a Friday, many of the students' families were leaving town for the long weekend. In a rare miracle, the rain stopped on his way home. It was the first day since he bought the Vespa that he had not been rained on in one direction or the other going to school. The new poncho worked better than he expected at keeping his clothes dry. He folded it and stashed it in the compartment of the scooter before walking upstairs.

Angela had left at noon for the weekend. Joe sat at the dining room table and wrote out the two letters that Nancy had given him the day before. They were done in less than an hour. As he wondered whether to start on the Arland papers or go for a ride, he heard the door open and his mother's heels hit the floor.

"Hi, Mom. You're home early."

"Not done, though. Almost everyone bailed out, so I decided that I could work in jeans and bunny slippers as easily as heels and a suit." She came into the dining room and stopped. "Wait a minute. You're early yourself. What happened?"

"So many parents called in about getting a start on the weekend, that Brother Roger made it a half day."

"Unusual," she said. "He rarely makes exceptions."

"Yeah, well, in the hallways they're also talking about the brothers going to a spiritual retreat at Terminillo." Joe winked.

"Right. At a ski resort." She grunted with good humor. "So, they loaded you down with extra homework to make up for it?

"Actually, no. I had a study hall last period this morning. Here are the two letters you gave me yesterday." He picked up the handwritten sheets and gave them to her.

"Thanks. One thing off my to-do list for today."

"Mom?"

"Yes?"

"Since you're busy, and I'm free, I'd like to go out tonight. Some of the guys at school are going to meet at Il Klub."

"The new discotheque on Via Salandra?"

Joe nodded.

"Nice place," she said.

"You've been there?"

Nancy laughed. "Of course. We take our out-of-town visitors to the clubs after business dinners. I think I have tried most of them."

"Makes sense."

"I like Il Klub because if you ask quietly, they'll leave the booze out of your drink discreetly. You can keep up with the others without getting drunk." She put the letters in her briefcase. "We don't go there much now. Too many students and the music has changed."

"Yeah. That's why we like it."

"So, who's going?"

"Aldo, Hans, maybe Matt."

"Your motorcycle gang." She arched an eyebrow but smiled.

"Uh-huh. Who else? Only Aldo and I know how to use the bus system."

"Well, if you want to stay steady on that new scooter of yours, ask the barman for a screwdriver *senza*. No one will guess it's orange juice."

"Thanks, Mom. I don't like vodka. Last time I had wine, they razzed me."

"Can't let your social reputation slip, can we?" She turned to go to her office but stopped at the door. "I'll be working late because I want a long weekend too. Don't worry about creeping in."

"Okay." He let out a silent sigh of relief because he had shoved the Arland papers into his bag just before she had come in. He took the backpack to his room to put it in the closet.

"Oh, Joe," she said as he passed the door to her study. "Here's another letter if you have time."

"Sure, I can do that before supper." He walked in and took it from her. Two pages. A cigarette was burning in the ashtray on her desk. Without saying a word, he cracked the window and closed the door on his way out.

Like the two he did before Nancy came home, Joe had this one written out in less than an hour. As he went to the kitchen, a Brahms symphony was playing on the phonograph in his mother's study. He put the roast chicken and potatoes that Angela had left in the oven to heat, then chopped up lettuce, celery, tomatoes, and a cucumber for a salad.

After supper, they did the dishes while Nancy brewed caffé. She went back to her study with a cup of coffee; Joe went to his room to change.

Il Klub would be easy to miss without the neon sign lighting up the back street next to the Forestry Corps building. The entrance was only half-height, with stairs leading into the basement. Joe parked his Vespa, checked his hair in the rearview mirror, and walked in.

Loud music came from speakers located in every corner. The excited voices of dozens of students matched the volume of the songs. Instead of a band, this place featured a disk jockey. The young patrons preferred to hear their favorite songs done by the original groups.

Comfortable couches lined the dance floor with its spinning disco ball. Joe recognized Aldo and Hans at the far side and started around the dancing crowd. Then he saw the girl from the embassy annex, the one he had held the door for back in September. She sat with another girl. He gave his friends a wave and turned to the two girls. The blonde had her hair pulled back into a ponytail now and wore a blue dress. Her friend had jet-black hair, dark skin, and black eyes. They both looked up as he approached.

"Hello. It's not a pickup line, but I *have* seen you before." He put out his hand. "Joe Lockhart."

She beamed with pleasant surprise as if finding an old friend in a party full of strangers. Her companion smiled politely.

"Sandra Billingsley." She held his hand slightly longer than necessary. "This is my friend, Sonja Sankar."

Sonja and Joe shook hands. Sandra patted the place next to her. Joe sat.

"You're the first person I've seen before in this place, even if we've only just introduced ourselves."

"This is supposed to be a hangout for international students," Joe said.

"I'm a student," Sandra said. "George Washington University – art history." Her stern glance told Joe that he should go along. "And you?"

"Notre Dame."

"South Bend or Via Aurelia?"

"The one here. What about you, Sonja?"

"GW also. I'm on a semester abroad until January."

"You don't sound like you're from DC."

"No, but my father is stationed at the British embassy there. We're from London."

"I'm meeting some friends." He indicated Hans and Aldo. "Would you like to join us?"

"Why not?" they said together. The three of them rose and went over to where his friends were getting out of their seats.

After introductions, he asked Sandra to dance. It was "The Twist." He admired the easy grace of her movements and the natural way she swung with him on the rock and roll numbers. Sonja seemed to be enjoying taking turns between Hans and Aldo. When "Blue Velvet" came on, Sandra moved straight into his arms for the slow number.

"I thought we'd never have a chance to talk," she said. "I'm delighted to meet you finally. When I see you working in the USIS library, I'm always running an errand and can't stop."

"I'm glad too. So, what's a working girl doing in a club full of college and high school students?"

"I *am* a student. Honest. Last semester, I came here. I got an internship at the embassy annex during the summer. They hired me to stay on, and I like working there. Now I'm taking time off to decide if I want to change majors or continue in art history."

"So, going back to DC next semester?"

"No. I can stay out for a year. After that, I must return or transfer to another school."

"Rome is ideal for art history. What else might you study?"

"Law or political science or accounting." Her face was expressionless.

"Interesting set of choices."

"That's what makes it so hard."

"What kind of work do you do?"

"Just a secretary."

"*Just* a secretary. It's the most important job in any office. Without secretaries, we'd have to shut down the embassy and break diplomatic relations."

Sandra laughed. "You're very observant for a boy." She looked into his eyes. "If you're a day-dog at Notre Dame, you must be here with your family."

"How do you know what a day-dog is?" he asked.

"I listen. Day-dogs aren't the only ones who go clubbing. Sometimes boarders go over the wall and sneak into town."

"Impressive."

"Back to my question. I never saw a Lockhart in the embassy phone book. Where does your father work?"

"He died when I was small. I live with my mother."

Sandra dropped her gaze and blushed fiercely. "I'm sorry."

"Don't worry." Joe gave her hand a gentle squeeze. "I learned about secretaries from her. She stunned the office when she arrived by hiring a woman from the outside instead of taking one of the men in the clerical pool. She says that Maria Grazia is the best secretary she's ever had. They're quite a team."

"So, your mother isn't the secretary."

"No."

"Let me guess: Nancy Ardwood Lockhart, VP for Operations at Smithson Italia."

Joe started. "How did you know?"

"I'm a secretary. I get the guest lists for every affair that my boss attends. Besides, I can count the number of female executives in this country on one hand – with three fingers left over. Your mother is a rock star among the working girls, as you call them."

Joe blushed. "Yeah, I guess."

The song reached the finale. She tugged on his hands and backed up her head to look directly at him.

"Joe, if you don't mind, don't mention that I work. No secret, but my friends only know me as a GW student."

"Okay, I can handle that. I've never seen you at work, y'know."

Back at the couch, Joe offered to make a run for drinks. Sandra asked for a glass of white wine, but the others had recently refilled. He went to the bar for his screwdriver senza and Frascati for Sandra.

The DJ was taking a break when Aldo shouted at the door. "Look who's here." Matt and two girls came across the floor, doing a silly soft shoe number. The girls were twins, taller than Matt, identical redheads with ponytails and green eyes.

"Uh-oh," said Joe. "The Irish invasion."

Cara and Kelly went to Marymount, the girls' international school close to Vigna Clara. They lived in the apartment building next to Matt's. Soon the party was in full swing and expanded to include students from Overseas American and the American Academy.

About midnight, Sandra was dancing another slow number with Joe. Sonja had disappeared with an English student whose family knew hers from the foreign service.

"Joe, tomorrow isn't a holiday in our office."

He leaned back, surprised. "I never asked you where you worked, but if it's in the embassy annex, I guess you must go."

"Yes. This has been great fun."

"How are you getting home?"

"The bus."

"There's a strike, you know."

"Doesn't that start tomorrow?"

"Yeah, but 'tomorrow' starts at midnight. The crews won't begin a run if midnight will come while they're out."

"I forgot the strike." She paused, thinking. "Not a problem. I can afford a taxi."

"Want a lift home? You'll be hard-pressed to find a cab with the buses not running."

"You have a car?"

"No. A Vespa. I can carry one more."

"On your scooter?" Sandra leaned back to face him, wide-eyed with her mouth open.

"Sure. Have you ever ridden one?"

"No. You're the first person I ever met who owns one. Let's do it!"

They said goodbye to the others. The guys gave Joe knowing winks, to which he rolled his eyes. There would be serious razzing on Monday morning.

Sandra collected her umbrella from the holder at the door.

"Where to?" Joe asked.

"Via della Giuliana, number eight."

"Not one of the usual expatriate enclaves. We used to live in that neighborhood."

"Well, I can afford it, and a half-dozen trolleys and buses stop just outside."

"Happens to be on my way home, too." They paused at his machine.

"This Vespa doesn't have a footrest, so you'll need to hold on tight. There's plenty of room to sit sideways, so you shouldn't feel like you're falling off."

"Okay."

He rolled the Vespa to the street, straddled it, and sat way up on the seat. He started it and motioned to Sandra. She put her arm through the umbrella strap, then sat behind Joe, putting her arms around his waist. *Funny*, he thought, *I don't get this warm when Mom gets on the scooter.*

Traffic was light, so he could move carefully to accustom Sandra to the motion. She balanced instinctively behind him. *Thank goodness, the rain stopped.*

Soon they were outside the *portone*, the large door to her apartment building. She slid off as if she had been born on a Vespa.

"Thanks, Joe." She took his hand and kissed him on the cheek. "Best time I've had in ages."

"I hope to see more of you."

"Me, too."

He waited while she pulled her keys from a pocket he had not seen before and let herself into the building. After checking for traffic, he did a wide U-turn to head up the Via Trionfale to the top of the Monte Mario.

ଔଔଔ

"You're home earlier than I expected for a night clubbing."

Joe coughed. The hall was thick with smoke. She had left the door to her study open again.

"One of the girls who has to work tomorrow forgot about the bus strike," he said. "I gave her a lift home." He coughed again. "Mom, you promised to keep the door closed when you smoke."

"I forgot," she said, focusing on the paper she was reading. "Sorry about that."

"Really?" Joe surprised himself with the bite in his voice.

Nancy looked up sharply. "Who's working, and who's playing here?"

"It's just that you know how I hate it, and forgetting doesn't make it drift away."

"It's my crutch, not yours. I get little or no support anywhere else in this world."

"Well, friends don't flock to ashtrays."

"Watch your mouth, young man." Nancy stood and faced him.

"You don't even smoke them that much. Most of them burn away in the ashtray like a joss stick. Why don't you take up incense? It would smell better."

Nancy took two steps toward him, eyes blazing. Joe grit his teeth and stared down at her. She took a deep breath, walked back to the desk, crushed out the cigarette, and opened the window.

"Crack the door and let it blow out," she said. "I'll close the door."

"Thanks, Mom." A hint of sarcasm colored the remark. He walked down the hall to his room.

As his anger ebbed slowly, he became aware of a different feeling, one of pain. His mother did work too hard and too much. Almost everyone else he knew smoked. The only guys in his class who did not were some of the jocks, Aldo, Hans, Benny, and himself. The boarders made a big show of it because it was forbidden at school. He figured that they did not puff as much as they pretended.

Joe walked back to the study and knocked on the door. Opening it gently, he saw his mother look up from the notepad she was writing on.

"About the smoking, Mom. I'm sorry. That wasn't fair."

"Accepted." The anger lingered in her voice. "I'm as upset at myself as you."

"Why? It's not that big a deal. Only old ladies don't smoke today."

"Because I don't like it either. It takes away my lung capacity. I can feel the air moving differently when I breathe. And I catch more coughs and colds."

"So why do you keep smoking? You never smoked before Dad died."

"Like you said, everyone's doing it. I tried it. After the initial hacking, it stayed down, and it felt good. But you're right. I do waste most of it. And I don't like the taste, or the holes in my skirt, or the smell."

"You could quit."

"We've had this conversation before. It's not easy. Every day, I tell myself that I won't smoke, but then a group goes out for coffee or drinks, and we all start smoking. Plus, it's kind of fun to watch the men try to outdraw each other with their lighters and matches."

"Even I do that. It's good manners."

"Well, you keep on being a gentleman. I need not to pull the cigarettes out. Until then, bear with me."

She got up, carried the ashtray to the bathroom, and flushed the contents down the toilet. After rinsing it, she returned to the study.

"So, since I'm taking an unscheduled break, did you enjoy Il Klub?"

"Yes. Lots of Beatles music and our favorite songs. I danced most of the time. And I had a couple of the screwdrivers senza. Thanks for the tip. I like the orange juice with a garnish much better."

"So, who needed a ride home?"

"A student from GW. She's on a year off from school and works somewhere in the embassy annex."

"Running with the college girls, now, are we?" Nancy grinned with raised eyebrows.

"God, Mom, not you too. The guys are going to grill me on Monday morning, I'm sure." He smiled. "Besides, we're the same age. She skipped two grades in school, then went to college early."

"Ooh, a child prodigy. Grab that one, Son. Does she have a name?"

"Sandra. Sandra Billingsley."

"Never heard of her, but I wouldn't know the parents of a student here from the States. Had you met her before?"

"Back in September, I held a door for her when her arms were loaded coming out of the Star and Stripes bookstore. We recognized each other from that."

Nancy looked at the clock over her desk.

"Well, I only have a little more to do, and I want to finish it before quitting for the weekend." She waved at the door.

"Good night, Mom."

Joe felt a warm happiness thinking of Sandra as he slipped into bed, but dark and dreamless sleep wrapped him as soon as his head hit the pillow.

# 7. Almost caught

"THIS MAY BE THE LAST ONE this year." Nancy handed Joe another letter from del Piave. "He's taking his family to Argentina for Christmas to visit relatives."

"This will put gas in the Vespa until he gets back." He put the letter in his room. Nancy went to the kitchen. Angela had set the table and fixed supper. She had not spoken about her family since Mario's funeral.

"Will you be going home for the holidays?"

"Sì, signora. We are all going to Pescara to see my father."

"Would you like a few extra days? Joe and I can manage just fine if you want to leave this weekend and come back after *Befana*." The sixth of January.

Angela put her hands to her face. "Oh, signora, you are too kind. My husband gets this Monday off. We had not planned on being able to beat the rush."

"Well, ask him. It's okay with us." Nancy smiled. "Now, don't miss your bus."

Angela seemed pleasantly distracted as she shouldered her purse and hefted three fishnet bags in each hand. Joe always marveled at how she shopped for two households every day. The Lockharts had kept American dinner hours ever since Nancy had hired

Angela. The housekeeper's family ate much later, which gave her time to get home with her shopping.

"Let's wrap their presents after supper," said Nancy.

"Angela's kids are going to love the jeans." They had prepared the surprise since the summer. Joe got the sizes from Angela on some excuse. His grandparents had mailed the clothes back in November.

Wrapping gifts for Angela's family put them both in a Christmas mood. They played carols on the record player. Presents for the relatives in the United States had been shipped long ago, so this felt like the beginning of the season for them. After the gifts were wrapped, Joe translated the del Piave letter. Then he worked on the Arland letters in his room while his mother worked in her study.

ଔଔଔ

Joe propped the hefty biology textbook on his desk. He laid an Arland letter against the open book, so it would appear to Brother Peter that he was following along in the text.

"Today, we will review the pattern research of Mendel…" the teacher began in his nasal drone. Joe opened his biology notebook on the desk and placed his note pad on top of it. He stared up at the board then looked at the letter. After he read the whole thing, he began to write.

> Dear M,
> With respect to your letter of the 13th last, I am pleased to inform you that the Directors of our subsidiary in Bergamo have agreed to travel to

Cologne for a meeting on the subject. They will meet us at the Bad Kreuznach Hotel on the 25th. We sincerely hope that you will be able to join us, and we invite you to repeat the presentation you made in Milan.

As mentioned in the enclosed, our work is of great interest to a wide variety of customers. The opportunity to expand the firm to include the participation of the Bergamo group should not be missed.

Best wishes and regards,
//signed// L

Joe turned to the clippings. There were three of them, from three different European news magazines, *Panorama* in Italian, *Paris Match* in French, and *Der Spiegel* in German. They all concerned the bombing in Milan, the one that killed Angela's brother.

*There must be some mistake*, Joe thought. He leaned down to his backpack and leafed through the manila folder.

"Mr. Lockhart!" Brother Peter's voice broke through his concentration. A titter ran through the class. Joe looked up, closing his pad over his work.

"Yes, Brother." His ears burned.

"You seem so intent on your notes, I assume you have followed my every word."

"I'm sorry, Brother." He scanned the board, desperately seeking some clue as to what the question might be. Benny shifted to the right up ahead, revealing the letters A-B-B-A in his notebook.

"The pattern, Mr. Lockhart, the pattern among the grandchildren plants."

"Uh, A-B-B-A, sir."

"And why is that?" the monk asked. Ben rolled his eyes to the ceiling. Joe punted.

"Because Mendel thought that they would possess traits from both sets of grandparents."

"See me after class and pull your head out of whatever you are doing that isn't biology."

The bell rang only two minutes later. Joe approached the teacher's desk.

"We're worried about you, Joe." Brother Peter gave him a ticket for "academic counseling." That meant staying after school. "We'll do this in Brother Roger's office."

*Oh God, the headmaster's office!* Joe took the ticket and moved to history class in a daze. He wondered which was worse: the threat of this getting back to his mother or being late for his appointment with Luke Arland.

The Arland file! *They're going to want to know what I have. This is the end. I'll never get another translation job again, and God knows what Mom will do.*

During lunch, Joe called Luke's office from the payphone, but the executive was at a meeting in another part of town. Slamming his fist into the concrete wall by the phone shot pain up his arm and shoulder. He should have gone with his instincts and warned Luke that four letters at once was too much with his schedule.

In the washroom, he cleaned his bleeding knuckles. His left hand ached as he recovered his bag from his locker.

At least he had not smashed his writing hand. Joe finished the second letter in study hall after lunch. He fretted through math and French after that until the bell rang for the end of school.

He ran to the parking lot and jumped on the Vespa. Two miles away at a red light, he remembered the ticket in his knapsack.

*Hell,* he said to himself. *No point in going back now. I'd be late for both Brother Peter and Mr. Arland. I'll think of something later.*

Joe waited self-consciously at the counter of the café at the Piazzale Clodio as he drank his espresso. After two waves of customers came and went, he ordered a glass of mineral water and sat at a table outside. Though he could afford these little luxuries now, he still felt uncomfortable, both spending the extra money and waiting.

He pulled out the third letter and a note pad and began to work. When Luke arrived just before four thirty, Joe had it half finished.

"Sorry I'm late," said the executive. "I had to park two blocks away. Do you have the letters?"

"Only two of them. My schedule has been too hectic."

Luke's expression fell. "I was counting on all four. Why did you say you'd do them?"

"I thought I could. I just didn't know." Joe took out the two completed letters. "I even got in trouble at school for trying to do them in class."

"Damn, Joe! You mean someone else has seen this stuff?"

"No, not at all. But my biology teacher caught me working on it. He didn't come over to see it, but I forgot to stay after for a meeting with him."

"This is serious. Maybe I made a mistake letting you do this. I can't afford for this work to be mixed up with your school life."

"I'm sorry, sir." Joe dropped his gaze. "It won't happen again. It was stupid to work on it in school."

"You're right. It was also stupid to say you could do it. I told you never to let this interfere with your schoolwork or the material your mother brings home."

"I know. I overestimated what I could do."

"You sure did." Luke stared up and down the street, his face grim. Then he looked back at the teenager. "I should fire you, but I can't turn to anyone else." He took the two letters. "I'll make do with these for now. Get me the next two as soon as you can. And don't ever run the risk of this being found out by anyone again. Is that clear?"

"Yes, sir."

Luke gave him two one-thousand lire notes and walked quickly away. Joe waited until the man was out of sight before putting the money in his wallet. *Is this what thirty pieces of silver felt like in Judas's hand?*

# 8. Expansion

JOE WAS IN HIS ROOM trying to concentrate on a painfully boring chapter about the Concert of Europe when he heard the front door open and his mother's heels hit the floor.

"*Ciao, tutti.*" Hi, everyone. Nancy's voice sounded cheerful.

"Buona sera, signora," Angela answered from the kitchen. "Dinner is ready on the stove."

"Thank you. I'm famished. We can eat as soon as I wash up. Where's Joe?"

Angela must have motioned because Nancy knocked on his door and asked to come in. "Two more letters from del Piave."

Joe did not want to see another business letter in any language. He put out his arm. Nancy pulled the letters out of her briefcase and held them.

"What's with you? Is the idea of work not always being fun catching up with you?"

"No, Mom. Just homework."

"I can do these two. You usually do that in study hall, but I can understand an occasional overload."

"I can do them, Mom."

"No, Joe. Not when there is homework outstanding. You're still a full-time student first."

"Oh, all right." He swung back to his desk.

"Well, I had a great day, and I won't ask about yours; I can tell. Wash up for supper, Son." She leaned over and kissed his head. He twisted away, and she laughed as she went out.

Joe slammed the book shut and walked to the bathroom to wash his hands. As he combed his hair, he noticed another pimple starting near the one on his cheek. He squeezed the older one and squirted pus on the mirror. Before he came out, he cleaned off the glass.

"I started without you," said his mother. "So, how was school today?"

"Okay, I guess."

"It must've been terrible. You don't pick your face unless you're upset about something."

"Mom, do you have to analyze everything I do?"

"Can't help it, Son. I'm a doctor, remember?"

Angela appeared with her incredible shopping bags. "Good night, everyone. I'm going home now."

The phone rang. Angela put down her load and answered it. She came right back.

"For you, signora, but I forgot to ask who."

"Thank you, Angela. See you tomorrow. Dinner is delicious."

"Grazie, signora, buona notte." And she was gone.

Joe picked at his food alone. Long ago, Nancy had learned to speak away from eavesdroppers, so he did not hear the telephone conversation. She was not as chipper when she returned.

"Do you want to explain why you stood up the headmaster this afternoon?"

His jaw dropped. He never thought someone would call home. It was not like Aldo, who was always in trouble. His parents got calls only after several incidents.

"Well?" his mother asked, spearing a piece of broccoli. *How could she be so cool?* He reached into his pocket and extracted the academic counseling ticket.

"I forgot that Brother Peter wanted to see me after school. I knew nothing about the headmaster."

"That was Brother Roger, not Brother Peter."

"We were going to use his office, but I didn't expect him to be there." Nancy raised one eyebrow. Joe felt his blood start to boil. "Honest, Mom. I got this ticket from Brother Peter."

"What for?"

"Not paying attention in biology."

"Hardly worth a ticket. What really happened?"

"I was working on something else."

"What?"

"Another subject."

"He said that Brother Peter has caught you before."

"Mom, Brother Peter is excruciating; he's so boring. And he never says anything that isn't in the reading assignment. I have to do something to keep from falling asleep!" Did he catch an uplift at the edge of her eyes? For a moment, he thought she would laugh. But she was serious again.

"So why miss the appointment after school?"

"I forgot."

"How did you forget? How often do you get these tickets?"

"First one."

"A big deal then. So, how do you forget?"

"Mom, I don't know! I just forgot. I've got too much going on, and I forgot!"

"You're whining." A quiet statement of fact. Soft and calm, but her voice could carry to the last row of bleachers in a stadium. It terrified Joe to hear that tone. "Since you seem to be having uncharacteristic problems organizing yourself, do I need to go over your homework with you each night?"

"No, Mom, please. I never had this problem before, and I'm all caught up now."

"You mean you won't do homework in biology anymore?"

"Right."

"Well, you explain it to Brother Roger. I told him you would be in his office fifteen minutes before school starts tomorrow." She paused when Joe's face fell. "Is there a problem?"

"No, Mom, but I'll miss breakfast with my friends."

"Oh, them. About your motor club in the mornings. So far, you guys have trodden lightly on the edge of trouble every morning." She smiled briefly, then frowned and pointed her fork at him. "I understand how much the breakfast meeting means to you. So, skip the *cornetto* and go straight to school for the rest of the week." Joe started to protest but caught himself.

"Yes, ma'am," he said quietly. He felt a major storm passing. His mother was not angry, and his secret about Arland's files was still safe.

Ten days later, as he walked from modern European history class to biology, Joe recognized the voice behind him.

"*Ué,* Joe," Aldo said. His English was excellent, except for not being able to pronounce "th." He and Joe grew up in Rome, so they fell easily into a mix of Italian and *romanaccio*, the local dialect. "It's my *onomastico* this weekend. Papà said I could invite you to come help celebrate. Can you come?"

"That sounds more like an American birthday party than an Italian name-day. Aren't you supposed to bring *bigné* pastries and champagne to your coworkers?"

"Can you imagine Brother Roger's face if I brought spumante to school?" They both laughed.

"I'll check with Mom tonight and let you know for sure."

The following weekend, Joe rode his Vespa to the Palazzo Lanzera, halfway between the Piazza di Spagna and the current Spanish embassy by the Tiber. Aldo's family had lived there since the first Count of Lanzera had arrived with the Spanish Ambassador to the Holy See in the fifteenth century.

The onomastico party turned out to be a small affair with the Lanzera family, a cousin Marisa from Naples and her parents, and Marcantonio Borghese, a family friend visiting from his job in Geneva. Conversation moved between Italian and English, with occasional French from Marcantonio. No one missed a beat.

The Lanzeras still had close ties with the royal family in Spain, Joe knew. Fifteen Counts of Lanzera had served the Bourbon Kingdoms of Spain and the Two Sicilies, since long before the idea of an Italian state ever arose.

The Borghese and Lanzera families were close, having been in the Papal court and Roman politics for centuries.

About six, Marisa's family excused themselves to go the Termini station, where they would catch the evening *rapido* back to Naples. Marcantonio had a dinner engagement with another friend and left with them. Joe's invitation included supper, so he stayed.

"Your Italian is amazing," said Aldo's dad as he poured Sandeman port in the study after the meal. "None of Aldo's other friends from school speak it so naturally. He tells me you're the class leader." Joe blushed and flashed a glance at his friend, who shrugged.

"Not really, sir. I think our friend Benny holds that spot."

"Just ask him, Papà."

The count considered his port for a moment, then looked at Joe. "Aldo got this idea when I was whining about my problems with the competition around Naples. You know our family has been in construction ever since the Piedmontese Invasion, don't you?"

Joe nodded. He knew that many people south of Tuscany had a different perspective on the "Unification" of Italy than the history lessons in his Italian elementary school. The count's grandfather had used all his deftness and diplomacy to make a new life when both the Papal States and the Kingdom of Two Sicilies vanished almost overnight. As a citizen of what was now the Kingdom of Italy, he moved into construction, which was booming after the destruction wrought by the Piedmontese armies. With his family contacts and property in both Campania and Lazio, he made himself an asset to the new masters in Turin and Rome.

"The papers have stories about the rise of the Camorra in building and trash hauling. Is this related?"

"Yes. The mafiosi and camorristi who came with the Allies in World War II keep the American commanders from seeing the criminal element around them. The Americans generally don't speak Italian, much less *napoletano.* They trust the people they do business with. Besides, the camorristi can answer the *bandi di gara* in English, which is required for submitting bids. Do you know what an RFP is?"

"Yes, a request for proposal." Joe's heart skipped a beat when Aldo raised his eyebrows in surprise. The elder Lanzera seemed not to notice.

"They keep winning the contracts because they have insider information. They cheat on the concrete mixing and use unqualified labor, but no one notices. One day, their buildings around Naples will start falling down.

"I can't find translators who can write in English well enough to explain our offer to the American Navy in Naples. There is a small base going up near the city, and I am sure we could do the job better than the competition."

"How can I help, *Signor Conte*?"

"Aldo thinks you could translate the offer, or at least work with our people if it's too technical. I'm willing to let you try. What do you think?"

Joe sipped his port.

"I have other translation clients, sir." Aldo looked surprised again.

"That does not surprise me," said the count, "even at your age."

"It's a coincidence, but I worked on a construction project – nowhere near Naples. The firm had a similar problem, but with a company in the US. I can only take on so much, but if you can show me some typical documents, I can tell you if I can help."

"We can arrange that. However, we also need confidentiality, so our plans do not leak to the competition."

"Of course. Do you have an NDA that you use with your suppliers?"

Lanzera put his glass down. "*Caspita!* You are a professional, aren't you?" He turned to his son. "Did you know this?"

"No, Papà. His English writing was the best in our class, so I guessed he could help."

"Joe, I'll give Aldo a package on Monday, which he can bring to school on Tuesday. It will contain our standard NDA and noncompete agreement in it, the executive summary of the RFP, and our draft response to it. Did you say you are also working for a construction firm?"

"Not directly. My client is the US company considering the bids – different sector."

"Discretion is important until the contract is awarded." Joe nodded, then remembered his problem with Luke Arland.

"One thought, sir. My mother does not mind my taking on translation work because I don't let it interfere with school. But I would like to be free to tell her about this. No details about what I'm translating, of course."

"That should not be a problem. When could you tell me if you can do this?"

"Probably by Thursday. If I can do it, I'll sign the two agreements and give them to Aldo. Do you want me to phone, or tell Aldo?"

"How about both? I'd like your answer as soon as possible."

They shook hands and joined Aldo's mother and sister in the living room.

ఇఇఇ

Nancy came in as Joe hung his coat in the armoire in his room.

"Hi, Mom. How was the dinner tonight?"

"Good, actually. Luke and I met with the management team from our new subsidiary in London. With everyone speaking English, he relaxed. I saw how effective he can be and why New York and Richmond think so highly of him." She took off her coat and slipped out of her heels. "And how was your party with Aldo?"

"Great. It turned into a business dinner too. I met his cousin Marisa and her family from Naples, and Marcantonio Borghese, who is an old friend of Aldo's dad."

"I met Borghese at an industrial conference. Doesn't he live in Geneva?"

"Yes, but he also has his home here and flies back and forth a lot."

"Nice guy. Never did any business with him. What did he want with you?"

"He left before supper. Aldo's dad wanted to talk to me."

"About what?" She headed for the kitchen. He followed.

"A translation job for his company. If I take it, there'll be an NDA, like the one with Smithson Italia. Are you okay with that?"

"What about the work for us?"

"It would still be a priority. And everything after schoolwork. I learned that lesson; I won't take more than I can fit in."

Nancy filled a glass with water from the faucet on the sink. She thought as she drank deeply, then drew some more.

"Well, you are a freelancer. The agreements make that clear, but you're still under twenty-one. I can cut you off if I get any more phone calls from Brother Roger." She put down the glass and gave him an intense look.

"I understand, Mom."

"Okay with me. I may not have to pay for your college at this rate." She smiled. He grinned back.

"I haven't agreed yet. This week the count will send me a sample so I can make sure I can do it."

"Smart." She put her arm around him and squeezed. "I'm bushed. How about you?"

"I feel keyed up, but it's been a long day."

She rinsed out the glass. Twenty minutes later, all was silent in the apartment.

◈◈◈

With a wink, Aldo passed the thick envelope to Joe while the gang enjoyed their breakfast to the sounds of "Love Me Do" on the jukebox. Joe contained his excitement until he got home that afternoon. Angela was in the kitchen fixing supper and singing a San Remo hit song.

Joe went into his room to open the envelope. The RFP was on US Navy letterhead and resembled the ones that del Piave had included in the proposals he submitted to Smithson. *A building is a building,* thought Joe. The draft statement of intent looked like one of del Piave's letters. He read the NDA and the noncompete agreement; they were almost identical to the forms from Smithson Italia. After signing them, he went to the phone in his mother's study, closing the door. He dialed the count's direct line, reading from the business card that Aldo's dad had given him.

"Signor Conte, I can do this. It is very similar to the material I did before."

"Excellent! There will be a lot of it. How fast can you work?"

"It depends, sir. I'm a student first, and my mother insists that my schoolwork comes first."

"Shall I intercede with *la bella dottoressa*?" Joe thought that he would never get used to the effect his mother had on grown men.

"Not necessary, sir. She has already approved my freelancing. But I must look at each assignment as it comes to be sure that I can fit it in with school and other work in progress. Something like what you sent me, I can turn around in a couple of days."

"We can work around that. The American Navy gives us generous deadlines."

"Do you want me to translate the draft? We haven't discussed cost yet."

"I should like to see your work and pass it around to my team. What is your rate?"

"Fifteen-hundred lire per page, sir. I don't type, so it will be handwritten."

"Fine. Please send it back with Aldo. Do you want cash or check?"

"Either, sir. A check should be made out to 'J.J. Lockhart'."

Only as he hung up the phone did it hit Joe that he had just gotten a 50 percent raise.

# 9. Leak

"*FLECTAMUS GENUA*," Father Bill intoned. Let us kneel. His pleasant baritone voice echoed off the frescoes in the nave and apse of Santa Susanna's Church. Holding the smoking censer steady, Joe knelt on the first step of the main altar in one motion, so that his cassock swung back neatly over his feet, covering his shoes. Five hundred sets of knees murmured as they hit the kneelers in the pews behind him.

Father Bill chanted the next prayer in the Midnight Mass. His spoken Latin normally had a thick American accent, but his singing was flawless. The pastor had contracted laryngitis yesterday. Father Pat preached great sermons, but he could not sing a two-note amen without messing it up. Joe gave the censer a short swing occasionally to keep the incense burning. The smell was one of his favorite parts of the liturgies of Holy Days.

"*...in saecula saeculorum.*" This prayer was over.

"Amen." Compared to the young priest, the congregation sounded clumsy. Joe put extra air into his notes, leading them in the response.

"*Levate.*" Rise. Joe heaved back on both feet at once and rose so that he never stepped on his cassock. Following Joe's lead, the congregation clambered to their feet.

Father Bill turned to Joe and took the censer from him. While the priest walked slowly around the church, blessing the congregation with incense, Joe stared at the fresco of the martyrdom of Saint Susanna. Meanwhile, a choir of nuns sang a Gregorian chant from behind the cloister screen over a side altar. Waving incense could take five minutes or more with all the people in the sanctuary. Midnight Mass ran two hours without a sermon.

Joe enjoyed the special liturgies. As the senior altar boy, he moved a lot during the service. He carried the missal from the Epistle to the Gospel side, washed the celebrant's hands during the Lavabo, rang the bells for the Consecration, and led the party in and out. And always, he recited the responses in a loud, clear voice. Most of the congregation counted on him to know when to stand, kneel, or say something. Even the ones who knew the Latin words often would lose their places. The frescoes on the walls, the stunning paintings in the ceiling, and the sculptures by famous artists of the Renaissance could be distracting unless like Joe, you happened to grow up worshiping in a sixteenth-century Roman church.

Rome glistened in the cold, wet darkness as Nancy and Joe walked to the car after Mass. It was two a.m.

"Traffic is light," she said, "but it still surprises me how many people are out."

"My math teacher said that if only one percent of Romans did anything outdoors together, it put 80,000 of them on the streets."

"Makes sense. Tired?"

"No. All that singing and moving around wakes me up. Besides, I'm still trying to figure out which present I'll open when we get home."

"To think, you get to act like this again in two weeks."

ଔଔଔଔ

Twelve days later, Joe woke up late. He sat on the edge of the bed and pulled on his socks. He always donned them first. Never warm in the summer, the marble floors were freezing in the winter, even in a heated house.

"Aren't you getting a little old for this?" Nancy mocked Joe as he padded into the living room, looking for his presents. "One of these years, the Befana isn't going to come."

"Never happen. She's older than Santa Claus. Aha!" He picked up the hiking boot by the tree. It was full of candy and small gifts.

"Why didn't I decide we would do either Santa Claus or the Befana when you were little?"

"You'd never have gotten away with it." Joe put his hand in the boot. "I just happen to be lucky enough to be an American kid in Italy." Grinning at her, he unwrapped a bite-sized cake and almost tossed it in his mouth but caught her look. "I know – after Mass." Although they no longer had to fast from the night before, fasting was still required within three hours of Communion.

"We're running a little late. Go get dressed."

They drove downtown because public transit shut down on the sixth of January. This was the big gift-giving holiday of the year, and Romans showed their appreciation to the city's workers by taking gifts to their places of work. Great piles of chocolate confections in fancy silver foil, panettoni, and gaily wrapped packages of every size and shape rose at the doorways and on the sidewalks outside the police and fire stations. A pile of presents from the neighborhood also covered the circular platform at each major intersection, where a traffic policeman usually stood.

"It looks like Santa Claus hit turbulence over the city and lost his load," Joe said, as Nancy drove around an especially tall stack at the Piazza Barberini.

"You sure it wasn't the Befana?"

"Maybe both. I wonder why no one ever steals this stuff."

"Maybe they do, and this is what's left. I have a hunch that the neighbors who brought this are watching it. Thieves have neighborhoods too. They're probably putting chocolate eggs at the doors of their own police stations." Nancy pulled into a parking space across from the church.

"That's a weird thought."

"I guess so, but it makes sense in Rome. Folks have had to learn to live together for a long time here. Even the burglars must get along with their neighbors."

○₹○₹○₹

The period after the Epiphany was always the least interesting time of the year. With no holidays to celebrate and cold rain for weeks on end, Joe wanted to hibernate like a bear. School days blurred into an endless string of homework assignments and quizzes, without a holiday, a major exam, or a standardized test to break the routine.

Only his three translation customers gave him something to look forward to each week.

In early March, he had just finished his homework when he heard his mother's heels hit the floor in the entrance hall and the briefcase land on the coffee table in her study. She padded into his room with a frown, but her eyes were bright.

"The leak I worried about finally happened."

He leaped up, his eyes wide and his heart pounding. "No, I swear, I haven't breathed to anyone."

"Relax, Joe, this leak is on my end." She smiled. "Cavaliere del Piave wants to meet you." He let out his breath.

"Who told him I was doing his letters?"

"You did, in a way. The people in New York complimented him about how well written his proposals were and how easy to understand. He thinks it clinched the deal with Smithson and his new investment partners, so he came to thank me. I had to tell him I didn't do it."

"Was he upset?" he asked.

"He might have been if he hadn't won the contract, but now he appreciates what you've done for him. He invited us to dinner this weekend. Want to go?"

"When? There's a basketball game at school on Friday."

"I remembered that. Saturday night. Either the Ostaria dell'Orso or Giorgio's."

He whistled. "Those are the two ritziest places in town."

"Standard fare for men like him."

Joe had a thought and grinned.

"What's he like, Mom? Is he after you?"

She laughed. "I don't think so, but just the same, I'd never get caught alone for the night with him. He seems stable enough, married with grown sons. Lives in a palazzo off the Piazza Barberini. Good-looking, but all business with me."

"Anyone else interesting at work?" He winked.

"What is this? You see the hours I keep. How do you expect me to find romance with that routine?"

"Well, since I'm your only company after work, anything that happens is going to happen at the office. The only place I can't protect you." She reached to the head of his bed, and he ducked the pillow that she swung at him.

"Since when did you take an interest in my love life, young man?"

"Since I met that new guy – Luke Arland."

"What about him?"

"He likes you. I can tell by the way he looks at you."

"Oh?" She considered what her son had said. "Point to you, Joe. It has been more fun around work since he arrived. But he's all business as far as I can tell. He did the same work in the States that I do here, so we have that in common. With him on the phone to New York so much, we hardly talk."

"He did ask us about playing tennis. Did you decide not to take up his offer?"

"We never did discuss that, did we?" She thought quietly for a moment. "Do you want to learn?"

"Yes."

"I could teach you; you never asked."

"I remember the trophy wall in the house in Richmond. I've always wanted to play tennis, but I thought that it was something that you wouldn't want to do. You never played once after Dad went into the hospital that last time."

"Well, your father and I were quite a team, and you were too young." She looked out the window, at something far away and long ago.

Joe knew that look and the slight sag in her shoulders. "Mom, it would be good to see you playing again." She straightened up.

"Okay. But when?"

"I think Saturday afternoons. You play Mr. Arland for a game or two, then one or both of you coach me for a while."

"What about the monthly campout with the troop?"

"There are two other assistant scoutmasters. I'll swap with one of them for a meeting or some other event – if they want me to."

"That might work." Her face suddenly went serious. "Are you matchmaking, or do you want to play tennis?"

He laughed. "Tennis. Mom. Honest." She relaxed. Then he said in an affected wink-wink voice, "Of course, what you do after the game is none of my business." She threw the pillow at him.

"Let me think about that. Meanwhile, what about del Piave? The Ostaria or Giorgio's?"

"The Ostaria, I've never been there."

"That would have been my choice too. I'll let him know."

ೞೞೞ

On Saturday, the rain stopped around noon, as it did for a few hours every day now. Delicate blooms appeared in the flowerbeds of the parks. The wind blew hard each afternoon, but by sundown, it was just a breeze. Nancy and Joe took a taxi to their dinner meeting with del Piave.

The Ostaria dell'Orso hid in a warren of narrow alleys a few meters from the Lungotevere Marzio on the Tiber River. It had been open since the Middle Ages; Renaissance artists like Michelangelo had patronized the place. *It hasn't had a face-lift since then either*, Joe thought as he escorted his mother to the door.

The deliberately worn exterior left him unprepared for the luxury inside. Dark silk damask covered the walls. Hand-carved hardwood furniture sat on thick Persian carpets that muffled their footsteps.

The maître d'hôtel showed them to the first room on the right of the entrance hall. The cavaliere was waiting for them at the bar. He was surprisingly tall, a muscular man in a tailored dark gray suit. His blond hair graying at the temples gave him a distinguished appearance. He gripped Joe's hand firmly and smiled warmly.

"It is a pleasure to meet you, Joe," he said in Italian. "Your work has exceeded my expectations, and I'm in your debt for the outcome." He held out a chair for Nancy as they sat.

"Thank you, sir." Joe's face warmed up.

They made small talk over aperitifs. Del Piave came from a long line of entrepreneurs and naval officers. His maternal grandfather had been the last commander of the Vatican Navy in the nineteenth century. He had attended the Naval Academy in Livorno and served in cruisers during the war. After the navy, he started a shipping line, del Piave Navigazione, which was still the core company of his business group.

For dinner, they moved to the Borgia Room, more than three hours after Joe's normal suppertime. He was almost past feeling hungry.

The decor in the dining room surprised him. A dozen tables for four shined in the yellow glow of a large crystal chandelier. Gold utensils lay next to the ornately decorated plates rimmed with gold. *I think I won't have pizza*, Joe said to himself. The menu had no prices on it.

The fare lived up to the Ostaria's reputation, though Joe did not remember a minute later what he ate. The meat was so tender that he did not worry about scratching the plate with his knife. After the fruit and cheese, del Piave brought up business.

"Joe, do you think you could translate a book for us?"

"It would depend on the book, sir, and how soon you need it."

"The text is easier than most of the material in my letters. It's a presentation book about our holding company. The kind you see on coffee tables. You would tell us how long it will take, and we'll base the production schedule on that."

Joe glanced at his mother and back. He had no idea how long such a job would take. *But I can figure it out*, he thought.

"I guess I can do it. May I see it first?"

The cavaliere smiled at his mother. "I knew I would like him, Nancy. He's a natural – and a careful businessman." He turned to Joe. "Of course. I'll have a copy sent over tomorrow." He held his hands out, suggesting they rise. "Shall we?"

The meal ended in the traditional way, with espresso in the bar and a walk. They strolled easily downstream along the river. The rain had not started back up. Other groups of Romans walked in the clean evening air.

Del Piave did most of the talking, but Nancy and Joe found him interesting. He talked about the changes in his city, about growing up before the Second World War. They compared the evening to walks by other rivers on other evenings: the Seine in Paris, the Thames in London, the Nile in Cairo. They agreed that the Tiber held a special charm this night. The city lights reflected on its slowing moving water. Headlights moving steadily in opposite directions on either bank set up a visual rhythm on the water. They paused on a bridge to admire the scene before turning back.

"This has been a delightful evening, Pino," said Nancy as he held the door of the taxi for her. "Thank you ever so much." Joe noticed a flash in the sky across the river.

The cavaliere bowed to take her hand. "It —"

A deep thump shook the night air over the noise of the traffic. They felt the impact of the explosion coming at them. The businessman slammed his hand on the roof loudly, shouting at the cabbie, "*Vai! Vai! Presto!*" Go! Quickly!

As the cab burned rubber heading into the street, Joe turned to look through the rear window. Flashing red and blue lights bounced off the clouds and the water. Sirens echoed off the river as the cab pulled into the traffic headed upstream.

"What was that?" Nancy asked, her face pale.

"Car bomb." Joe was surprised that his own voice was so calm.

"How do you know?"

"I've heard it before." Too late to catch himself.

"You what?" Nancy shouted, swinging to face him. Joe told her about the bomb in September. He finished as the taxi pulled up in front of their building. Nancy stopped on the sidewalk and stood there while he paid off the cab. When he turned around, she was shaking, with her arms wrapped around herself.

"Why didn't you tell me before?"

"I don't know. It didn't seem worth bringing up." He started toward her, but the rage and fear on her face terrified him.

Nancy took several deep breaths. She fumbled in her purse for her keys. Joe left his hand in his pocket around his keys and let her take her time. He was taking slow breaths himself. The Cavalieri Hilton across the street shed more light on the scene than the streetlamp.

"We should go home," she said, looking a little dazed.

"We are going home." He started toward the door.

"I mean back to the States. It's getting dangerous here." Joe stopped.

"Mom, it's dangerous everywhere. You just said yourself that we couldn't take an evening walk like we just did in Washington or New York."

"Yes, but – "

"I don't want to move." Joe turned and planted his feet apart. "At least not before I leave for college."

Nancy sighed. "I'm scared, Joe. The work and worrying about whether you're okay while I'm gone is wearing me out. And now this."

"It might be mostly the work, Mom. You haven't had a proper vacation since I started high school."

Nancy looked at him for a while, then smiled. He saw the tears welling in her eyes. "You're right, son. Let's take that trip to England as soon as school is out. We've talked about it long enough." But she was deep in thought as she opened the door to the apartment.

# 10. Friendship

"BYE, MOM. SEE YOU LATER."

Nancy watched Joe's scooter roll down the street as she waited for the number 96 bus on the corner. The sun caught his windblown sandy hair, making it blonder. Her heart skipped a beat for the umpteenth time since he had bought the Vespa. It was natural enough to worry about him as he rode off to school alone, but watching him deal with the terrors of modern life, perhaps better than she, filled her with a jumble of emotions.

Her neighbors on the corner and the passengers on the bus did not help matters. All conversation focused on the bombing the night before. A car had exploded outside the Palace of Justice, across the river from the Ostaria dell'Orso. No one had claimed responsibility yet, so everyone argued for their preferred terrorist group. Nancy sat quietly, breathing slowly to calm herself.

"Buon giorno, signora bella!" Luke Arland's voice surprised at her as she walked into the café between the bus stop and their office building.

"Good morning, Luke," she said. "Your accent is getting better."

"Grazie." He beamed.

"But don't call me *bella*, please. It sounds like a clumsy pickup line."

He bowed, still smiling. After they finished their coffees, they walked to work. Neither spoke in the elevator. The receptionist greeted them both. Luke responded in Italian cheerfully; Nancy nodded and went straight to her office. While she hung up her coat, he stood at the door.

"I don't think I've ever seen you bring a storm cloud to work. Is everything okay?"

Nancy flared her eyes at him. Then she took a deep, slow breath.

"Fine." She smiled at him. "As for your Italian, at the rate you're going, we'll have you translating the board correspondence before Joe goes to college."

"I thought I would have to fight you for that."

"No way. When the time comes, I'm pulling seniority on you." She considered his silhouette, then shoved aside the thought. "New jacket?"

"Yes. You're the first one to notice, or at least, the first one to say anything. But the idea is to stop standing out like the new guy on the block, isn't it?"

"It looks good on you." Nancy picked up the papers in her inbox and held them, waiting for him to leave. He gazed steadily at her with an intensity that did not match his easy smile.

"Thanks. Hear about the bombing last night?"

"Yes. Luke, I really need to finish these before the ten o'clock meeting."

He tipped his fingers to his forehead in a casual salute and went to his own office.

The weekly staff meeting took rather longer than usual to start. Nancy did not participate in the general speculation about the bomb at the Palace of Justice. She felt relieved when Moretti finally called the meeting to order. The business took less time than the chatter.

After the meeting, Nancy called Maria Grazia into her office and asked her to close the door.

"Maria Grazia, when did I last take a holiday?"

"I could check, signora, but I am sure you took one week three years ago." She tilted her head with a motherly look, clearly indicating it was time to do something about that. Nancy found that ironic, considering how much younger her secretary was than she.

"So long?" Nancy gave Maria Grazia a sheet of notepaper on which she had written down some places in England. "Could you make arrangements for Joe and me to be gone for the last two weeks in June?"

The secretary scanned the list. "No problem, signora. I can do the company paperwork and make the bookings for you too. Since you want to go to England, would you like to tack your holiday on the end of the quarterly meeting in London?"

"Excellent idea. Thank you."

As Maria Grazia left, Luke came in.

"Join me for lunch?"

"Is this social?"

"Only partially. I get low blood sugar about the middle of the day. Food helps."

"Okay, I guess, but I need to finish the Santorini report to Richmond before I go home today."

"My report to New York on Santorini is almost done. We can compare notes as part of the agenda." He held his hands out in a gesture of innocence. "I promise not to carry you away."

Nancy gave him an eye roll.

"Meet you in reception at twelve thirty. Do you know where you want to eat?"

"Table's booked. See you at twelve thirty."

Nancy sometimes hated his self-assurance, and sometimes she liked his attention. She wondered what was so important that he needed a meeting outside the office.

Luke's role in the company did not fit the usual organization chart. Officially the vice president for Strategy and Investment, he served mainly as a liaison between the Italian subsidiary of Smithson and the New York office. The people in New York stayed close to the major Wall Street investors. Although Smithson's world headquarters was in Richmond, Virginia, the money was in New York. She and Luke worked together to avoid disconnects between Richmond and New York. She knew that he also had impressive negotiating skills, which his lack of Italian (or any language but English) had blunted.

She liked Luke. *Hell, everybody likes Luke,* she thought. She found him personable, pleasant, trusting, charmingly naïve, and smoking-hot. It wasn't fair that he was a coworker. *Easy, girl. He's a sexy bachelor, and you're the mother of a teenager.* She was not sure why he put on the charm with her, but she carefully fended it off.

Two hours later, they were seated outdoors at the Taverna Giulia. To keep things short, Nancy ordered grilled fish and a salad, Luke the penne al pesto. House white wine.

"So, what do you need to discuss?" As they waited for their food, she sipped her wine.

"You tell me." He tipped his glass toward her. "You're out of character today."

Nancy bristled. "How would you know? You only met me in August."

"People tell me I'm good at sizing people up. You are arguably the most consistent, levelheaded person in the company." He took a sip of wine. "I also work more closely with you than anyone else. I can't help noticing details. Something's bothering you."

"It has nothing to do with work; I'd rather not talk about it."

"Fair enough, but in case you haven't noticed, I would like there to be more than just work between us."

"And in case you haven't noticed, I don't do office romance." She took another sip of wine. "No offense. Frankly, I wish you weren't a coworker."

"I'm not talking romance. I'm talking friendship."

Nancy arched her eyebrows and gave a small laugh. "Now *that* sounds like a pickup line."

He chuckled. "I guess it does." His expression leveled out. "Still, I wish I had someone I could confide in, someone I could trust."

"Is there something bothering you?"

"As a matter of fact, there is. I have wanted to ask you for some time now: how have you managed to live here in Rome for so long? Every week since Christmas, I ask myself if this job is worth it. Sometimes I just want to pack it in and go home."

"I never suspected."

"My dark secret: I'm not the happy-go-lucky guy everyone thinks I am."

"Perfectly normal." Nancy smiled at his surprise. "Ever heard of culture shock?" He shook his head. "It's the disorientation that happens when you leave your hometown or home country. It can be worse if you go to a place where you don't speak the language. The symptoms can range from mild homesickness to clinical depression. It hits hard between three and six months after arriving."

"Did you go through this?"

"I moved around a lot as a child, so I never established a 'home culture.' But every time we moved, I found myself missing the last place a lot during the first year."

"Is there a cure?"

"Learning the language and having something interesting to do are the best antidotes. You naturally see the good in people, so you'll learn to appreciate Italy faster than most Americans."

"I hope so. Thanks."

They both fell silent while the waiter brought their food.

"*Buon appetito*," said Nancy.

"*Grazie. Altrettanto,*" he replied with a smile. Thank you, same to you.

After a few mouthfuls, he asked, "Don't you ever want to go back to Richmond?"

She put down her fork and looked away for a long while.

"Yes." She picked up her fork and stabbed some salad.

He let the silence hang, waiting for her to fill it. She met his eyes.

"Every day," she said, then paused. "But I can't yet, and it's not as if I don't like it here."

"What keeps you here? After what you've done with Smithson Italia, you could write your ticket to the head office."

"Personal reasons." She paused again. Inside, she was desperate to unload her fears. *Why are his eyes that color? I can't get enough of them.*

"Joe?"

Nancy blinked, then nodded.

"Maybe after he leaves for college, there won't be as much to hold me here."

"There are fine high schools in Richmond."

"Sure, some of the best. But it's unbelievably disruptive to move as a teenager. Rome is Joe's hometown. I can't change that now."

He thought for a moment.

"Let me guess. The bombings aren't just yesterday's news for you."

Nancy smiled, but he saw the fear in her eyes. "Damn you, Luke Arland. I wasn't going to talk about it." She took another sip and spilled some wine putting the glass down. "You're right. The bombings are scaring the hell out of me. What's worse is that Joe is taking it better than I am. Last night, we were down by the river when the bomb went off. Joe recognized it before I did. It turns out he was one block away from the Via Bissolati bomb in September. Then our maid's brother died in the Quinsana bombing in Milano. I'm scared for myself and for Joe. I wonder how important keeping him in one place for high school is compared to the danger."

Luke reached out and put a hand over hers. She closed her fingers tightly around his thumb.

"What does Joe say?" he asked.

"It isn't any safer anywhere else."

"And?"

"And he's right, dammit. But it doesn't make me feel any better. It's a mother thing.; you wouldn't understand."

"Why not? I had a mother."

"You're making fun of me." She pulled her hand back.

"No, I'm not. Last time I saw my mother, my parents were waving goodbye as I left on the troop train. I'll never forget her face. My father was all wistful pride, but my mother was scared shitless. That's the face in my dreams – and my nightmares."

"I'm sorry." Nancy reached back for his hand. He squeezed.

"Not your fault." They sat silently for a while longer, then Luke looked at his watch. He waved for the bill.

"I promised not to carry you off. We have our Santorini reports to finish."

# 11. Tennis

"ARE YOU STILL SURE you can handle a full-sized book?"

Cavaliere del Piave's thick eyebrows and his height, even seated, put more fear in Joe than perhaps the man intended. Behind his desk, with the view of the city out two picture windows and surrounded by the space and light of his office, the magnate exuded power more directly than in the intimacy of dinner the week before. "Business letters are between me and my correspondents. This book has to cut a *bella figura* – make the group look good – to the world."

"I think so, sir." Joe gripped his hands together below the level of the desk, where del Piave could not see them. "If I have any difficulty, I will certainly call you immediately, hopefully in plenty of time for you to give the job to someone else."

"I sincerely hope that won't be necessary. I like the work you have done for us."

The conversation took place in the corporate headquarters of Gruppo del Piave. They spoke in Italian, which was more formal sounding than English. Del Piave addressed Joe with the *tu* pronoun, which adults use with children, and *padroni* with employees, while Joe used the *Lei* denoting respect for elders and employers.

The man continued. "Your mother must countersign as required for transactions over 100,000 lire, but the contract is between us. We'll pay you 800 lire per page; half on delivery, the balance upon approval of the reviewer. You can keep the typewriter and the dictionaries. I added two weeks to the timeline you gave me. Your deadline is the twenty-fifth of July, typed and hand-delivered to my office. Is that understood?"

"Yes, sir." Joe signed the three documents. He placed the original with one copy in his backpack. Del Piave put the other copy in a desk drawer. "My mother said she would sign it this evening. I can bring it by tomorrow or Monday, as you prefer."

"Monday would be fine." He stood, indicating that the interview was over. Joe got up and shook the businessman's hand. Del Piave smiled. "I hope this goes well. I would enjoy doing business regularly with a young man like you."

"Thank you, sir. Arrivederci."

Del Piave pressed a buzzer as Joe turned, and the secretary, a man in his late twenties, appeared and held the door. With a smile and a word of thanks, Joe made his way down the hallways lined with Roman statues and frescoes from the Renaissance to the wide marble stairway leading to the entrance. The portiere nodded approvingly at the Vespa as Joe drove off.

൯൪൪൪

Traffic was light getting home. The Friday before Palm Sunday was the first day of Spring Break. Many had left town to spend Holy Week and Easter with relatives.

Joe heard the phone ringing as he came home. Angela answered it.

"For you, signorino. Your mother."

"Thanks, Angela." He put the handset to his ear. "Yes, Mom?"

"I'm glad I caught you. Luke and I are getting out of a meeting at the Hilton. Would you like to join us in the coffee shop?"

"Sure. Be right over." Joe dropped his backpack in his room and went to the bathroom to wash his hands and face. As he combed his hair, he thought again how grateful he was that his suit was not sweaty and dirty.

As far as he knew, Luke and his mother never met outside the office. When he walked into the coffee shop, they were seated at a table but had not ordered yet.

Nancy asked for a glass of wine, and Joe took a *chinotto*, the traditional citrus soft drink. The latter intrigued Luke, so he ordered one too.

"This is an interesting taste, Joe. An adult soft drink."

"It's not very sweet, so it makes a good aperitif."

"Well, TGIF," said Nancy, holding up her glass. They clinked their glasses.

"I guess the conference was successful?" Joe said.

"Not a conference," she said. "More of a progress meeting with our European affiliates. I'm ready for the weekend."

"Speaking of weekends, Joe, you never answered my question about tennis. I can't talk your mother out on the court either." His mother must not have mentioned their conversation.

"Come on, Luke. You're the jock in the office."

"And you need to get out of it more," he countered. "Why don't we meet every other Saturday or Sunday. We'll keep it fun and easy."

"I don't know," Nancy said. "I try to spend weekends at home. Monday to Friday is such a rush for us." Joe sensed her instinctive push.

"I'm talking about both of you. What do you say, Joe?"

"I think I'd like it, sir."

"Nancy, why don't you play? I've read the stories. Rising star in the US Lawn Tennis Association, then you disappeared."

"I lost my partner." She stared at the Eternal City through the picture windows.

"I'm sorry. I forgot."

"Don't worry about it. Little things like this make me wonder if I ever will."

"Let's try, Mom. I did say I wanted to learn."

"Well, okay." She punched Joe on the shoulder. "I have a different reason to play now. Might be fun." He thought her smile was a little forced, but he also thought that Luke could not tell.

"Great," said Luke. "Let's start simple. I'll meet you both here tomorrow at about two. I have a dinner engagement, so we'll stop on time." Nancy sighed so softly that Joe almost missed her expression of relief.

ଔଔଔ

"Mom, it's just a tennis lesson for me." Joe stood there as Nancy fretted over a half-dozen outfits laid on her bed. "You already play, so it shouldn't be a big deal for you."

Nancy stopped. She sighed and sat on the bed. "You're right. It shouldn't be a big deal, so why am I a nervous wreck? I haven't played since your father died. This all feels very strange. Does this make any sense to you?" She reached for her purse on the dresser.

"You promised me not to smoke in your bedroom."

"I know, Joe, but –" She got up to take her purse to the study, looked at her watch, and threw the purse across the room. "Dammit, Joe, why did I let myself get talked into this?"

He walked up to his mother and put his arms around her. She buried her face in his shoulder, trying not to cry or scream. Then she hugged him so hard, he almost couldn't breathe. He felt her tears dampen his shirt.

"Mom, it's not that important. I can go tell him you can't make it."

She stopped crying and stood back. "No, Joe. You and Luke are right. I must play tennis again. Remember what your father said after you fell off your bicycle and broke your arm?"

"He made me ride again as soon as I got out of my cast."

"Right. And look how you recovered. You're fearless on two wheels now."

She went to her dresser and got out a tennis outfit from the bottom drawer.

"Another outfit?" Joe asked.

"No. *The* outfit. I wore this the last time we played before your father got sick."

☙☙☙

"Hi, Mom. I just started the water," Joe shouted as he heard the apartment door open.

He had left Luke and Nancy on the Cavalieri Hilton tennis courts, having hit more balls in his first lesson than he expected. He also discovered his upper body muscles, and they were not happy with him. After watching them play for a set, he offered to start supper and walked home.

Secretly, he wanted to see if the Tiger Balm in the medicine cabinet still worked. He had not used any since he ran track last year.

Nancy tossed her tennis bag into her room and came into the kitchen. Except for a stray hair or two, she did not look like she had played two hours of tennis. Not even scuff marks on her shoes.

"What's for supper?" she asked, stretching her arms behind the back of her head.

"*Pasta al mistero.*" Spaghetti with mystery sauce. Joe winked as he tossed some dried oregano in the saucepan without looking. She sniffed the vapors coming out of the pot.

"Uh-oh, creative heartburn."

"C'mon, Mom. It's not that bad."

"Of course." She mussed up his hair. "What's in there besides tomatoes, sausage, onions, and garlic – anything green?"

"Not yet."

"Okay." Opening the refrigerator, she pulled out some fresh parsley and a green pepper. She chopped them up while Joe stirred his sauce and put the water on to boil for the spaghetti.

"Did you say you had the book contract?"

"Yep. I told Mr. del Piave I'd return it to their offices on Monday."

"Great. How do you feel about it?"

"A little scared. It's so long, although I know I can translate it." He took the cutting board of green things and poured them into the sauce. "You need to countersign the contract. On your desk."

She rinsed off her hands and went to the study. When she returned, the pasta was al dente. Joe poured it into the strainer while she set the table. Nancy wolfed the first few bites, then stopped herself.

"I can't remember when I was this hungry."

"You were pretty impressive on the court with Mr. Arland. Burned a ton of calories for sure."

"Don't tell my shoulders and legs. They won't believe you."

"You too? The Tiger Balm in my bathroom didn't dry out from last spring."

"Thanks. What about you? How did it feel?"

"I was surprised that I returned so many balls. I thought I'd be swinging at air the whole time. Probably beginner's luck, but it felt good."

"You're more of an athlete than you give yourself credit for."

"Are you glad you played?"

"Yes, I am. Thank you for pushing me yesterday. I needed this."

"So, can we do this every other week? Shouldn't I be practicing?"

"Since we're both sore, we should go back out there tomorrow afternoon, then maybe again on Tuesday or Wednesday. Not let our soreness go stiff on us."

"Lucky me, two teachers."

They ate in silence for a minute or two.

"About the book translation," Nancy said. "Aren't you worried that our vacation trip to England will interfere?"

"No. I have almost a month after we get back."

"What about your other client? Aldo's father."

"Lanzera Edilizia submitted its bid last week, so I'm all done – for now."

"Okay, I won't nag you. The book is between you and del Piave."

"I know, Mom." Joe did not stifle his annoyance as well as he meant to. "Let's talk about the trip. Will we drive or take the train?"

"Surprise, I think we'll fly."

"Wow! How'd you swing that? Plane tickets cost a bundle."

"True, but the company will fly me to the quarterly meeting in London. If you can stay out of trouble for a couple of days, I could afford your part of the fare for the price of two train tickets."

"Neat-o. I've always wanted to fly."

"For some of us, it's not so hot."

"You mean you get airsick, too?" His mother had not come out of their cabin for most of the voyage to Europe in 1956. SS *Independence* was a big, stable ship.

Nancy nodded. "C'mon, let's do the dishes. Then I want to change. We should go walk these screaming legs of ours."

ଔଔଔ

The following Monday, Joe found a large, heavy package at the portiere's window when he came back from dropping the contract off at the Gruppo del Piave offices. Inside were two brand-new dictionaries and a black Underwood typewriter, made of steel, like the boxy typewriters in black-and-white movies and history books. He checked the plate on the front: "U.S. Patent Reg. 1896."

He hefted it out of the box and set it on the table. *Dr. Mom was right.* His arms did not ache as much today as they had Sunday morning. They had played easily, just to keep moving. Joe missed more returns at first until he figured out that Nancy was serving him a predictable rhythm he could match.

"Angela, *vieni a vedere*," he called. Come see. As she came from the kitchen, he pointed. "What do you think?"

"Oh, signorino, that's a nice one. My sister Vittoria worked on a machine like this in Florence before she got married."

"Your family works all over the country."

She shrugged. "We go where the work is. My father and one brother can run the farm. Is this the typewriter from the businessman?"

"Yes."

"Seems he could spring for a newer one."

"I thought so, too, but maybe he thought I needed the American keys. See, it has J, K, W, and Y in different places because we use those in English and but not in Italian."

"Perhaps. I can't type, so it would not make any difference to me."

"Me neither, but the cavaliere del Piave doesn't know."

She patted his arm. "You have fun with it, signorino, I have fish to fry." He laughed. "What's so funny?"

"Oh, nothing, except that in English, *pesci da friggere*, 'fish to fry' also means to take care of business, which is exactly what you're doing."

Angela waved her hands in mock disgust and went to the kitchen, smiling.

Joe arranged some room on his small desk for the machine. He tried typing something, but after getting the keys stuck twice, he moved the typewriter to a table and finished his homework by hand.

After lunch, Joe considered the typewriter, then took out a writing pad like he always did. He picked up the del Piave book. It measured about twelve-by-fourteen inches and contained many beautiful photographs. Gruppo del Piave SpA executives would give it to important investors and others that the group wanted to do business with. The group owned many companies. Joe recognized the one that built the Cavalieri Hilton Hotel across the street from his home.

The Italian resembled the language in del Piave's letters, so Joe used the same kind of English style. He did not need to look up much in the *Dictionary of Economics and Banking,* which del Piave had given him. *This will go quickly.* He finished drafting the introduction before his mother came home. After supper, he translated some of the material in the Arland file, while his mother worked in her study.

This latest batch was giving him trouble. The letters back in the fall were straightforward, but now there were more letters enclosing clips from magazines and newspapers about Smithson. Most had handwritten notes in the margins. Some of the articles had sidebars from other articles in the same magazine stapled to them, with hand-drawn circles around pictures or words in the sidebars. Joe had not had a chance to ask him about these strange excerpts, but Luke had told him the handwritten stuff was important because it gave him background.

The abbreviations drove him nuts. The sidebars, especially, were full of acronyms about politics and the military. Some, like NATO (North Atlantic Treaty Organization) and MEC (European Common Market), he knew. But SIFAR, MI6, BR, B-M, and FT-9 stumped him. Some abbreviations were hand-written and not always easy to read.

He could not ask Luke about them yet. The few that he had gotten turned out to be in Italian, which explained why Luke did not recognize them. Joe deciphered OTAN (NATO in French or Italian) by himself, so he kept working on these alone too.

*I need help*, he thought, *but this stuff is confidential.* That the company would consider a magazine article confidential annoyed him, but he guessed that the handwritten material made it secret.

*And why did Smithson Italia care about this?* Luke said his mother had read it all, but Joe wondered if she had read the clippings or these very pages with the handwriting on them. They were from national magazines. He wished more than anything that he could ask her, but, for now, his promise seemed more important.

Joe wrote out the words and abbreviations in alphabetical order. He would carry the list around without the clippings and check libraries and experts until he found answers.

*I'll start with the history teachers*, he said to himself as he compiled the list. *Brother Mark is a current-affairs freak. He could get me started.* It was almost midnight when Joe finished the four-page list and went to bed.

# 12. Research

IT WAS ONLY EARLY MAY, but it had been hot since mid-April. Attention spans shriveled, and teachers' tempers flared as interest in academics melted. Brother Roger relaxed the dress code to let students leave their jackets in their lockers, but sweat drops still ruined handwritten assignments and lecture notes.

Joe stayed behind after history class to show Brother Mark a half-dozen of the acronyms.

"I found these in magazine articles, but I can't figure them out."

"I recognize all but this one," the monk said. He took a pencil and wrote the expansions in Joe's notebook. "They're about military intelligence."

"Spying and such?"

"And armies and terrorism. It's been in the news a lot. These are specialized abbreviations. Where did you read them?"

"Different places. *Panorama*, *Espresso*, and magazines like that."

"Are they like *Time* and *Newsweek*?" Brother Mark had arrived from the United States in time for the school year.

"Yes, Brother. Where could I find out about this?"

"I'd check the USIS library at the embassy. Try 'intelligence,' 'military science,' and 'counterespionage' in the card catalog. I think 'terrorism' is too new an idea to be there yet. That should give you a start."

"Thanks." The bell rang, and Joe ran to his next class.

At dinner, he told his mother that he wanted to go downtown the next day after school to look things up at the USIS library.

"Leave a note for Angela," she said, "so she knows not to expect you. I'll save your supper."

ଔଔଔ

The holdings in the USIS library did not impress as much as the marble statues or the wall friezes of the sixteenth-century palazzo that housed it. Most of the military books covered wars in ancient Greece and Rome. Joe did not even find much on World War II. The few volumes under "espionage" were about spies during the American Civil War. The place had served him well for school reports, but he felt discouraged looking for current material.

"Most of these things are too recent to be here yet," explained the librarian when he showed her his list. "There are always new books coming out, but they don't show up here until a few years after publication. Try the British Council library. If they can't help, you'll need to go to a bookstore and buy new books."

The British Council library near the Piazza di Spagna held even less than its American counterpart, but he did find a book about espionage in general. It was interesting reading and helped him understand why countries spy on each other. He did not decode a single abbreviation, however.

Two weeks later, Joe rode downtown to visit bookstores. First, he tried the English-language Lion Bookshop on Via del Babuino off the Spanish Steps. It carried things aimed at tourists and fiction from British and American authors, but nothing that he found helpful. Next, Joe checked the big Libreria Internazionale near the Termini train station, which sold books from all over the world.

"May I browse?" he asked the manager. "I can't buy anything today."

"Sure, go ahead. You can't fill in your gift list if you don't know what's here."

Relieved, Joe darted into the stacks. He found several books on NATO and Communist politics and two on the rising threat of terrorism. Noticing some abbreviations on book jackets was a lucky break. He went back to the front.

"I like all your books, especially the ones on the third stack back, but I can't ask for them all. They seem so expensive. Why is that?"

"Mostly taxes and customs duties," said the manager. "There are some used bookshops in the neighborhood, but you won't find anything on current affairs."

"Don't the books ever go on sale?"

"No, never. If you need more than one or two, you'll need to go to England. They have the best prices in the world. Not much help, is it?"

"Actually, it gives me an idea. Thank you, sir." Joe left the store more excited than ever about the coming vacation.

He picked up two more acronyms in the newspaper the next day. He scanned the major daily newspapers in English and Italian more carefully now, as well as the magazines that published the articles with Luke's letters. He had the Arland file almost finished by the weekend.

The material in the files provided background for what Joe was seeing in the press each week. *Whoever collected this stuff is seriously worried about the bombing groups.* That triggered two more worries: had his mother in fact read all this, and why was it in the files at Smithson Italia, a pharmaceutical company?

Joe found none of the abbreviations in the handwritten notes. They only appeared in the margins of articles or letters where someone had circled the name of a person or group. He concluded that they must be code words for those people. Or someone used them for telegrams or telexes.

He had done enough, though he wished that he had found everything. He copied out the list of abbreviations, so he could look for the missing items. *Besides, I don't want to look these up again later.*

He typed one short letter, making a copy by placing a sheet of carbon paper between two sheets of typing paper. But it took so long, he did the rest of the job with a ballpoint pen. He pressed as he wrote, and the carbon paper made a nice dark copy on the bottom sheet. Now he would have the copies for reference as he researched the abbreviations.

"Mr. Arland," Joe said on the telephone. "I finished the whole batch you gave me."

"Great, Joe, but I thought you were going to give them to me as you finished them."

"There were so many abbreviations that I couldn't finish any of them. When I got those figured out, the letters and enclosures all came out together."

"Next time, call me. Some are internal company codes you wouldn't find. The others aren't important."

"I guessed as much. Sorry."

"Don't worry about it. I have another pile for you. Can you do these a little sooner?"

"Yes, sir. School is out."

"I forgot. We can meet during the day. Are you at home?"

"Yes, sir. Do you want to pick this up today?"

"Perfect. How about the hotel lobby in a half hour?"

ଔଔଔ

"I have a luncheon appointment back downtown," said Luke as he walked into the lobby. "Here's the second batch." They exchanged the thick folder for the finished file.

"One letter is typed, but it took so long, I went back to handwriting everything. Also, there's a list of six abbreviations I couldn't find. If you tell me which ones you don't know, I'll keep looking for them."

"This is fine, Joe. Thanks for trying to type, but like I said, we can type them. I would rather see the translations back any way you can get them."

"Yes, sir. Remember, we're going on vacation this weekend, but I should be able to work on some of this while we're gone."

Luke started. "I don't want your mother in on this. You both need the vacation."

"She won't know. The book for Mr. del Piave gives me a reason to be translating. This is interesting. I don't mind."

"Well, okay." Luke put the translated files in his attaché case. "Just remember our deal: the stuff for your mother first. How many pages was this?"

"Fifty-nine, sir."

Luke took a one-hundred-dollar bill from his wallet.

"Ever see one of these?"

"No, sir." Seeing the face of Ben Franklin, Joe felt a rush. "This is thirty-five hundred lire more than you owe me."

"You'll lose that much exchanging it at the bank, so it comes out even. I would have had to go change it myself, but I'm running late. Is that all right?"

"Yes, sir! I wish I could keep it."

"I think you'll see a lot of Mr. Franklin. You're a good worker." He shook Joe's hand and turned to walk quickly out the door.

Joe looked about himself nervously as he walked from the hotel lobby past the boutiques to the bank branch. But no one robbed him.

# 13. First Flight

"C'MON, SLEEPYHEAD!" Joe's mother shook him gently. He struggled from a groggy fog. It was dark outside his bedroom window. Then he remembered why he had taken so long to fall asleep. He leaped from the bed wide awake as his mother headed for the kitchen to put out breakfast.

Two hours later, the sun was still struggling to clear the Apennine mountains when the taxi left them at Rome's domestic and European airport in the suburb of Ciampino. Nancy could have asked for a company car, but she did not want the driver to have to go to work that early. They carried their luggage into the lobby and joined the line.

"Is the line always this long?" asked Joe after a few minutes.

"This one is moving well for a change," she answered. "As long as we don't have a passenger with a problem ahead, we'll be done in ten minutes."

After checking their bags and collecting their boarding passes, they went through opaque doors into the duty-free customs zone, then past a newsstand to the waiting and observation area. The place resembled a large bus terminal. Plastic seats bolted to the floor faced the window.

The view made up for it.

"Mom, this is an Air Force base."

"Yes, the airport, such as it is, sits on the edge, like a small civilian corner."

Joe watched military jets from various NATO countries land and take off on the runway on the other side. He recognized a Fiat F-91, Italy's newest fighter-bomber, from its short, stubby shape. A half dozen of them were lined up by a hangar on the far side of the airfield.

"Mom, look at that! Those are American." He pointed to a twin-engine jet that dwarfed the other fighters already on the ground. "That's an F-4 Phantom. It deployed this year on the *USS Enterprise*."

"You seem to know a lot about military aircraft," said Nancy.

"They're all over the news magazines. Hey, that one's a navy plane!" The roar from the military jet shook the windows. As it turned, its engine exhaust aimed at the civilian terminal. The building shuddered.

"God, they're loud!" Nancy held her hands over her ears.

"Here come some more." Four of the powerful fighter-bombers landed in quick succession. All conversation stopped, and the waiting passengers turned to watch the Americans taxi to their parking places near the F-91's. They moved in formation, turning into their final position together.

They did not shut down, but with their sides to the building and their engines idling, conversation resumed. A flight attendant from British European Airways came out and announced that the flight to London had been called during the interruption, and would everyone please follow her. Another attendant by the door collected their boarding passes as the passengers filed out onto the tarmac.

Outside, the military and civilian jets and turboprops filled the air with a pounding din. Joe and the others tried to hold their hands over their ears, but their carry-on luggage made that impossible.

The line turned right. The first attendant led them to a BEA Comet jetliner. Joe had seen them in the sky, easy to identify with the four engines inside the wing up against the fuselage. He was not ready for its size up close. They climbed the ladder to the door, as high as the second story of a house.

When the flight attendant closed the doors, the cabin seemed to fall into a hush. As he sought his seat number, walking down the center aisle, Joe could hear conversation over the engine noise.

"Here it is, Mom."

"Good, near the front. I find the ride is rougher in the back. We stow our bags above and buckle up." She pointed to the seat near the window. "You go in first. I've seen the view."

"Thanks, Mom." After swinging his backpack onto the open shelf, Joe slid in. He found the two ends of his seat belt. "These look like the belts in the new American cars at the embassy."

"Actually, the car makers copied the airplane belts. Do you know how to work them?"

"Sure." He made it click and cinched it down. Then he took out the colorful brochure of safety instructions in an elastic pouch in front of him, while the other passengers found their seats and flight attendants edged around them, helping the less experienced get settled.

Joe studied the booklet. He felt a nervous excitement as he read the procedures for sliding out of the plane if it went down over water. He located all the exits and tried to imagine what it would be like to open one in the dark. He practiced holding his knees in the brace for an emergency landing.

"I hope we won't need that position," his mother said with a smile.

"Just checking it out."

"If you don't mind, I'll take this." She reached over to remove the airsickness bag from Joe's literature pouch. She carefully arranged both bags, so she could grab them in a hurry.

"You already know you'll be sick?"

"Well, I held it down once before. These jets don't bump around as much as the propeller-driven models."

"What if I get sick?"

"I'll give it back, and we'll order more."

Joe heard a change in the sound outside. They began moving. Nancy pushed her head against the seat back and breathed deeply. *Wow*, he thought, *she is really afraid of this*. Then he noticed that he was gripping the armrests with white knuckles; he put his hands in his lap.

He looked out the window. The traffic on the Via Appia ran parallel to the airport. The relative motion of the cars disoriented him a little. The vibration of the aircraft throbbed up through his legs and rear, a strange, new sensation.

A flight attendant began giving instructions over the public address system. Joe thought she went too fast, considering how many Italians might not be able to follow her English. Then she repeated everything in excellent, unaccented Italian.

At the end, she asked if there were questions. About half the people raised their hands. The flight attendants moved from chair to chair, showing people how to work the seat belts and pointing to the instruction booklets and the little doors for the oxygen masks. He was glad not to be the only new passenger on board.

The jet came to a stop. After a while, the buzzing under Joe's seat changed as the engines sped up. The plane moved again, turning onto the runway, opposite the way they had taxied. He forced himself to take deep breaths to stay calm.

The engines accelerated even more, but the plane did not move. The attendants sat out of sight. Joe wondered if something were wrong. He saw nothing but grass at the edge of the tarmac. The wings and fuselage shook, but still the aircraft did not move. The turbines reached a deafening pitch as they strained against the brakes. Joe did not understand why everyone was so calm. His mother was the color of marble, pressed against her seat back. She smiled at him weakly.

"Mom," he said. "Why –" The pilot released the brakes.

Joe's body slammed back into the seat. He gripped the armrests so hard his hands hurt. He closed his eyes and prayed. He made the Sign of the Cross, and he was not alone.

The tarmac seemed much rougher than Joe had expected. The engine noise penetrated every cell of his body. *We have to be running out of runway.* He wondered if he should be in that brace position. His heart raced, and he alternately opened his eyes and shut them again.

Suddenly, Joe's stomach reached under his seat. He tried to pull into the brace position, but the cabin swung backward and tilted up. He held his breath to keep from hyperventilating. The cabin pitched back even more. Odd pieces of luggage and debris rolled down the aisle. The sunlight changed in irregular flashes through his window. Bright. Dark. Fuzzy. Bright again.

Joe's throat closed. He squeezed his eyes shut.

He felt his mother's hand on his. He turned his head to the left. She was still pressed to the chair, but there was more color in her face. She smiled.

"You okay?" she asked. He nodded. The tension drained from his body like a bucket of water sliding off his clothes. The takeoff noise abated after the landing gear retracted with a crashing thud. The roar was steady now, but tolerable.

He looked out the window.

"Wow! Look at those clouds go by. This is better than driving fast in the mountains."

"At least there are no hairpins turns or oncoming trucks here."

Pain shot through Joe's eyes as they broke into the blazing sunlight above. He squinted to take in the expanse of puffy, snow-like billows.

"Incredible! Like snow or magic, like you could walk on it." He found the sunglasses in his pocket and put them on. He stared at the white wonderland that continued to fall away below them.

At last, the jet leveled off. It was not as sharp as the takeoff, but Joe's mother clenched her teeth and dug her nails into his arm as she pressed back into the chair. He forced himself not to wince or cry out. She let go of his hand when she got control back. He pointed at the window.

"It's beautiful. Is it always like this up here?"

"More often than not, but sometimes there are terrible storms on the way up here. And once I flew through a high-level storm all the way. It terrified me and most everyone else."

"Do you always have this much trouble, Mom?"

"Yes, Joe. This is a good trip. See? I still have my breakfast."

"Why do you do this?"

"I try not to whenever I can, but with the packaging subsidiary we bought in England, I have to fly to London at least every three months. Business is picking up everywhere. I'd lose my job if I couldn't be at the meetings where they need me."

"Is it worth it?"

"Yes, it is," she said. "Sometimes I tell myself we need the money. But we could live on less. Fact is, I like my work. After you leave home, I may go back to the States for a job without so much travel, but we don't want to move now, right?"

Joe shook his head. The flight attendant announced that the passengers could unbuckle their seat belts and move about the cabin but that they should keep the belts loosely fastened when in their seats. Joe chuckled at the rush of clicking noises as many stood and stretched or visited their friends and relatives.

A flight attendant came by and gave them a menu card and served them drinks. They both chose Coca-Cola.

"We get lunch?" He marked the ham sandwich on his card.

"It's supposed to be a snack, but it's more like a cafeteria lunch." She checked the pasta.

After the attendant passed by, they sat in silence for a while. Nancy read a newspaper. He looked at the in-flight magazine from his literature pouch. It was not as interesting as the Arland file in his suitcase.

The food came about twenty minutes later.

"Joe, I got the strangest call from Luke Arland just before we left the house."

Joe's pulse went up. He made himself concentrate on opening his mustard.

"Oh? Why strange?"

"He started out asking for you, which was odd enough. When I said that you weren't home, he chatted with me about unimportant office matters. I could tell that he was agitated about something."

Joe did not answer. *What am I in for now?*

"Why would he want to talk to you?"

"I don't know, Mom."

"Have you been seeing him for anything?"

"Well, he did ask me to translate a couple of letters a while back. Simple stuff, really. Is that okay? I didn't think to ask you about it."

Nancy thought for a moment. "It didn't hurt your schoolwork, so I guess it's all right. I wonder what he's up to – sometimes he acts so odd."

Joe kept silent, focused on eating his sandwich. His mother seemed thoughtful but said no more about it.

He had just about gotten used to the steady flying when the plane began banking to the right, straightening, and tilting to the right again.

"Why all the turns?" At that point, the captain announced that they were beginning their descent to London's Gatwick Airport, and the seat belt sign came on. Those walking around hurried back to their seats.

"The plane makes a racetrack pattern coming down. It takes a while, but it's gentler than the takeoff." She nodded to the window. "You'll be able to see when we break below the clouds."

Joe stared in amazement as the clouds lifted above them, revealing southern England as a patchwork of different shades of green. First, he made out the motorways, and then the highways and villages, and the urban sprawl that had to be London. He saw the landing pattern as they flew back and forth over the country west of the capital.

The captain made a cryptic announcement that caused the cabin crew to take their seats. Outside, the ground came slowly closer. Soon, Joe saw tarmac under the wings. His mother pushed against her seat again, but her face was not as pale as on takeoff.

Only when the nose tilted down slightly did Joe realize that they had landed. Some passengers applauded, but they were interrupted by the scream of the engines and a sudden deceleration.

"What's that, Mom?" Joe shouted. His seat belt pulled him back as his body tried to move forward.

"I'm not sure how it works," she said, "but someone explained to me that the pilot reverses the turbines in the engines, which works like an enormous brake. Some racket, isn't it?" She no longer seemed troubled, now that they were on the ground. The roar lasted less than a minute, then they taxied calmly to the edge of the airport terminal.

Debarkation was the reverse of boarding in Rome, but the lines at Customs and Passport Control were longer and slower. The separate entrance for British citizens had no line. He found the variety of people in line and the advertising displays in the terminal so interesting that he jumped with surprise when his mother tapped his shoulder. They showed their passports to the Frontier Police and went to claim their suitcases.

An hour later, they were checking into a suite in the London Hilton, still known locally as the Great Western Royal. Nancy's meetings would be held there for the next two days. They had plenty of time to change and take in some of central London together.

# 14. England

"I WANT TO CHECK OUT THAT BOOKSTORE." Joe pointed to a store occupying most of its block on Piccadilly, its dark wooden façade contrasting with the pastel stuccos and white columns of the rest of the building.

"Okay. I'll meet you there in a half hour. I want to see about Maria Grazia's present." Nancy had ordered a wool suit for her, the nicest gift she had picked for anyone in the office.

Joe stepped into Hatchard's and stopped at the door. All the way back, tightly packed bookshelves rose to the ceiling, even along the stairways to the upper floors, and disappeared into the far wall on each level. He remembered pictures of places like this in old prints and photographs, but to see it live, and full of shiny new books took his breath away.

"Good day, sir. Is this your first visit?" Joe jumped at the kindly sound. A man with wire-rimmed spectacles and a tartan waistcoat beamed at him, looking like an old print of Father Christmas.

"Oh, yes, sir," Joe stammered. "It must be obvious."

"If I may say so, young man, what is obvious is your love of books." He came around the counter. "May I help you find something in particular?"

"Well, yes, no, I mean, I think I want to see everything, but I do have a list here." Joe searched for his sheet of abbreviations while explaining that he hoped to find current information on military affairs, intelligence, and perhaps terrorism. The bookseller seemed to understand exactly what he needed and led him upstairs.

"I dare say that we are seeing increasing interest in these things. We may have to expand our modest holdings and bring them to the ground floor. Several titles are already on various best-seller lists." He paused at the top of the stairs to consider the wide-eyed youngster in front of him.

"Would you care for some tea?" he asked. "You may be here a while."

"Thank you, sir, but no. My mother will be meeting me here in a half hour."

"I will watch out for her. Perhaps we could take tea when she arrives or at a future visit. Here is the section that I think you will find most useful. Out to the corner and along the far wall. There are more titles on the next floor up if you still can't quite find what you need." He turned and stepped lightly down to the main floor.

Joe raced along the shelves. This was a bibliophile's cornucopia: books on spy craft, intelligence organizations, glossaries of military and intelligence terms in every major European language. He settled on a small military dictionary and a NATO glossary. Between them, he found all the words on his list. He went back to the books about terrorism and Interpol, the international police organization.

"Joe, where are you?" Nancy's voice reached him from the ground floor. He glanced at his watch and jumped up; he had been lost for more than an hour. He grabbed his books and ran downstairs.

He found his mother and the bookseller going over new releases on the European Common Market and a scholarly monograph about a new line of drug research. A tea service sat on the counter. The man winked at him behind her back.

"Would you like that tea, now, young man?"

"Yes, thank you."

He poured a cup and put it near Joe on the counter, then slid the sugar bowl toward him.

"Mom, I have to come back here. This place has everything." He took a sip of the tea.

"I think you're right, Son. I could go broke in here." She turned to the merchant. "Do you publish a catalog?"

"Yes, we do, ma'am. A complete edition quarterly."

"Excellent." She gave him a business card. "Could you add us to your mailing list? I can pay for the extra postage."

"Not necessary, ma'am. Most of our list members are on the Continent." He tilted his head toward Joe. "Shall I mark it for an additional copy?"

"Yes, thank you."

Joe put his books near the register. "Mom, I still would like to come back."

"We will, but I need to buy more traveler's cheques before we do."

Joe fished out his wallet of American Express cheques. He only needed one. "I love this place."

England was famous for its rain. They barely made it to the hotel before the skies opened. The shower settled into one of those steady downpours that could go on for days. They chose to stay indoors, Nancy attending meetings and networking with her colleagues, Joe translating the del Piave book as fast as he could.

During the day, Joe worked in the suite. The rain beat steadily and gently on the windows, setting up a comfortable rhythm as he wrote for hours. The translation did not pose any problems, and he made notes as he went along, rather than stop.

After dinner each night, they took refuge in the reading room. A nineteenth-century railway hotel near Paddington Station, the Great Western Royal retained the somber air of a gentlemen's club downstairs. Overstuffed armchairs with floor lamps and heavy writing desks with brass lamps allowed quiet comfort and a change of scenery. They could order coffee or drinks and relax in more space than their suite.

The second evening, Joe pushed back his chair and exhaled a sigh of relief. Seated in an armchair, his mother looked up from the monograph that she had purchased at Hatchard's.

"Finished?"

"First draft. I have to check everything I wasn't sure of and fix the mistakes."

"That's the way writers produce books, Joe. The hard part starts now."

"It still feels good to get through the whole thing once."

Nancy closed her book. "I'm supposed to be the one working. My meetings end tomorrow, and you've been burning overtime on this book."

"But I like this work."

"I like my work, too, especially since you freed me to concentrate on it. But neither of us is getting a break. Tomorrow, I think we should take a tour of the city. Then I'd like to get out of London."

Joe packed his work into his backpack.

"Could we see Stonehenge?" he asked.

"Sure. We could tour the Salisbury Plain and the Cotswolds, then come back."

They checked out two days later and took the train to Salisbury.

ଔଔଔ

"I want to stay here, Mom. It's raining."

"It's always raining here. That hasn't stopped you before." Her gaze went to the backpack, hastily stashed against the wall by the bed. "Have you been working again?"

"A little."

"I thought you finished" She started toward the pack. "What's in there?"

He leaped in front of her, grabbing the bag. "Just the book, Mom. Leave me alone."

"Joe, this isn't healthy. Are you hiding something from me?"

"I want something that's mine. And I don't want to go out."

Nancy sat. He hated that. Whenever she got upset or ready to argue, she would sit quietly and think, never taking her eyes off him. He sat on the bed, clutching his backpack and staring at the floor. This time he would not crack. He would make her talk first.

Time slowed down. A car with a defective muffler drove by, whining like an overworked lawn mower. The chambermaid knocked on the door down the hall, then went in. Water ran through the pipes. *She must be cleaning the bathroom*, he thought.

*How quiet this English village is.* Rome was a crowded, bustling metropolis. He was surprised by how such plain sounds stood out here. The sound of his mother chuckling softly snapped his attention back to the room. He scowled.

"Go ahead and say something," she said. "You win."

"What's so funny?"

"It's hard to stay angry with you. You're so much like your father and me."

"Not that again, please."

"Then let me ask this. Do you really not want to go out, or do you want to work on what's in the backpack more? – no, ten seconds."

Joe almost burst for five seconds. This was another trick he hated, mostly because it worked. When the time was up, he said, "I want to work."

"I understand. I know you mean it, but we promised ourselves a real vacation. We both know we need it."

"I know."

"Are you afraid of missing your deadline?"

"I still have the typing."

"But you can't type here anyway."

"Well –" He stopped. *She's going to find out about the Arland stuff if I keep talking.* "Okay. Let's go."

"Leave the backpack closed until we get home?"

Joe nodded. He held it a little closer.

Nancy stood. Stopping at the door, she faced her son still sitting on the bed. "Joe, relax. I won't look inside. Is there anything in there besides translation work?"

"Just my camera and film."

"Bring it and leave the rest behind."

Hiding Arland's translation work from his mother bothered Joe even more than getting caught in class last year. It was bad enough with the guilt. Now he worried about what his mother and her company might be involved in. He did not know for sure what she did when she traveled, or whether it was a normal amount of travel or not. Nancy did not discuss the details of her work outside the office. As often as not, he learned about it from the newspapers.

On the way to the cab stand on the corner, he forced himself not to dwell on it. The taxi driver offered to accompany them to visit Stonehenge and bring them back. He included a stop at Woodhenge, which was much smaller and not as well known.

On the way to Stonehenge, the rain stopped.

Accustomed to the man-made wonders of the Eternal City, Joe thought Stonehenge looked like a natural formation. That humans without tools and advanced machinery laid massive stones on one another with such precision amazed him. He appreciated the grandeur and acoustics of Salisbury Cathedral, but Stonehenge left him breathless. He walked among the stones and noticed how the sun traced a line between them. When the summer solstice came, that line would run perfectly up the center of the avenue at sunrise.

They tarried in Stonehenge for an hour, after which their driver took them about two miles north to what resembled a park. Woodhenge was a collection of concrete cylinders in circles, sitting in an open field with no signs or the usual collection of hawkers and tour buses. Down the slope, sheep grazed in the tall, uncut grass. The driver explained that the two henges were roughly contemporary. Woodhenge had been built with large timbers. Concrete forms provided a visual indication of what had been in the holes.

The next day, they took a train to Bath, where Nancy hired another cab to take them through the Cotswolds. In a little village on the edge of a ravine, Joe pointed to a sandwich board on the sidewalk.

"Hey, Mom, read that fast three times."

"Bar Food. Barfood. Barf food." They laughed so hard they had to wait to calm down before going into the pub. The substantial and delicious fare went well with the locally brewed beer.

They spent an extra day in London, walking the downtown area, and collecting the shopping being held for them. Both felt rested and glad that they had left everything normal behind for a few days.

☙☙☙

Joe gripped the armrest again as the plane plunged. The storm had struck south of Milan, only an hour from their destination. Lightning flashed outside, turning the portholes of the airplane cabin into big strobe lights. It froze the passengers in a variety of poses of terror and misery. He thought of the engravings in the illustrated copy of the *Inferno* at home. *This would be one of the circles of Hell if Dante were alive today.*

His stomach fought for a chance to fill a bag like his mother. Most of the passengers were using the airsickness bags and pushing the call buttons for more. Joe gave his bag to his mother and hoped he would not regret it.

A flight attendant worked her way down the aisle with a handful of bags. She gripped seat backs and luggage racks, falling twice by the time she ran out of bags and started back to the galley.

The storm stopped as suddenly as it had begun. The attendant walked back to the galley for a cart to collect the trash and the bags. Joe looked out the window. The plane came out of the clouds. Below him, the Agro Pontino lay between the Alban Hills and the Tyrrhenian Sea in a vast patchwork of farms. Sunlight bathed the countryside, with no hint of the cloudy horror behind them. Despite the lingering smell of vomit, he breathed deeply as the fear drained from his body.

The captain announced their descent to Ciampino airport. He reminded the passengers about their seat belts, but they were already as tight as they could be.

Customs in Italy proved a lot smoother than in Great Britain. The finance guard at the exit asked them if they had anything to declare and marked a big X on their suitcases with chalk. Joe wondered what that accomplished, but it was soon forgotten. He was grateful to be on the ground and home again.

Nancy went into the ladies' lounge while Joe went out to the sidewalk with a porter. They had accumulated several boxes of shopping in London.

"Joe! Over here." Luke Arland stood near a company car.

"Mom'll be right out," Joe said as he pointed out the car to the porter.

The driver and the porter put the luggage and boxes in the trunk while Luke and Joe waited at the door to the terminal.

"How was the trip?"

"It was fine going up, but on the way back, we hit a storm. Most of the passengers got sick."

"Sounds lousy." Luke glanced around. "Did you translate any more of the files I gave you?"

"Some. You didn't tell me what you wanted first, so I started on the letters. Is that okay?"

"Fine." Luke's tone made Joe uneasy. "Did you go over the rest of it?"

"Yes. I found a book in London, which should help me figure out the NATO gobbledygook."

"Do you know what this is all about?"

"Company business, but I don't understand all the other stuff. Did you find any mistakes in the last batch?"

"No, it was perfect." Luke relaxed. He put his arm on Joe's shoulder. "You keep working the way you have. Oh, here comes your mother."

She had her normal color back, and she had fixed her hair and makeup. The driver held the rear door for her. Joe sat up front while Luke went around to sit with Nancy.

"Joe said the trip back wasn't fun."

"Terrible. I may never fly again."

"We got the Procter and Gamble contract after you called from London. I – "

Nancy held up her hand to cut him off. "That call was the start of my vacation. I don't come to work until Monday. Can it wait?"

Luke laughed. "Of course. What are you doing this weekend?"

She put her hand on Joe's shoulder. "If my son isn't *too* thoroughly sick of being stuck with his mother for two weeks, I'd like to hang around the house and do nothing at all. But we'll think of something."

Joe twisted around. He thought he caught a flash of disappointment in Luke's face, but the man recovered.

"Well, del Piave called several times. Maria Grazia said he wants to do dinner again. Is he work?"

"Pino is work. I'll return his calls Monday."

Nancy kept her word. The farthest they strayed from home for the next two days was to go to church on Sunday. Saturday morning, they rose late and walked across the street to the Cavalieri Hilton, where they enjoyed a couple of sets of tennis and had lunch overlooking the Eternal City. They ate at home the rest of the weekend.

Nancy read the journals and monographs she had bought in London. Joe read *The Art of Espionage*. They played *Monopoli* (the Italian version of the board game) Saturday night. Sunday afternoon, they walked to the Parco della Vittoria at the top of the Monte Mario.

At the park, they each ordered a granita from the refreshment stand at the overlook. Rome looked like the scale model of the ancient city at the Museum of Roman Civilization. The cars on the Via della Giuliana and in the Piazzale Clodio moved like lines of ants. In the far distance, the white buildings of E.U.R., the 1939

World's Fair that never happened, rose from the dark green trees of the open country southwest of the city. The late afternoon sun washed over the palazzi and churches of the city, painting them gold and pink.

A rush of emotion enveloped him.

"Mom, this really gets to me," he said, choking slightly as he took in the view.

Nancy stood closer to him. "Beautiful, isn't it?"

"It's more than beautiful. There's something special about this city. I've never felt like this about a place."

"Like you've come home?"

"Yeah, that must be it. It feels good to be home."

# 15. Gruppo del Piave SpA

MONDAY MORNING, Nancy went to work. Joe cleaned up breakfast. Then he laid out his translation of the del Piave book on the dining room table. He put a Beatles record on the phonograph and sat down to correct the draft. The text was much simpler than the letters and articles he had been working on. He adjusted the style to be less stuffy and more like the coffee table books he had seen in bookstores and people's homes.

He jumped when the front door opened.

"Mom?"

"*Oddio! che sorpresa!*" God, what a surprise! Angela came into the dining room. "I forgot you would be here, signorino. Your voice startled me."

"You surprised me too. I'm working on the book for the cavaliere. You go on with whatever you were going to do. If you need this table, I can move."

"Mondays I usually clean, but with you two gone, there's not that much to do." Angela headed for the kitchen. Joe followed. "I thought I'd go out and do some shopping now that there are mouths to feed. Will you be home for lunch?"

"I hadn't thought about it. Today and tomorrow, yes, but probably not every day."

"Well, I'll shop for every day. It will help if you tell me the night before or leave a note if you go out before I get here in the morning."

"I can do that."

When Angela came in the next morning, Joe was still working on the book. She went straight to the kitchen with her bags.

The fourth Beatles record ended, and the player shut off. Joe got up to turn the stack over. He heard Angela's voice singing an aria from an opera that he could not remember the name of. The sound of knives on cutting boards and silverware on tabletops, mingled with the tragic lyrics of the song, made him chuckle. He left the record player off and finished correcting the last two pages of the book.

He had just brought the heavy typewriter from his room to the dining room table when Angela came out to call him to lunch.

They ate in the kitchen. A light soup, followed by a *fettina di manzo*, a thin slice of beef, and a salad.

"You're going to spoil me, Angela." She beamed. "I'm used to sandwiches and school lunches."

"It will be simpler most days, but I don't do American-style sandwiches. You know that."

After lunch, he went back to the dining room table and started typing up the draft translation. Two hours later, he had pages one and two done. Then he called the Liu house. They were home this summer, a lucky break because the family traveled whenever they could.

"Benny, I need help, bad. I need more typing lessons." He explained his predicament.

"You got a typewriter?"

"Yeah."

"Portable?"

"Kind of. I mean, I can strap it to my Vespa on a board."

"Well, I can't teach you, but I could show you again. Meet me at the gallery."

Among other things, Mr. Liu imported Chinese artwork and artifacts and sold them all over Europe. He had a store off the Via del Tritone in the heart of downtown Rome. Joe borrowed a board from the portiere and strapped the Underwood typewriter to the seat behind him on his scooter. Traffic was mercifully light. Benny stood outside.

"I have an idea," he said. "Dad wants me to mind the store with Jerry Yang for two weeks. I don't have to be in the showroom unless Jerry must go somewhere, which isn't often. We could work up in the office area overlooking the shop."

"Hasn't Jerry worked for your dad for a long time?"

"They came out of China together. Jerry's been with the Liu family since before I was born."

Setting themselves up as a team, Joe walked around the large teak table covered with dictionaries and paper, dictating from his manuscript. His friend typed furiously, never looking at the keys. So it went from morning until supper. For lunch, a trattoria next door served cheap, home-style Roman cooking.

☙☙☙

The next day, Joe came back before Angela left.

"Signor Arland called you many times today, signorino," she told him. "He asked that you call him before five." She gave him a number on the back of a cash register tape from the supermarket. "I hope I got it right. His accent is so thick, I had trouble."

Joe smiled. "It *is* pretty bad, isn't it? That's his office number. I'll call right away. Thanks."

Luke was out, but Joe left a message that he would be home and would try again tomorrow from the Galleria Cinese if necessary.

The phone rang fifteen minutes later.

"You're hard to get hold of." Joe explained the typing project at the Liu store. "Somehow, I thought my translations would move a little faster in the summer when school let out."

"Everything is moving faster, sir. I finished the review of the del Piave book in one day, and the typing may take a week or so. My friend Benny and I are working as a team. You told me always to work on the stuff from Mom first. Wouldn't the del Piave book count like that?"

"You're right, Joe," Luke said with a hint of resignation in his voice. "I just feel like I'm missing something, and it might be in the letters you have now."

"The book is due on the twenty-fifth. The letters will go quickly after that."

"Okay. It's all we can do."

Joe felt bad about not being able to share the Arland work with his mother, but after the scene in the Salisbury hotel, he would never bring any of that material out at all. He even resolved to translate in the reading room of the USIS library downtown rather than risk having Angela or his mother discover those files.

As Joe had predicted, they had the book in a rough typescript after five days. They began trading places. Benny mostly stood over Joe's shoulder as he tried to imitate Benny's ten-finger style. Joe still looked at the keyboard when he typed more often than not, but with some nagging, he got better each day.

Joe started checking the typed draft alone, passing the pages to Benny to type for the final draft.

"Hey, Joe," said Benny after about a half-hour. "What's this sentence on page three: 'The Monte del Piave firm don't –' It's 'does not' and what don't they do?"

"Oh, hell, the second half of the paragraph is missing."

"What's worse is you didn't catch it going back over it."

"What am I going to do? I can't be skipping big chunks like that."

"Why don't I read it too?"

"Take too long." Joe got up and stretched. He walked to the rail and looked down. Cases filled with gleaming jade jewelry and hand-carved ivory spheres made the gallery look like a museum instead of a shop. Jerry Yang sat by the cash register, reading a book. Joe watched him for a while because readers who moved their lips fascinated Joe. Though Jerry did not read out loud like the old man on the number 8 trolley, he obviously read slowly.

"That's it!" Joe turned back to the table. "Remember what Mr. Santoro said in English Composition class about checking a story."

"Yeah, read it aloud."

"Let's each take half and read, moving our lips to slow down. Then the mistakes should stand out."

This pass only took two more days, and they took turns typing the final draft. Joe used three times as much paper as Benny, but he never would be as neat as his friend. On the twenty-third and twenty-fourth of June, Joe read the final typescript aloud to Benny, then called the del Piave offices to let his client know that he would deliver the next day.

The next morning, Joe put on a fresh suit after his mother left for work. He bundled the typescript of the translation in wrapping paper and stowed it in the compartment of his Vespa. Then he drove to the del Piave building near the Circus Maximus.

In the courtyard of the palazzo, del Piave's secretary was waiting for him.

"The cavaliere would like to see you, Signor Lockhart," he said in a clipped Northern Italian accent. They walked up the marble staircase to the businessman's office. Del Piave rose and came around his desk.

"Joe, what a pleasure!" He motioned to the couch by the coffee table. Joe set the package down. They sat together. The secretary produced a Swiss Army officer's knife and carefully opened the bundle. He called out for coffee, while the businessman inquired about Joe's mother and the trip to England. Joe knew that the bar had been forewarned because the delivery boy showed up in less than a minute and a half. After the young lad left the tray with the cups of espresso on the coffee table, he departed with his tip. Del Piave turned to the stack of typewritten pages and began turning them over.

"I am excited to have the translation ready so soon," he said.

"But it's only on time, sir, not early."

"Ah, yes. We are so accustomed to deadlines that slip, that I expected you to need more time. I only dared to hope for this after you returned from England and your mother told me that you had finished the first draft. Now I will be able to turn it over to the production people before the *Ferragosto* holidays instead of September. Thank you."

"You're welcome, sir." Joe felt a little uncomfortable being praised for just meeting the deadline. "It should be error-free. I had a friend review it with me more than once."

"We have hired a professor from the British Council for the revision, and the production department has professional copy editors. I am sure that it will be fine."

"I enjoyed this, sir. Let know me if you need anything else translated." Joe smiled.

"Certainly. As per the contract, the check for half the amount is waiting downstairs. We'll send the balance as soon as the reviewer reports to us."

"I hope that you still intend to let me see the galley proofs. I am told that little things happen when typesetters are not working with their native language."

"Of course. Armando here will keep you informed as this progresses."

Del Piave stood, and Joe jumped up with him. They shook hands. Armando escorted Joe to the main office on the ground floor, where an envelope was waiting. After shaking hands with the secretary, he walked to his scooter. He drove with special care back to the Cavalieri Hilton, lest anything keep him from depositing the check safely. Then he parked the Vespa under his apartment building and went home for lunch.

# 16. Things get complicated

AFTER LUNCH WITH ANGELA, Joe collected his backpack and rode to the USIS library to work on the Arland file. He had been excited to deliver his first book translation, but now he felt a different excitement: the anticipation of jumping back into the mess of papers he found so challenging.

*Where do I start?* Joe looked at the folder of clippings and correspondence in front of him. He would need one of the long, massive oak tables all for himself.

Sorting the material into piles, it felt like seeing it for the first time. There were weekly news magazines like *Espresso* and *Panorama*, letters from various Smithson offices in Germany, France, England, and Northern Italy, a couple of postcards from islands in the Indian Ocean, and what seemed to be articles copied from encyclopedias or scientific journals.

*This will be tough, and he is already acting like it's late.* His heart sank, so he stood back for a minute. Then he noticed the librarian staring at him, a stern-looking woman of about forty. Joe walked over to her station in the center of the room.

"*Scusi*," he said. Excuse me. "It is quiet today. May I spread out on the table? Just for a while. I promise to pull it all together if anyone comes, or as soon as I figure out where to start."

The woman's face softened. "You let your summer assignment catch up with you, didn't you?" Joe shrugged, letting the misunderstanding go. "That's okay," she continued. "You should see this place in late September before school starts – packed with procrastinators. Go ahead. I'll let you know if it becomes a problem."

"Grazie, signora." Thank you, ma'am. He went back to the table. Now he had an excuse for working at the USIS library so much.

"Libraries and bookstores are your natural habitat," his mother had told him once.

Spread out, the piles intimidated him less. He decided to review all the printed material chronologically first, then go through the correspondence. That should bring out the common subjects. He would translate the letters first.

Like the magazine clippings in the first folder, the items in this one were not related. He found news reports on events between 1960 and 1966, everything from the Olympics in Rome to the assassination of John F. Kennedy, and one about paramilitary groups training at a Soviet naval base in Syria. The articles about new drugs from Smithson and its competitors came as no surprise. The travel pieces about vacationing in the Seychelles made him scratch his head. After taking about an hour and a half to scan them all, he got up to stretch.

He was not going to be able to interrupt all this to go home for lunch. Angela should not have started cooking yet. He checked his pockets for a telephone token: he had one left. Catching the librarian's eye, he held up the slotted brass slug and pointed to the payphone outside the door. She nodded. When Angela answered, he told her that he would eat downtown.

"Thank you, signorino," she said. "Everything can keep until tomorrow, and I can use the fresh greens for supper."

Back at the table, Joe scanned the letters. They covered the same period as the clippings, but only two of them referred to the enclosures. Those two enclosed articles about Smithson products. Otherwise, there seemed to be no connection between the letters and their attachments. Almost all the letters introduced new drugs in markets throughout Western Europe, but mostly in cities in Italy.

The encyclopedia-looking excerpts came from *Farmacologia,* a scholarly journal on pharmaceuticals. Each one reported the results of clinical trials of new medicines, most of them drugs mentioned in the magazine articles. The journal issues were not new: Joe recognized two of the products as over-the-counter remedies sold in stores.

Hand-drawn circles in different colors appeared on the clippings. *Curious*, he thought. *They don't relate to anything or even to each other.* He assembled the material in chronological order, keeping any printed material with the correspondence that mentioned it. He counted forty-five carbon copies on onion-skin paper in the folder.

By now, his stomach was growling, but he could safely restack the piles in order. He did that and put everything in his backpack before making his way to the grill in the basement.

ೞೞೞ

Back at the big table in the library with a happy stomach, Joe slipped a piece of carbon paper under the top page of his writing pad and started to translate.

The first few letters from 1960 concerned the introduction of a new drug without a name. They never named the disease either, except by reference to meetings held earlier. Growing up with a pharmaceutical company executive, he knew that the firm shrouded new initiatives with more secrecy than a military weapons project. It wasn't until after development moved far enough along to file patents that the company's tight security would relax enough to admit that they were working on something.

By 1962, things had progressed enough for the product to get a name: Securinon. After translating about six letters, Joe decided to hold on to the whole lot until he finished them. They kept referring to each other, and he needed to change word choices in earlier pieces as he discovered new insights in the later ones. *Mr. Arland won't be thrilled by this. If I can't finish a draft by the weekend, I'd better give him a call.*

At four p.m., he quit, having written first drafts of the bodies of half the letters. A square with a number at the top and the bottom of each translation would tell Luke or any potential typist what letterhead, salutation, and closing to use. He packed his bag and headed for the

Vespa parked on the sidewalk. The librarian smiled and returned his "arrivederci" as he left.

When he got home, he let Angela know that he would work through lunch every day. She assumed he was doing schoolwork too.

"You be careful you don't become a stressed-out manager like your mother, signorino. She skips too many lunches. Lunch is the main meal for a reason. It breaks up the hard day to make it bearable. Remember that."

"Yes, Angela. Just this week. I'm enjoying the hamburgers at the American grill. It's fun for a change, though I wouldn't eat them every day."

She snorted something about barbarian cuisine from German cities like Hamburg and gathered up her shopping. Joe laughed gently and went to his room to put away his backpack.

After washing his face and hands, Joe went to the living room. While reading *Hornblower and the Hotspur* in the living room, he listened to Rossini's *L'italiana in Algeri* on RAI, the State Radio. He wished that he had read the Hornblower books before taking Modern European History. It would have helped him understand the whole Napoleonic era better. Hatchard's catalog listed all the novels both by publication date and in the internal order of the series. He was following the fictitious naval hero's life and enjoying himself immensely.

The opera ended on the hour. *Giornale Radio,* the news, came on.

Two more bombs exploded that day, one at the Ferrari plant in Modena and another outside Camp Ederle in Vicenza, home of US Army Southern European Command (SETAF, Joe now knew). The pundits came on to guess which right- or left-wing group was responsible. Most agreed that a Communist cell would target the American installation, but opinion split on who would bomb the iconic racing car factory. It generally took weeks for the police to figure it out unless someone claimed responsibility. That did not stop the commentators from filling the program slot with speculation.

*This will surely start another discussion about going back to the States,* he thought. He reached up and turned off the radio, just as he heard the front door open.

"Hi, Mom. How was your day?"

ೋೋೋ

On Tuesday, he came across two letters referring to some of the clippings about new drugs. These letters had circles like the clippings he had seen. He wondered about the circles as he worked. There were six different colors. He pulled out the older material and looked for circles. He found circles on only six letters. They were all recent. Each had only one circle, and each circle was in a different color.

"Securinon," the new drug under development, was circled in purple. That color in the clippings surrounded phrases like "D-day, launch-time, coordinated assault," and only occurred in articles about paramilitary operations or military movements, except for one group of words. Purple circled the words Rome, Turin, Milan, and Naples, each on a different piece of paper.

Joe leaned closer as he moved quickly through the file. Blue circled the word "Robbins" in one letter, then a photo in a *Panorama* magazine article. He recognized

General Ettore Arcibaldo, Commander of the Carabinieri Corps, Italy's military police. The general had retired since the issue came out. He was now running for parliament from a district in Rome.

Green surrounded "Production Department" in one letter and parts of separated words in clippings in a way that made no sense to Joe: Hofbräu (a German beer), Frankfurt-am-Main (the city) and "Carlsbad" in a story about the caverns in the American Southwest. Yellow, brown, and red did not make any more sense than green.

*I need to call Arland*, he thought. This time, he packed up his work and went to the Stars & Stripes newsstand to buy more telephone tokens.

Luke's line was busy. When Joe tried again, he got Luke's secretary.

"*Dottor* Arland is out," said Giacomo. "I expect him in about an hour. May I take a message?"

"Yes, tell him –" Joe paused. "No, Giacomo. Thanks, don't tell him anything. I think I'll see him tonight anyway. Don't bother him." They hung up.

Joe had not eaten. It was now almost one. He went to the grill and sat to think and eat. *If I don't know who's doing what, I should not worry about the circles. Once Mr. Arland has the translations of the letters, I won't need to do the articles unless he doesn't know what the file is about and asks for the clippings to be translated too.*

Feeling better, Joe finished lunch and went back to the library. He found it hard to concentrate. The later letters were much longer, some over six pages. He still had three to draft by four o'clock when he quit. Still, he thought he could do them in two days, so that night, he left a note for Angela that he would come home for lunch.

About eleven the next day, Joe picked up the last letter. Although in Italian, it was on the letterhead of the Munich office of Smithson's German subsidiary. As he read, his pulse quickened. He grabbed his pencil and wrote as fast as he could.

Dear Mr. Robbins:

As agreed in our meeting last March, all arrangements will be completed for the delivery by 15 June of this year. We will make final deliveries to all sales teams in Milan, Naples, Palermo, Florence, Venice and Genoa no later than 30 July. We will meet your team in Rome on 7 August for the formal launch of the new Securinon product...

By now, Joe knew that Securinon was a code word for a military operation of some kind, not a new drug. He threw down the pencil when he reached the end of the letter and pulled out his lists of words and colored circles. His heart was pounding.

*There's going to be a coup d'état on the seventh of August!* Rumors had been running in the press about a coup for almost as long as Joe could remember reading newspapers, but no one took the pundits seriously. Here was proof that it was really happening!

# 17. JOE REPORTS

JOE SCANNED THE LIBRARY to see if anyone was interested in him. The librarian was shelving books on the other side of the room. A college student was sleeping head down on a thick book two tables away. A gray-haired pensioner sat in one of the armchairs with his back to Joe, reading the *International Herald Tribune*.

Joe spread out his notes and the copies of past letters. His hands shook as he traced the path of circles in the correspondence and the clippings.

*What do I do now?* The only person he could think of who would know what to do with this was Doug Redwood's father, who was the FBI liaison in Rome. *His office should be here in the annex.*

Joe packed his bag and walked around to the heavy doors that he had held for Sandra so long ago. He checked the building directory across from the American newsstand concession. The FBI representative's office was on the third floor. Joe almost ran into the spacious lobby and up the broad staircase to his left. He took the steps two at a time and arrived at room 335 a little breathless. He knocked on the door and opened it gently. The office contained a mix of rich wooden furniture and US Government-issue metal file cabinets. The walls were a neutral color, with the ubiquitous portraits of the president and J. Edgar Hoover, the FBI Director.

His jaw dropped.

Sandra stood behind the desk in the waiting room, sorting papers. She wore a white angora sweater with a plaid skirt and had her hair in a ponytail. She gasped and beamed a smile as wide as the Mississippi.

"Hello, Joe, what a wonderful surprise. How did you find me?"

"I didn't know you worked here. You never told me."

"One of the reasons they like me. I don't blab about where I work." She winked and smiled.

"I'm looking for Agent Redwood. Is he in?" He thought her eyebrows sagged a little then perked back up.

"No, he's at lunch. Did he tell you to come?"

"No. An emergency came up. Will he be back soon?" Joe's stomach growled. He had completely forgotten about food until now.

"In about twenty minutes. You could wait or come back. He has a busy afternoon. Can I make an appointment for you?"

"I guess so. Can it be right after he gets back?"

"Yes, but only for fifteen minutes."

"Okay, thanks." He returned her smile. "You know Doug, too, right?"

"Of course. He likes your Vespa. I heard him pestering his father for one." The way she looked at him made the heat flow up Joe's neck to his ears.

"I hope it hasn't gotten him in any trouble."

"No. Just wishing. You don't need to stand there." She pointed to the couch behind the coffee table.

"Thanks, but I think I'll run down to the grill in the basement. I missed lunch, and I don't get burgers at home." He started for the door, then remembered Angela. "May I use the phone for a minute?"

"Sure." Sandra turned her telephone around on the desk.

Joe asked the embassy operator for an outside line and dialed home.

"Angela, I'm sorry. I got so busy at the library, I forgot to come home. Now I have an appointment here, and I can't make it."

"No problem, signorino. I'll make you eat it tomorrow." Joe could picture her smile. She always acted tough. "I hope she's cute!"

"She is, Angela." Catching himself by surprise, Joe looked at Sandra and blushed. Angela said goodbye, and he hung up.

"You're pretty fast with the Italian," Sandra said. "After a year, I'm still learning."

"I grew up here. It's no big deal for a little kid." Joe felt relieved that she had not understood the high-speed exchange with the housekeeper. "Have you eaten?"

"Yes, thank you."

"I'll be right back."

Down in the grill, he ordered two cheeseburgers and fries and paused after paying. Doug's father was eating at a table against the wall facing the entrance, reading the *Rome Daily American*. Joe walked over.

"Hello, Mr. Redwood."

"Hi, Joe." The agent pointed to the other chair at the table. "I was just finishing up. You can have the table."

"Actually, sir, I need to see you. Sandra gave me an appointment right after lunch."

"You interested in the FBI?"

"I hadn't thought about it. I came to show you something I came across that bothers me. I'm not sure what to make of it."

Agent Redwood glanced around the room. "Want to tell me here?"

"Probably not. It's a collection of correspondence I translated and my notes. I need to let you look at it and ask me questions."

"Well, finish your burgers. I'll wait for you upstairs. Okay?"

"Yes, sir. Thanks."

The FBI man took his tray to the counter, even though there were busboys cleaning up the tables. Joe watched him fold his newspaper as he headed for the stairs. He did it in one swift movement. Folded into a tight club, the paper would be easy to throw. In the movies, Joe had seen boys on bicycles delivering newspapers. Much as he had wanted to do that, living in a city of apartment buildings and news kiosks made the business model unworkable.

Joe ate fast. Agent Redwood was still talking to Sandra in the front office when Joe walked in.

"Come in, Joe, let's see what you've got." He motioned to his door.

In the large office, the afternoon sun picked up the reds of a hand-woven Bukhara carpet and gave the walls a pink cast. On one wall hung dozens of plaques and pictures, mementos of a career that spanned the globe and twenty years. It occurred to Joe that this assignment might be considered a reward for top agents.

Redwood waved at the six-foot-long conference table across from the desk. Joe emptied his book bag.

"Are you aware that I do some translating for my mother's company, sir?"

"Smithson Italia. No, but it doesn't surprise me. You're more fluent than some Italians I know."

"Thank you, sir." Joe arranged the letters in order on the table, with his code word notes next to each one. "There's a new vice president at Smithson, Luke Arland."

"I've met Luke." The FBI agent motioned for Joe to go on.

"Mr. Arland speaks Italian well enough, even if the accent is thick, but he doesn't read it fast enough to go through the backlog of files he needs to read. He's the only one in the office who isn't bilingual, and he said he doesn't want the others, especially my mother, to find out how weak his Italian is. So, he hired me to translate the stuff in the files that he can't read."

"I take it this is between you and him, and your mother isn't supposed to know."

"Yes, sir. Mom brings other materials home, and the deal is that I always do the official Smithson work first. It has taken a long time to translate some of this."

Redwood read the letters as they talked. He stood over the neat rows and read without picking them up.

"Are you sure your mother doesn't know about this?"

"If she does, she has me fooled. It's been the biggest strain in my life to keep this secret with Mr. Arland. I got in trouble in school and almost lost it on our vacation in England."

"This is *very* interesting, Joe."

"It all came together this morning when I translated the April thirteenth letter from Munich." He pointed to his draft. "Until then, I couldn't understand why all the military information and details about neo-Nazi groups meant anything to an Italian drug company."

Agent Redwood let out a low, long whistle. "Jesus, Joe, I think you've stumbled on something really big here." He leaned closely over the Munich letter. "This backs up indications we've been getting elsewhere about both the timing of a right-wing coup and about foreign leftist cells active in Italy."

"At this point, I knew I had to tell someone; you were the only person I knew who could tell me where to take it."

"You're in the right place, Joe. My job here, besides recruiting bright young men like you for the bureau," he winked, "is to fight terrorism and conduct counterespionage. A lot of the information the bureau uses comes from Italy, and it flows through my office. Classic international police work in action."

"Doesn't the CIA do that?"

"No. That's a common misunderstanding. They spy on other countries; we try to catch foreign spies working against the US."

"I guess your paths don't cross much."

"Not at all, unless there are double agents or moles involved. Then it gets complicated."

"I get it." Joe recognized the concepts from his recent readings. A double agent in the CIA would be a threat that the FBI would want to uncover. A sleeper or mole, a spy hiding in one's own organization, was every intelligence agency's nightmare.

"What about this stuff, sir? Is Mr. Arland in trouble? Should I take it back to him?"

"You must not give him *any* hint at all that you've seen me or anyone else with this. We need time to check him out and to check this information. He may be perfectly innocent. This looks like real company correspondence. Do you have any reason to worry about him?"

"I don't think so. He gets awfully uptight sometimes, but I can't turn his material around quickly and secretly when new correspondence comes in from Smithson."

"Okay, then. You keep up the work as normally as possible. Could I make copies of this?"

"That would take me a long time, sir, but I could do that for you. I'd rather not leave any of this behind as long as I have undelivered work."

The policeman laughed. "I meant we would copy it. Sandra!"

The secretary opened the door. "Yes, Mr. Redwood?"

"Show Joe here how to use the new Xerox machine. Poor lad has been hand-copying all this as he works. We need a complete set of it."

"Yes, sir. You have a meeting across the street." She and Joe gathered the papers on the table while the FBI agent collected his notes from the desk and put them in his briefcase.

"Sandra, I want Joe to be able to turn to someone with his material if something happens to me. Would you introduce him to Steve Wolcowski if he's in? Make an appointment for him if Steve is out, and I'll go along."

"Mr. Wolcowski will be at your meeting this afternoon. I'll set this up for later in the week."

Agent Redwood moved swiftly out the door, with an athletic grace that explained where Doug got his ability on the basketball court. Sandra led Joe to a small room next to the reception area. She showed him the shiny Xerox Model 660.

"I don't know how we won the Second World War without this," she said. She fed the sheets in one at a time. Warm copies spilled out slowly from the bottom of the machine. Joe peered in and saw the glow coming from a red-hot wire stretched across the paper path.

"Why doesn't the paper catch fire?" he asked.

"Special paper. Kind of expensive, but still cheaper than paying me to retype everything. And it copies the pictures and handwriting."

"Amazing." Joe put the originals back in his backpack. "Thanks. Could I come use the copier again?"

"Please do. We will need copies of all your work. Besides, I wouldn't mind seeing you in here again." Joe felt that heat under his ear again. He managed a small wave and left.

He floated down the stairs and out to where he parked his Vespa. The feeling crashed when he saw the clock outside the embassy annex. His mother would be home soon. He preferred to beat her back to take the spotlight off his own activity. He did not need any close calls like the scene in Salisbury.

He passed long lines of jammed traffic on the way home. About halfway there, he noticed a man on a Vespa 125 behind him. *Odd*, he thought. *People on larger scooters don't usually pass like that.* Joe caught a yellow light at the river, and the 125 ran the red. *Very odd*, Joe thought again.

The Vespa driver seemed to be of medium height, slim, with black hair and a pale complexion. Under the high cheekbones, and the sharp, aquiline nose typical of native Romans, he wore a dark leather jacket. That seemed too warm for a summer day.

Joe took a few turns among the buildings around Viale delle Milizie, heading first toward Piazza del Risorgimento and the Vatican, then back to the river and Castel Sant'Angelo. A bus crossed between them at Vicolo del Campanile. Joe switched back into an alley and slipped into the courtyard of an apartment building. Parking the scooter, he walked back to check the street. The stranger had stopped at the corner and was looking around. He finally drove up the Viale della Conciliazione toward Saint Peter's Basilica.

Joe pulled back into traffic and moved upriver through the side streets. He took the smaller back road that climbed Monte Mario rather than the Viale delle Medaglie d'Oro favored by most. That gave him a clear view of the street and sidewalks around his house as he approached. But he had lost the stranger.

"Ciao, Angela," he shouted as he let himself in. "Is my mother home?"

"Not yet, signorino."

He stashed his backpack in his closet and went to the telephone in the living room.

"Mr. Redwood's office." Sandra's voice bounced like her hair. He smiled at the image. "Hello, *pronto?*"

"Hi, Sandra. It's Joe. About the appointment with Mr. Wolcowski."

"Can you come in Thursday about ten?"

"Sure. Uh. By the way, I was followed coming home today."

"Are you sure?"

"I think so. This guy on a Vespa tailed me in and out of traffic from Piazzale Clodio. I even wandered around the neighborhood across from Piazzale Flaminio, but he was always right behind me."

"So, he knows where you live?"

"Not from following me. I lost him behind the Castel Sant'Angelo and took the back road up Monte Mario."

"Very good, Joe." The way she said it made Joe's ears get warm again. "I'll tell Mr. Redwood."

"Where is Mr. Wolcowski's office?"

"If you come here about nine forty-five, I'll take you there."

"Okay. See ya." They hung up.

The front door opened. The heels hit the floor in the entrance hall.

"Hi, Mom. How was your day?"

# 18. Burglary

TUESDAY MORNING, Joe stayed home. He called Luke Arland and made an appointment to meet at a café near the Smithson offices the next day. With the rest of the morning, he carefully proofread all his translations. So much was marked up that he decided to type up what he had.

Angela fed him the meal he had missed, as promised. She had turned the pasta into a cold salad, and the stew-like *spezzato di manzo* was as hearty reheated as fresh. After lunch, he went back to work in his room. He told her that he would not be home for lunch the next day. By the time Nancy came home, he had typed all the letters and half the clippings.

Joe finished typing the magazine articles the next morning after his mother left for work. About ten thirty, he gathered all the translations and the source files. He put everything in his backpack, along with a file folder and an oversized safety pin.

೧೩೧೩೧೩

Joe looked out for the stranger on the Vespa, but he was nowhere to be seen. *I hope this means they don't know where I live.*

He drove to Termini, the main train station downtown, where he put the full set of carbon copies and his handwritten drafts in a locker. He planned to visit the lockers at odd times during the week. The safety pin secured the key inside his bag, so it would not fall out accidentally.

Then he rode to the embassy annex. Sandra was busy with a delegation of visitors, but she pointed him to the photocopier. He made a set of copies, put them in a manila envelope, and marked it for Agent Redwood.

After lunch in the grill, Joe walked up the Via Veneto to his appointment with Arland. The Smithson executive was waiting at a table at the Café de Paris when Joe arrived. Joe ordered a double espresso and pulled the translations from his backpack.

"I hope you don't mind if I start typing these things. Since finishing the coffee table book for Mr. del Piave, I can type faster than I can write. Not pretty, but more legible. What do you think?"

"It looks good. This is a lot of material too. Can I write you a check?"

"Sure, as long as it's in lire, sir. Make it out to 'J.J. Lockhart'."

Luke had another thick file for him. Within a few minutes, Joe was on his way. No sign of the man on the Vespa 125. The main office of the Banca Nazionale del Lavoro was across the street from the embassy annex. Joe deposited his check, then crossed back to the USIS library.

He worked at the library for about a half hour until he realized that he was finishing the drafts faster than he expected. His dictionaries and his typewriter were at home. His mother never came home during the day, so he packed up.

Still a little nervous, he checked his rearview mirror often and glanced back when he made turns. Only a two-wheeled vehicle could have kept up, so he was reasonably sure that no one followed him.

The next day, Joe put on a light sport coat and a tie and rode downtown. He parked a block away from the annex and walked to the FBI office. Sandra was intent on some typing. Her face brightened.

"Hi, Joe," she said. "How's the word sleuth today?"

"Okay, thanks."

"Have you met Mr. Wolcowski?"

"I was his son's den chief when he was in Cub Scouts."

Sandra picked up a file and came around the desk. She squeezed his hand. "Come on, let's walk over to the embassy. Agent Redwood had to go to a meeting with the Italian State Police."

First Minister Steve Wolcowski was the senior professional foreign service officer in Rome. Joe and Sandra waited in the anteroom until the diplomat arrived from the ambassador's office. A tall, slender man with broad shoulders, he made Joe think of Clark Kent in the Superman comics.

"Hello, Sandra, Joe. Sorry I'm running behind a little. Won't you please come in?" He motioned to the door. "Claudia, would you please hold all my calls except the ambassador?"

Inside, he closed the door and paused.

"Please, sit down." Wolcowski took a chair around a coffee table across from them. "Joe, it seems strange to see you in civilian clothes. Louie likes you a lot."

"Thanks, sir. He's turned into a good patrol leader."

The older man leaned forward on his knees. "I've read Agent Redwood's file. We've been trying to crack this connection for months. This is the most serious crisis this country has faced since the Second World War, and you may have saved many lives."

Joe blushed. "I couldn't just sit on the information."

"You did the right thing." Wolcowski checked his watch. "Any questions?"

"Do I come here if I can't reach Mr. Redwood for some reason?"

"Straight here. Tell no one about any of this except Agent Redwood, Miss Billingsley, or me. My secretary has only been told to interrupt whatever I'm doing if you show up."

"What about after hours?"

"Go to our homes. Do you have our addresses?"

"Yes, sir." The foreign service officer looked from Joe to Sandra.

"I took care of that already," Sandra said.

"Good," said the first minister. "I hope we can help the government head off this coup smoothly and without trouble, but we don't know all the leaders yet."

"Isn't General Arcibaldo the boss, sir?" asked Joe.

"Not quite. He is the principal public figure, but the real power is a narrow field of suspects behind the scenes. So far, our best information is what you translated. They may be identified in some letter or clipping you haven't gotten to yet."

"A scary thought," said Joe. "What if Mr. Arland never gives it to me?"

"Then we can say we did the best we could. Does there seem to be any order to the way he's pulling the material out?"

"By customer and vendor accounts, I think. Usually, everything in one file is about the same company."

The diplomat smiled. "Of course, Joe. Our people are too fixed on the political and military subjects. These are business files. Sandra, pass that on to Jim, would you?"

"We noticed, sir. It supports the point that Mr. Arland may not be in on this."

"Or that he is very, very clever." Wolcowski looked at his watch again. "Anything else?"

"No, sir. Thanks for being available. I know how busy you are."

"You and your work are a top priority now. Keep the copies coming and press on as naturally as possible." He stood. Sandra and Joe rose, shook hands with him, and left.

They walked back to the embassy annex, stopping at the newsstand in the entrance. Each bought a copy of the *Rome Daily American* and the *International Herald Tribune*. Sandra paused outside the newsstand.

"You have my number now." She smiled. "Call me sometime when we're not working a case."

The heat crept up the back of his neck. "Sure, thanks. See ya." He felt like he had four left feet as he walked out the door into the street.

Still looking out for the stranger on the Vespa, Joe drove home. He wondered if he was becoming too edgy. He decided he was not when he saw two police cars outside his apartment building. Somehow, he knew they were not there for one of the neighbors.

Inside, a police private tried to console a distraught Angela, seated in the hall. Every piece of furniture had been moved aside and left askew. Every drawer and cabinet door was open, the contents on the floor.

A plainclothes detective came out of the kitchen. He was about Joe's height, but dark-haired and muscular under the nondescript gray suit he wore.

"Scusi, signore," Excuse me, sir, "what happened?"

"And who are you?"

"I live here. Joe Lockhart. Do you need my documents?"

Before the officer could answer, a wail came from the housekeeper.

"Oh, signorino," Angela cried. "I only went shopping. No more than two hours."

"Calm down, Angela, this is *not* your fault." Joe put his arms around her shoulders. "In fact, it has nothing to do with you."

"He's right, signora," said the police private.

"I won't need your passport, Mr. Lockhart," said the detective. "It looks like a sloppy burglary attempt. We won't know until you inventory everything. Your housekeeper saw two men running from the apartment as she walked up the stairs, so she did not surprise them. They finished stealing whatever they came for."

Angela took some more deep breaths. "I must pick this up. The signora must not see this mess."

"We called her at work," said the detective. "Please do not put anything back until we finish here. We will need a statement from each of you."

At that point, Nancy Lockhart arrived. The detective introduced himself and questioned her, while

Angela recovered. He waited while they went through the mess in the house.

"We won't know for sure until we put everything away," Nancy told him, "but I don't see everything from my jewelry box on the floor."

"Value?"

"A couple of bracelets and a string of fake pearls. Not worth a lot, they'll find."

"Where is your television?" asked the detective.

"We don't have one."

The detective nodded to the sergeant who had just packed his bag after taking photographs and lifting some prints from the front door and some cabinet doors. "I think that is all for now. Please come to the station no later than tomorrow evening to sign your sworn statements. That should give you time to see if anything else is missing."

"Thank you, Lieutenant." Nancy held the door for the policemen as they left.

As their footsteps receded on the marble outside, Nancy, Angela, and Joe stood motionless, staring at each other. Angela turned quietly toward the kitchen.

Nancy blew out a powerful breath. He had never seen her so angry.

"We have to go back to the States." Her glance cast about the entrance hall of the apartment as if looking for something. She strode off to her room. Soon, Joe heard her going through drawers and purses. Then she stormed into her office, slamming the door. More crashing about. He wavered, not sure whether to stay to offer some kind of comfort, start an argument about leaving Rome, or go to his room.

"Mom, it isn't any safer there," he mumbled, half hoping she could not hear him. He paused with his hand on the door handle. His mother threw the door open and came charging out. Joe jumped aside.

"Angela!" she shouted, heading toward the kitchen. "*Abbiamo delle sigarette?*" She wanted a cigarette.

"Mom –"

"Get off my case, will you?" she snapped. "I need a smoke and –"

She crashed into Angela coming to her call. The shorter woman fell against the side table, knocking a statue to the floor. The arm broke off, leaving the fallen figure looking like the *Venus de Milo*.

"*Signora, mi dispiace!*" I'm sorry. Turning to her signora, Angela froze, caught between fear and bewilderment.

"Mom – "

"Don't 'mom' me! Why don't you hide a butt or two like other teenagers?"

Joe did not recognize his own voice. "You know I don't smoke, and you know I don't like smoke. Neither does Angela here. That was not fair, Mom."

"Don't you raise your voice to me!"

"Well, you're having trouble hearing me!"

Nancy's championship backhand crossed his cheek like a two-by-four. Joe staggered to the wall. He tasted blood in his mouth. As he raised his fists, he heard a cry behind him.

"Angela!" He turned to the sobbing servant.

"*Ma che fate? Che succede?*" What are you doing? What is happening?

They stared at Nancy. She stood like a statue, her hand still raised over her shoulder at the end of her follow-through, shock across her face.

"Oh, my God! What am I doing?" She rushed to Angela and hugged her. "I'm sorry. Joe, I'm so scared now." The anger emptied out of him like a flood. He put his arms around the two women.

"Mom, I can run across the street for some cigarettes," he said in English. "It will only take a minute."

Nancy disengaged herself and reached for her purse. Angela's sobbing changed to heavy breathing as she gained control of herself.

Nancy drew out a ten-thousand lire note and extended it to Joe. He let go of Angela and stood.

His mother suddenly pulled the bill back and shoved it into the purse.

"No!" she said in Italian, looking at them. "That's part of the problem, not the solution. Let's talk about this after we get the worst of this mess put away." She picked up the sculpture and set it back on the side table, laying the broken arm next to it.

As if on cue, Angela and Joe went to their parts of the house and started putting drawers and shelves back in their places and picking up the scattered items. With something to do, they began to recover. Each worked silently, knowing that they would need to resume the conversation, but not wanting to bring it up.

By the time Angela was supposed to go home, they had the apartment more or less in order. They offered to get Angela home in a taxi, but she declined.

"I want to sit and think. I can do that on the bus." She hoisted her shopping bags and walked slowly out to the street.

Nancy and Joe ate in the kitchen. Neither felt much like talking. Each brought something to read to the table. But they had the same thing on their minds and kept looking up from the unturned pages of their books to catch the other staring at them.

"You're right about not moving back to the States," Nancy said at last. "It's not any safer, and you need to finish high school here."

"I wish there were something I could do, Mom." Joe closed his book. "It tears me up to see you so upset. More than any fear of mine."

"I understand, son, but I must deal with my own fears. You can't do it for me."

That night Joe could not find his transistor radio. They made another careful pass through the house, but only the cheap jewelry and the radio were missing.

Nancy went to work late the next morning. She wanted to see how Angela was. The housekeeper seemed fully recovered and intent on planning Joe's lunch and doing some deep cleaning.

After Nancy went to work, Joe walked to the Cavalieri Hilton Hotel and used a public phone to call Agent Redwood's office.

"Hello, Sandra. This is Joe. Our flat was burglarized yesterday. I couldn't –"

"Oh, that's terrible. Hold on." After a pause, she said, "Could Mr. Redwood meet you in the coffee shop in a half hour?"

"Sure, great. Thanks."

"Bye, Joe. Be careful." She hung up quickly, which surprised him. Then he realized that Sandra had managed the call so that anyone listening would not know where Joe was or any details about the burglary. There had not even been time for a trace. *She's good.* He smiled as he walked to the coffee shop.

Exactly thirty minutes later, Special Agent Redwood took a seat at Joe's table.

"Tell me about it."

Joe recounted as much detail as he remembered. The FBI man quizzed him about what he knew about the two men, from what Angela had said.

"The fact that they were so thorough means two things. One, they didn't find what they were looking for. Two, the missing stuff is a cover-up. Real burglars wouldn't go through the whole house. They would concentrate on the bedrooms and living room, and spend their time loading the high-value items they found easily."

"I thought they worked at night."

"Another reason I don't think this is a burglary. Burglars sometimes work during the day, but not in a house with a domestic servant who is likely to return at any time. They probably had Angela and you under surveillance for some time. When they saw her go shopping, they knew how much time they had."

"They left such a mess." Joe shivered involuntarily.

"Part of the show. They are trying to scare you while making themselves look amateurish. Was there something that wasn't where it belonged? Where's your translation work?"

"In the backpack with me."

"Is there a wastebasket in your room? Where's your trash from translating?"

"I get rid of it away from the house, like here at the hotel, your office, or the library." Agent Redwood raised his eyebrows. "To keep Mom or Angela from discovering what I'm working on," Joe continued, "since the scene in England."

"Anything that *wasn't* moved?"

Joe thought for a moment. "My typewriter. Something strange."

The agent motioned for him to go on.

"It was getting faint, and I meant to buy a new ribbon. Today it typed fresh and dark."

"You must have a cloth ribbon."

"Why, yes. Why is that important?"

"It proves my point. When was the last time you had the typewriter out of the house?"

"In June. I took it to the Galleria Cinese to work on the book for Mr. del Piave."

"They've been watching you for a long time if they brought a ribbon with them and tried to make it look like the machine hadn't been disturbed."

"Why steal my typewriter ribbon, sir?"

"A mistake, Joe. Modern electric typewriters use plastic ribbons that only go under the keys once. They work like carbon paper. You can read what was typed by looking at the letters in the used part of the ribbon. Whoever sent them probably told them to replace the ribbon, not knowing it was an old-style typewriter. The thieves did what they were told by bringing a compatible ribbon and stealing your old one." Agent Redwood signaled the waiter for the bill. "Are you and your mother going to be okay?"

"I think so. I mean, what can we do now?"

"For one thing, change the locks on both doors, not just the damaged one out front."

"The police detective told us to do that."

"And keep the door to the balcony locked when no one is home. They can still get in, but not without your knowing that they were there."

"Angela or I are always the last to leave during the day. We can make sure of that."

"For now, let the world keep thinking this is a burglary, but don't take anything for granted. These people are experts at what they do. I don't think they'll harm you directly. They can't afford the publicity." Doug's father stood and shook Joe's hand. "Call me anytime – about anything. They may be good, Joe, but you're not alone."

"Thanks, sir."

Joe walked home. Angela was dusting in the living room. After closing the door leading to the small balcony off the kitchen, he went to his room to read.

When Nancy returned home, the Lockharts and Angela walked to the *commissariato*, the local police station in the piazzale, at the end of the street. They told the police what they had found, or rather, what they had not found, which was not much.

"Amateurs in a hurry," concluded the detective lieutenant. "Just to be safe from any others, remember to lock all the doors when you leave, including the balcony."

It took an hour for the police sergeant to type their statements on the long, official paper required for such things. They signed the affidavits and left the station. Angela caught the bus outside.

Joe and Nancy chose to eat at the trattoria in the piazzale. Neither wanted to go home. Home felt different.

# 19. Wednesday Morning

THE NEXT WEEK, Nancy and Luke had to go to Cologne for meetings with Smithson's German subsidiary. Joe was relieved because he could work late on the translations. The USIS library closed at ten p.m.

As she snapped her suitcase shut, he came out of his room.

"That's new," he said, pointing to the tennis racket case.

"It is. We'll have a little free time, and isn't this week when we play? Unlucky you, you miss your lesson." She smiled, gave him a hug, and went out to the waiting company car.

Joe closed the door and turned toward his room. His mother's cigarettes and lighter were on the side table in the hall. He picked them up to run after her.

The car was gone. He shrugged and put them back on the side table. Then he recognized them as the same pack that she had bought at the *tabaccheria* when they walked home from the trattoria after signing their statements at the police station. The seal was still unbroken.

ଔଔଔ

Nancy leaned back in the rear seat of the car and took a deep breath. *Joe should be fine by himself with Angela coming in every day.* Though she had left him countless times before, it would take some time for the stress of the home invasion to abate. Analyzing her feelings did not always help.

She felt violated. A home should be a place of safety, but she may never feel safe in her own home again. Her tension was getting worse, not better.

The car sped up on the Via Appia, heading against the flow of the morning rush hour. Nancy stowed her feelings about the burglary, unhappily aided by the consideration of the coming plane trip to Cologne.

Mostly, she wanted a cigarette. Her body was not happy with the choice her head had made. But she could sense the difference on the court now that she was playing tennis again. Luke may not be the champion player that Jason had been, but he was a worthy opponent, and he was improving quickly. She had not appreciated how much she missed the game all these years.

It was not as if she needed the smoke. Unable to light up in the office, and with Joe becoming more adamant at home about smoke-free zones, she hardly got many chances to enjoy the habit. Women smoked freely back in the States, but here in Italy, ladies did not light up except in social situations with people they knew. She had smoked less in the last month, and already she could detect the stale smell on her clothes. She was ready to quit – she hoped.

"*Eccoci, signora.*" Here we are, ma'am. The driver pulled up next to another black Alfa Romeo Giulia. The other chauffeur waved as he backed out. "Dottor Arland is here too."

"*Grazie, Adriano. Arrivederci a sabato.*" See you Saturday. Nancy let herself out while he removed her suitcase and tennis racket from the trunk and carried them to the check-in counter. Nancy collected her boarding pass and walked into the waiting area.

Luke stood at the window, staring at the mix of military and civilian traffic. He looked comfortable, with his right hand in his pocket and his left hand holding his briefcase. Nancy paused to consider his broad shoulders and the way his hair fell over the back of his head. The crew cut he had brought from New York had grown out completely, and whichever stylist he was using had turned his head into a model of male elegance. With his tailored suit and the Gucci case, he no longer looked like a naïve American. She walked up behind him and stopped again.

"You still nervous about this?"

He smiled even before turning slowly toward her. She moved up to the window.

"Frankly, yes."

"Don't be. First impressions count, and you'll make a good one."

"Says the Amazon who can fight in four languages." He knew that she had heard that crack about her negotiating skills. "I'm finally following a little Italian, and we're off to Germany."

"The discussions will be in English, Luke."

"But not the side talk. I never appreciated how important your ability to overhear the muttering was until I watched you working with the del Piave group."

"Only one of us has to be a spy. I'll keep you up to speed."

"I never had occasion to ask before: how did you learn all those languages?"

"Army brat. My father was the military attaché in Berlin and Rome before the war. With no American bases in Europe, we lived on the economy and went to local schools. My mother is French. When the war broke out, we moved to Montreal to stay with cousins. Quebec is for me as Italy is for Joe, I guess."

"Amazing."

"Not for a little girl using different languages every day."

A Lufthansa flight attendant called their flight at the door to the tarmac. Soon they were buckling themselves into their seats. Nancy insisted on an aisle seat.

"Are you going to need that?" she asked, pointing to the bag sticking out of his magazine pocket.

"No. Do you get airsick?" Luke's surprise was written all over his face.

"Yes, although these modern jets ride more smoothly than the propeller-driven planes." She plucked the bag and put it next to hers. "I need to be ready."

"I never figured."

"We all have an Achilles' heel. Mine is motion sickness. It hasn't come up because I've never flown with someone from the company before. Seems fair to warn you, in case we hit turbulence."

Luke smiled, his eyes taking a gentle depth that Nancy had never seen before. "My co-pilot carried four of those on every mission, and he filled every one. I can handle it."

"You mean they let him fly bombers when he got airsick?"

"Recruiters couldn't be picky towards the end of the war. Once the flak started, we were too busy for him to notice. All that mattered was getting back."

The engines began their roar, and the plane trembled, straining against its brakes. Nancy leaned back, closed her eyes, and gripped the armrests until her fingers hurt.

Warmth flowed over her left hand as Luke put his hand over hers and held it firmly. It ran up her arm like an IV injection. She relaxed her shoulders and realized that she had been holding her breath. Focusing on her diaphragm, she breathed steadily and slowly as the brakes released and the jet barreled down the runway.

When the pilot leveled off at 30,000 feet and turned off the seat belt sign, she sighed and turned her head to look at Luke. His gentle expression had not changed.

"Thanks. That helped."

"You're welcome. I should have held my co-pilot's hand, but I never thought of it."

She laughed. She had forgotten her stomach during the takeoff.

The flight was calm at altitude. Nancy leaned forward and looked out the window. He backed into the seat to let her lean in front of him.

"So beautiful up here," she said. "I never let myself take a good look before."

Luke seemed to be staring far away, past the clouds. "It is. I never stop loving the view or the feeling of flying my own aircraft."

"Flying is fun?" Nancy's expression surprised him. He saw fear and disbelief.

"Hard to imagine perhaps, but nothing can top it – except maybe sex." She laughed, then turned serious.

"Not my experience, believe me."

"It might be different if you were in control, like steering a boat instead of sitting in it. People who get car sick as passengers often don't when driving."

The clouds thinned, and Nancy looked down at the Alps crawling in the other direction.

"Maps can't capture this, can they?"

"Nope."

After they passed the Alps, the cloud cover disappeared. She saw the patchwork of farms in Luxembourg and northern France, and the watery flatland flanking the Rhine River. As the jet descended, Nancy sat back. This time she reached out for Luke's hand. He put his other hand over hers and smiled.

"I noticed how this pilot controls the plane. He may have trained as a *Luftwaffe* bomber pilot. I'll bet he makes a long, slow approach, and you won't even know when we touch down unless you're looking."

Nancy squeezed his hand.

"You look. I'll breathe." She looked briefly into his eyes, gave him a quick smile, then fixed her gaze on the "No Smoking" sign at the front of the cabin. Talking with Luke put her at ease. She tried to think of something besides her fear.

"Did you fly over Germany?"

"Yes, but not over Cologne." He glanced out the window. "My bio mentions that I flew bombers. Do you think it could come up at the meetings?"

Nancy thought for a moment.

"It could, but I don't think anyone will mention it. The war affected everyone here more than perhaps you can imagine. Some don't want to be reminded; others would consider it bad manners to bring it up; still, others wouldn't want their views to come out in public."

"I still can't square the BDA photos with the postcard pictures of German cities today."

"BDA?"

"Sorry – bomb damage assessment. The fighter pilots covering our exit would take photos if they could." He fell silent.

She tapped his hand. "Focus on what we're doing here, and everything will be fine. You don't need to feel guilty or worry about our hosts. Europeans learned long ago to put war behind them and get on with life." She smiled again.

"That worked."

"What?"

"Look out the window. I told you he would come down gently."

Nancy gasped to see the fence of the airport outside the window. The pilot reversed the engines and slowed the big jet as the terminal came into view.

"I don't know whether to slap you or thank you."

"Let's thank each other. The war thing has been eating at me. I needed someone to explain my options. Thanks."

"Thanks, yourself." She squeezed his hand again and let go to unbuckle her seat belt.

As they collected their bags, Nancy recognized a slender man in a chauffeur uniform, holding a placard that read "Smithson Italia." She touched Luke's shoulder to get his attention, then walked over to the driver.

"*Guten Tag*, Manfred. You did not need to draw a sign for us!"

Manfred drew himself up stiffly but also smiled.

"Guten Tag, *Frau Doktor*," he said. "I was not sure who would be coming."

"This is Doctor Arland," she said in English. "I think that we're the only arrivals on this flight."

Manfred gave Luke a brief bow, then reached for their bags. He led them to a black Mercedes limousine parked at the curb. Luke held the rear door for Nancy, while Manfred loaded the luggage. He started the car and pulled into traffic.

"Do you wish to stop anywhere in particular?" he said in English, looking at them in the rearview mirror.

"I think the hotel directly would be fine," she said. "Do you have other pickups today?"

"Not until this evening, Mrs. Lockhart."

"Maybe you can take a nice long break."

Manfred smiled quickly, then concentrated on the drive.

They were silent during the short ride. The doorman opened Nancy's door. Luke got out on the other side and walked around. The hotel manager was waiting.

"Doktor Lockhart, what a pleasure to have you visit us again!" the manager beamed. He waved at the bellboys, who were racing to the trunk.

"Thank you, Hans, it's good to be back." Her reply in English was all the hint the hotelier needed.

"Doctor Arland, I presume." The two men shook hands. "Hans Ulsdorf. We are delighted to have you staying with us. I arranged for adjoining suites; in case you need to confer privately between meetings."

"Pleased to meet you, and thank you. Whatever arrangements suit Doctor Lockhart are fine with me." He nodded toward Nancy.

"Of course, sir."

In the lobby, the manager gave them their keys, then accompanied them to the elevator.

"Please deposit your passports at the reception at your convenience."

"Hans, do you mind taking care of it? Here's mine. Luke?"

Luke pulled his passport from his coat pocket and handed it to the hotelier.

"Thank you. I will bring them back myself today unless you want to pick them up."

"We'll get them later," Nancy said. "I expect that we won't go out until this evening."

As they walked to their rooms, Luke said, "You have them eating from your hands, Nancy."

"Companies like Smithson and Bayer spend a lot of money here. It's not just the rooms; it's the conference facilities. When we use a big hotel like this, they attend to the details, like security, PA systems, and such."

"I know about that, and you know what I mean. They genuinely like you."

"They can tell that I care about them as people. You learned that in med school. They react to it. And it pleases me to see them enjoying our company."

"Still, you have an amazing bedside manner, if that's all it is."

"Don't ask Joe's opinion. Teenagers are tough patients." They both laughed. "You're no slouch yourself. People relax around you. I've seen it – and after the flight today, I understand it."

They paused outside their rooms. Nancy unlocked her door.

"Tennis, lunch or a nap?" she asked. "We need to discuss the dinner tonight with our German counterparts, but that shouldn't take long."

"I was thinking of all three in that order. Shall I reserve a court?"

"Maria Grazia already did, but I'll give them a precise time, so they can free it up after us. Meet you there in a half hour?"

"Give me an hour. I want to check out any info they left in the room."

"Okay. See you in sixty."

Inside her room, Nancy found her suitcase sitting on the luggage caddy. She called the front desk to confirm the court for two hours, then unpacked. She had used this suite before. The door in the wall was one of two doors between her room and Luke's.

She smiled as she freshened up. *Europeans are so clever and discreet*, she thought. She gave herself a mental slap. *Business is business, and Luke is part of business*. With a sigh, she changed into her tennis outfit. Having him along for one of these conferences would be more enjoyable than the lonely sorties she had made in the past. At least she hoped so. Sometimes he was so sharp, and sometimes, what he did not know amazed her.

# 20. Cologne, Wednesday

NANCY AND LUKE PLAYED HARD AND FAST, not stopping for the whole two hours. After sitting in cars and airplanes all day, they reveled in the exercise. They were both high on endorphins when they quit at two p.m.

"You didn't say a word," he said as he wiped his face. "Are you angry?"

"Not at all. I feel great. I haven't had a match like that in years. Were you holding back on me in Rome?"

"I don't think so, but how could I tell? I never had coaches and scouts looking at me."

Her face darkened just for a second.

"You played with a passion I've never seen before."

"Well, I haven't played quite like this in a long time. This is even more fun than I remember."

"Can you stand lunch? I haven't eaten since dawn."

"Neither have I. Knock on your door in a half hour?"

"No. Coffee shop downstairs. I want to check the concession shops on the way there." She picked up her tennis bag, and they headed for the elevators. "Would you bring your copy of the schedule too? We might as well get some planning done."

"Okay." Luke watched her breathing. "How's your wind?"

"Not as good as it used to be."

"Think we can play like this every day?"

"Sure. I might let you win one or two." She punched him and went into her room. Inside, she flopped on the bed and took a long series of low, deep breaths, counting four seconds in and four seconds out. As her heart and lungs slowed down, she knew that she would never pick up her cigarettes again. She loved the feeling on the court. She resolved never to lose it again.

She decided to phone Joe later. The shower was tempting, but she did not allow herself to luxuriate in it. She changed into a skirt and blue-green blouse, which brought out her eyes, and a pair of pumps. She folded the schedule into her purse. Giving the door in the wall a wistful look, she went downstairs.

She walked slowly through the shops in the hotel concourse, not meaning to buy anything, unless something for Joe jumped out at her. Thirty-five minutes after she punched Luke in the hall outside their rooms, she entered the coffee shop and joined him at a table against the far wall. He seemed relaxed, casually looking at the people in the restaurant. Blue polo shirt and tan slacks.

"Sorry, I'm late," she said, smiling as she sat.

"Late?" he said, returning her smile. "You're right on time. I'm the one who needs to be early." Nancy wondered how he could make irony sound so positive. "Shall we look at menus or schedules first?"

"Menus." She signaled to the waiter and ordered steak and eggs and coffee.

"The same," he said, handing the menu back to the waiter. "A Texas breakfast. I'm surprised."

"Then you're in for more surprises," she answered. "I'm not only hungry, I need protein after all that tennis. A croissant or a salad won't cut it."

"I'm going to enjoy seeing new sides of the boss this week."

"Luke, we're both Americans. We understand teamwork, and I'm not your boss. The other participants may need to perceive someone in charge, but I'm keenly aware that you're the negotiating expert on the team. It's why Richmond sent you to us."

He motioned with his hand for her to go on.

"I've worked with these men for years now. I can tell you anything you want to know about them. I can take charge of a meeting. But to push this to the next level, we need a one-two punch. You in your 'manly' role making it clear that we're working together and me letting you make points so that we score as a team. Though I understand the side-chatter, you can size them up with a different perspective. That may be crucial. What do you think?"

"That was my hunch about coming with you on this trip. It's a relief to have it confirmed."

"More like partners in a squad car, eh?"

"Sure, 'pard.'" He grinned. "Who do we take down first?"

They paused as the waiter came back with their coffee and some sweet rolls.

"Let's discuss our own team first," she said after the server left. "They've been working on this deal between my visits."

"Why do I get the impression that this is a not a gung-ho bunch?"

"They aren't. It's unusual for an office of men working at their level. There are two who carry most of the load, but even they need me or someone else from the head office to come in occasionally to confirm arrangements and make commitments. All the others do is lay the groundwork for the next meeting. That is why I asked to have only three representatives for this negotiation with Bayer. It makes five of us, and two of them are the ones we can count on."

Over lunch, they discussed the three men who would be joining them for dinner later. They took notes on their schedules. Several cups of coffee after the steak and eggs, they had an understanding about how best to interact with the management of Smithson Deutschland GmbH. Luke signaled for the bill and put it on his room.

"Okay," Nancy said. "The third item on the list was a nap. See you at five?"

He yawned. "I never thought I'd ever take naps in the afternoon, but it sounds like a wonderful idea. See you after siesta."

As she unlocked her room, Nancy thought that they might need the rest each day to make it through the business dinners at night. She didn't feel the coffee at all.

Through the adjoining door, she could hear Luke on the phone. She wondered who he might be calling, but then remembered that he had family back in New York. She knew so little about him.

☙☙☙

"Thanks, Operator, I have it." Luke tapped the cradle of the phone for a new dial tone and asked the hotel operator for another international line. He listened patiently as the switches closed in Cologne, Brussels, Paris, Penmarch, Clarenville, and New York. Electricity flowing over the continents and under the Atlantic.

"FBI, New York Field Office, may I help you?"

"Special Agent Worthman, please."

"Whom may I say is calling?" *So formal these government operators*, he thought. He gave her his name. She asked him to wait.

"Luke, you old dog, is that you?" Bob Worthman did not sound a day older or less bubbly than he had in college.

"'Tis I, good man, and brother to ye all, Bob." The old fraternity greeting.

"You still with Smithson?"

"Yes, and that's partly why I need to talk to you."

"What about?"

"Something weird in my company – or not. I'm not sure."

"Can you tell me about it?"

"I'm not sure about that either. Let me tell you what I have, and you tell me where to turn next."

"Okay. You talk. I'll listen."

Luke sat. He paused to put his hand to his eyes and took a deep breath.

"You remember that I was sent to Rome last summer?"

"Nice promotion, as I recall. And a nice party before you left."

"Right. Well, one of my duties, if not the principal assignment, is to be a liaison between the Italian subsidiary and the major investors in New York."

"Insiders?"

"No, not really. Headquarters in Richmond set it up. We owe our biggest shareholders some special treatment and a little extra reporting. Most of them are either headquartered in New York or maintain major offices there."

"Makes sense. So, what's weird?"

"They all have Italian-speaking staff. I happen to be the only one in the Rome office who's not bilingual. So, I find it strange that I must send copies of certain files to New York in Italian. I can't read them. They're marked up in our various offices throughout Italy, with multiple copies for different files: by operating division, geographic area, and a copy for New York."

"Everything?"

"No. The correspondence for major investors has a code on it and comes in three copies. Only about three or four pieces a week. Each letter has attachments, usually magazine or journal articles about our products." He paused.

"And?"

"Sometime in April, I noticed that the attachments were almost all from the regular press, and certain words or photos were circled. Also, only one word is circled in any cover letter. About six different colors are used. I never paid attention before because my Italian only improved enough in the last month to spot common words in Italian."

"Coded messages?"

"That's what I thought. I've been having the files translated for my own reading, and the English translations don't have the circles on them, of course. But now that I can read some of the Italian, I see that most of the circles are around words about military targets, NATO bases, and security issues. It worries me."

"I would be worried too. How can I help?"

"Any idea who could help me figure this out? You're the only FBI person I know, so I thought I would start with you."

"It sounds serious, and I can tell you who can help." Luke heard him shuffling a Rolodex file on his desk. "Did you know that we have an FBI Office in Rome?"

"No."

"It's a dream assignment, believe me, as good as this one in New York. We maintain close relations with our allies' police forces. Our man in Rome is Special Agent James Redwood. He's top-notch, and you can trust him. Want the number?"

"I've met him. Yes, a number would be helpful. I'll call him as soon as I get back. I'm at a conference in Cologne this week."

Bob read him the number. "A Miss Billingsley will answer the phone. If Redwood isn't in, tell her to tell him it's about what Bob Worthman reported. I'll call them myself to give them a heads-up."

"Thanks, Bob. I hope this isn't anything, but it has me worried. My translator is just a kid. His mother works with me at Smithson, and I wouldn't want anything to happen to her, either. I don't know if they know anything about this, except the translator, and he hasn't mentioned the circles, yet."

"Whatever you do, don't do anything different until you talk to Redwood. We don't want to tip our hand if this is important."

"Got it. Thanks again. Give Patsy a big hug for me." They hung up.

Luke slipped off his shoes, then lay down on the bed, feeling some relief. He remembered Jim Redwood from the American Chamber of Commerce luncheons. He had never mentioned being FBI, but then Luke had never had a close conversation with him.

ಊಊಊ

The alarm woke Nancy at four thirty. She felt disoriented at first. It had been years since she had taken a nap in the afternoon, and the deep sleep following the exercise and lunch made the experience even more unfamiliar. She slipped into a pair of slacks and a blouse then called home. No answer.

"Strange," she said to herself out loud. Then she remembered that her son would be out of the house for any of a dozen reasons. *Silly to worry about him*, she thought, even if it was perfectly natural for a mother.

The phone interrupted her musings. It was Luke.

"Your place or mine? We never discussed where to meet at five."

Nancy looked at the door in the wall. She would not mind either place.

"How about the coffee shop again? Or maybe the terrace by the pool. The others won't be here until seven, so we'll have plenty of time to change for dinner." Silence on the line.

"Okay. See you at the pool in ten minutes." Luke sounded more chipper than Nancy felt.

By six, they had laid out their plan for the meetings with Bayer and exchanged notes about the participants from Bayer. All that remained was to hear what the local Smithson people had to say and enjoy the meal.

༺༺༺

Nancy came out of her room to find Luke standing by her door in the hall.

"I thought maybe we should go down together. What do you think?"

"Just don't take my arm."

He laughed and followed her to the elevators.

The Cologne team were at the bar outside the hotel restaurant, as agreed. Nancy knew that they had all arrived within five minutes of each other, between six fifty-five and seven p.m. *Such precision is easy*, she thought. *All they need are orders.*

"Helmut, good to see you again." She shook hands with the shortest of the trio, a fifty-something man with gray hair combed back and a rosy face. Then she said in English, "This is Luke Arland, our vice president for Strategy and Investment. Luke, Helmut Gottlieb."

The two men shook hands, and Gottlieb introduced the other two. Hans Schmidt, VP for Operations, stood as tall as Luke, with thick blond hair carefully styled. He stood with an easy grace, like an athlete. Klaus Durst stood ramrod straight and jerked slightly as if remembering just in time not to click his heels. His handshake was short and formal.

Introductions done, the three Germans looked at Nancy.

"Shall we dine, gentlemen?" The group left their unfinished beers and accompanied her. A back room had been set aside for the occasion, so they were assured of both privacy and security. The restaurant jealously maintained its five-star rating; the dinner and the service set a tone of comfort and pleasure.

The usual pleasantries about backgrounds and favorite places occupied the first two courses. Nancy and Luke asked about the work of the subsidiary as they worked through the meat, dessert, and fruit and cheese. Men love to talk about their work, so it was easy to keep them engaged until the coffee came out with the port. The wait staff discreetly drew back. By then, the German executives had warmed to Luke like an old friend.

"It seems that we're about as ready we can be," said Nancy, turning to the main course of the conversation. "Bayer is hoping that we can undercut your competitors in Germany, France, and the UK for their new generics contract. They also want representatives from the American parent group, which is why Doctor Arland and I are here, instead of our Italian colleagues. Doctor Moretti is in on this arrangement, part of which was his idea." She paused. "What is your sense of the competition and our ability to win the contract?" She let the silence hang.

Helmut spoke first. "I think that it will be tight." The other two nodded. "Roche, Merck, and Schering can each match our production capacity. Can we undercut their bid enough?"

They were looking at Luke. She indicated for him to go ahead.

"I think so," he said. "Everyone knows what our labor costs are, especially in Southern Italy. No one in Europe can produce such high quality as cheaply, in almost any industry, from movie-making to automobiles."

"Yes, but pharmaceuticals have stricter regulatory and safety issues than most industries," Klaus said.

"But we are already meeting those requirements." Luke looked around.

Hans leaned forward and spoke to both Americans. "To achieve the unit costs needed in the proposal you are planning to present tomorrow, I think that we would need to increase production by at least twenty-five percent. We don't have the infrastructure for that here in Germany. And if we did, we could not attract the workforce needed to man the plants."

"Granted." Luke paused. "What if I told you we could do it in Italy?"

Helmut looked sharply at Nancy. Hans straightened up, and Klaus sucked in a short breath.

"There has been no news of an increase in capacity," said Helmut.

"And there won't be. Some very confidential negotiations could be accelerated if we win the contract from Bayer."

"What would our role be in this?" asked Klaus. "It looks like a Smithson Italia show."

"Same as now. You would provide the product and collect the revenue. Smithson Italia would send the product to you as an intra-group transfer. Win-win, I think."

"So, you do not intend to change the working arrangement between Smithson Deutschland and Smithson Italia?" Helmut said.

"Not at all."

The three Germans seemed relieved and pleased.

"Now we understand better why the numbers seem so risky," said Hans.

"But not impossible," said Helmut. "I think we can pitch this to Bayer tomorrow in a convincing way."

Luke sat back.

Nancy brought their attention back to her with a slight cough. "One extremely important point. This extra production capacity is well along in negotiations, but we cannot allow any hint of it to reach Bayer. We only want you to understand why Smithson Italia is confident that we can deliver, but we want Bayer to continue to work with our currently known figures. Is everyone clear on that?"

"Ja, frau Doktor." Helmut grinned. "It will be a pleasure to beat out the other contenders in this one." The others nodded and grinned.

Nancy rose, which caused a general jumping out of chairs. Luke stifled a grin as they all shook hands. Luke accompanied them to the door, while Nancy signed for the dinner.

"That went well, I think," he said, as they walked into the cool air of the night.

"I thought Hans would hug you during the meat course, he got so excited that you play tennis."

"Speaking of which, did you hear him ask about playing doubles with his wife before we leave?"

"No." Nancy drew a breath. "Did you accept?"

"I told him that I would check with the boss and tell him in the morning." He winked and grinned.

"I haven't played doubles since – "

"I know. That's why I didn't make a commitment."

"Have you played doubles?"

"Yes, but I didn't have a tennis partner in Rome until recently."

"Let me invite the Schmidts myself tomorrow. I want to make noises about my lack of recent experience."

"Of course. Hans is going to get an earful from his wife about committing her to play a champion."

"They'll never let it show, will they?"

"Nope."

They turned into the park at the end of the block and made a relaxed circuit among the lovers on the benches and some teenage boys playing soccer on the grass near the center.

Back at the hotel, they rode in the elevator in silence. They paused at the doors to their rooms. Nancy felt the pull as much as he did.

"Luke."

"Yes." He stepped closer. Nancy's eyes widened.

"You were good today. I hope that you can charm the Bayer team as well."

"I'll do my best." They both glanced at her door.

"Good night, Luke." Nancy put the key in.

"Sleep tight, Nancy. See you in the morning."

On her side of the liaison door, she leaned against it and breathed deeply. Then she sighed and got ready for bed. It was too late to call Joe. *At least, he'd better be asleep in bed,* she thought with a smile.

# 21. Rome, Thursday

THE DAY AFTER NANCY AND LUKE LEFT, Joe typed at home while Angela worked in the kitchen. He missed the open space of the library. After lunch, he gathered up all his papers and rode down to the USIS library to work on the last few letters. The heat of the day only began to ease as he made his way through the afternoon rush hour.

There were new people in the colored circles in this collection. The letters themselves dealt with an old medicine, one that went out of patent protection a few years ago and now sold as a generic drug. Unlike the politicians and General Arcibaldo, he did not recognize any of these people.

He bought a snack at the Star & Stripes Newsstand before it closed and went back to the library. A steady rain began outside, muffling the sound of the traffic and rinsing most of the tourists off the street.

"We close in fifteen minutes, you know." Joe started, then relaxed. Being alone this week, he could finish in the morning and go to the train station to stash his copies.

He packed up and stepped into the hallway to go to the exit. A familiar perfume caught his attention. Sandra and Agent Redwood were coming through the swinging doors.

"Working late?" Joe smiled.

"So are you, it seems," said the FBI agent. "Unfortunately, this happens more often than I like."

"It's only four p.m. in Washington," said Sandra. "They keep the phones and telexes busy as long as they can."

"And your case is big, Joe."

"Speaking of that, I'm working on the last of the current batch of letters. I don't recognize some of the people in the colored circles. I'll bring it all up to you tomorrow."

"Wonderful. I look forward to it." They stood at the door, looking at the rain, which was heavier.

"Where's your umbrella, Joe?"

"I got so used to getting wet, that I keep forgetting to carry one."

"You can share mine," offered Sandra.

"Come to think of it, Joe, I wouldn't mind if you walked her to the bus stop. I usually do when we work late, but I want to catch at least the fourth quarter." Joe would normally have been at the game too.

"I'd be happy to."

Agent Redwood shook Joe's hand and headed into the rain, crossing the street to the embassy, where he parked his car. Sandra gave Joe her umbrella and wrapped her arm around his. Warmth ran up to his shoulder and neck. Trapped under the umbrella, her perfume made his head swim.

They started up the Via Veneto. The rain beat a soothing rhythm on the awnings over the few late-night patrons sitting at the sidewalk cafes. Otherwise, the street was almost deserted.

"You take the number eight trolley, don't you?" They neared the Pincian Gate at the top of the hill.

"That's right." She pulled him closer. It was a lady's umbrella, not a golf umbrella.

"There's a transit strike again tomorrow. What do you do when that happens?"

"For something like that, the embassy sends a car around for me and some other secretaries in the annex. If there are no embassy cars, we find a cab or a friend with a car." They made their way briskly through the gate and across the Viale del Muro Torto. The rain would alternately come down hard and drizzle.

Sandra huddled closer under the roof of the stop. Joe felt a warm rush as the entire length of her body pressed against him up to his shoulder. He could not stay out of the downpour without putting his arm around her, so he did. She snuggled in.

"This is worth getting wet for." She laughed. A small, gentle laugh.

"Yeah." Joe tried to sound confident, but his face burned. *Could she feel his pulse?* He hoped he had enough layers of shirt and jacket.

Couples came and went from the Villa Borghese park behind them. They stood at the stop for about twenty minutes, but neither a bus nor a trolley came by.

"I think the strike started," he said.

"But it's more than an hour until midnight."

"But the yard's at the other end of town from where you live. Maybe the crew decided not to start the last run."

"Now what do I do? Can we find a taxi?" They looked at the empty stand across the street.

"They'll be pretty busy." Joe gave her a short squeeze and grinned. "I can take you home again, but you'll get wet."

"We're already drenched. Let's do it."

Huddling under the umbrella, they walked back down the Via Veneto to where he had left the scooter near the annex.

Fifteen minutes later, they were outside her building.

"That was fun." She slid off the Vespa, "But now we're soaked. Come on up and dry off, will you?"

"I'm used to it. I should be getting home." Joe waited, but she did not take out her keys to open the portone, the heavy outer door. She seemed surprised. She eyed him with a crooked frown for a moment. Then she brightened up and fished the keys out.

"Joe, get off your scooter and come inside for a minute. You don't need to come upstairs."

He parked the machine and followed her into the building. Only one light worked, on the next floor up. The portiere had closed up and gone home.

Sandra turned and put her arms around him. He hesitated. She kissed him, hard, on the mouth. His head spun, and his ears pounded. Her wet hair dripped on his shirt. He held her close and opened his own mouth.

Suddenly, it made sense. He relaxed and held her tighter. He returned the kiss. He no longer cared what went on around them. There was just Sandra and her kiss, warm, wet, and hungry. Sandra touched his lips carefully with her tongue while still kissing him. He imitated the gesture, surprised by the smoothness of her lips.

They parted and stared into each other's eyes. They kissed again, not as long, but with the same effect. When they stepped back, the world flowed in like an unruly crowd mobbing his soul. He yearned for the timeless bliss of that kiss, but reality crashed loudly outside.

"I need to go on home," he said. *Hell,* he thought, *what for?*

"I know, thank you – for the ride and, well, everything."

"Anytime." He heard someone else talking. That somebody turned toward the portone while his heart tried to follow her up the stairs to her apartment.

"Sandra," he called. She stopped and turned around. "Could we – uh – would you like to go for a ride to, say, a movie or something sometime?"

"Yes, let's – and soon." She paused. "I thought you'd never ask."

"Good. Uh, I'll give you a call, okay?"

"Sure."

"And if that embassy car doesn't make it, call me. I can take you in."

"I'd like that."

"G'night, Sandra."

"Thanks, Joe. 'Night."

Joe did not know if the rain had stopped. He daydreamed of Sandra in a hundred different adventures while the scooter took him home. His body went to bed without him.

# 22. Cologne, Thursday

"HOW DO YOU DO THAT THING with your clothes and the eyes?" Luke asked as they rode down in the elevator. Nancy considered his tailored Italian blue suit and his patterned tie.

"Not hard with hazel eyes," she said. "They seem to change color depending on what I wear. Speaking of which, do you pick your own ties? That one brings out your hair and eyes."

"It does? I chose it from a selection the clerk at the men's store showed me."

The doors opened, and they made their way across the gleaming marble floor to the coffee shop. Nancy ordered muesli, yogurt, and coffee.

"No steak and eggs this morning?" He used his hands to tell the waiter to bring him the same.

"Can't make a habit of it. This gives me the protein I need to get through the morning. Let's see what I eat after tennis this afternoon."

"What about doubles with the Schmidts?"

"I'll catch Hans before the meeting this morning and propose tomorrow afternoon. That should give him time to talk to his wife during one of the breaks."

After breakfast, Nancy called home.

"Signorino Joe is not here, signora," said Angela. "He left a note. He would be home late. Working at the USIS, whatever that is."

"The American library near the embassy. He uses it for his summer homework research. Thanks, Angela. I just called to say hi. How are you and Mr. Ceccarelli?"

"We're fine, signora. My sister is with us again until she can find an apartment. We share the shopping and cleaning."

"I'm happy for you. I must go now. Arrivederci." She hung up. After staring at the liaison door again, she gathered her briefcase, checked herself one last time in the mirror, and walked to the elevator.

Luke met her at the lobby level.

"Do you want to go in together, or make your own entrance?"

"Did you see the others?"

"I snuck a peek at the conference room. Everyone's there, standing around chatting."

"Good. They won't stand when I walk in. It took three meetings to break our team of the habit. They solved it by learning not to sit down until they had all arrived. I like that better for a lot of reasons." She turned toward the stair leading to the mezzanine. "Let's go in together."

The chief operating officer of Bayer stood at his place to welcome everyone. He was a tall man, slender and strong with the manner of a born aristocrat. Nancy read "Otto von Kracken" on the place card in front of him.

He started with introductions, which she appreciated. The name cards were helpful for spelling someone's name right, but hearing them say something created a first impression beyond the visual.

The Bayer COO explained that they would meet for two consecutive mornings, so the parties could confer between sessions. He invited them for cocktails that evening and reminded everyone about the absolute confidentiality of the meetings. He then asked his procurement manager to outline the contract bidding process.

No one had questions, so the count asked Nancy if they were prepared to make their presentation. She asked Luke to join her at the lectern. She watched von Kracken closely as she worked through the operational aspects of the proposal. He kept his face still, but the others betrayed their familiarity with the details.

"Thank you, Doctor Lockhart," said the COO when she paused. "So far these are facts we know. What is different today?"

Nancy nodded to Luke. "I would like Doctor Arland to give you the economic aspect of the proposal."

Luke projected a color viewgraph on the screen behind the lectern. The COO's face did not change, but Nancy heard him take an extra breath.

"Gentlemen, this table shows our proposed pricing for your generic drug lines as outlined in your request for proposals. If you want to add additional quantities or other products to the RFP, we can offer similar economic conditions." He left the slide up, while the Bayer representatives scribbled notes. One pulled a slide rule from inside his jacket and began to run calculations furiously.

"Doctor Arland, could you have produced this for us on paper?" The procurement manager seemed to be trying to write down everything.

"We will be happy to provide this and all the other details of the proposal in writing tomorrow afternoon." He tipped his head to Nancy.

"As Count von Kracken reminded us," she said, "this meeting is highly confidential. We would not want to risk having this information in any form that we cannot track until tomorrow. By then, of course, we should have reached an agreement, and we will adjust the formal proposal accordingly."

Von Kracken nodded solemnly. Nancy thought the edges of his mouth turned upward ever so slightly. She suspected that he kept a sense of humor amid the business battles.

The rest of the morning consisted of volleys of questions and answers. Sometimes, Helmut would provide specifics on how the products would move from Italy to the Bayer facilities in Europe. Hans gave examples of how additional quantities could be ordered and how the orders would affect the price. Luke and Nancy answered the rest of the questions. Except for a break at ten thirty, the conversation continued unabated.

Each representative tried to make his mark, both for themselves and because their boss was watching. Nancy had seen it before, many times. At one point, she caught von Kracken's glance and a knowing arch of his eyebrow.

At noon, the Bayer COO stood. Conversation stopped.

"This has been a most productive session. Doctors Arland and Lockhart, thank you. We will now adjourn until this evening." As everyone rose, he turned to Nancy and asked for the pricing just until the evening. Nancy reached into her briefcase.

"This is the page we used to make the viewgraph. We will need it back in the morning because assuming all goes well, we'll have the proposal printed in the requisite number of copies tomorrow afternoon."

"I am impressed by your efficiency, Doctor Lockhart, and your flexibility."

"Nancy."

"Otto." The COO took her hand to his lips with a bow, then strode from the room, gesturing to the procurement manager to catch up.

Nancy turned and saw Luke and Hans in an animated conversation with the Bayer representative who had pulled out the slide rule. Klaus and the other Bayer executives had left.

Nancy caught Helmut's attention and approached the trio.

"*Herr* Scherer is it?" She proffered her hand to the Bayer man.

"Ja, Frau Doktor. Siegfried Scherer. Operations Plans."

"I was impressed that someone in the room actually did some calculating" She switched to English. "How do our numbers stack up?"

"It is what I discuss with Doctor Arland and Herr Schmidt. It seems to me that you need more production capacity than you have, even after the explanations."

"What are you using as a labor factor?"

Scherer cited three different wage levels. Nancy smiled.

"Why didn't you mention this during the meeting?"

"Alas, a slide rule can only slide so fast. Count von Kracken adjourned us just as I was finishing up."

"Luke, shall we tell him?" He nodded.

"Herr Scherer," she said, "those are the Western European averages for pharmaceutical workers. Our numbers for qualified workers in southern Italy are just over half of that."

"What happens when you start having labor problems because everyone else is being paid more?"

"Things take longer to happen in Italy." Nancy gave a slight shrug.

"By then," said Luke, "we could increase our production capacity and our plant efficiencies to accommodate the new labor costs."

"Which would still be lower than German, French or Swiss pay scales," added Nancy. She winked at Helmut.

The German subsidiary president put his hand on the Bayer planner's shoulder. "Siegfried, what are you doing for lunch?" Helmut led him out, switching to German.

"You two are remarkable," said Hans, smiling broadly. "It felt like watching a tennis match the way you took turns answering the questions. I look forward to a real challenge tomorrow afternoon." He shook their hands and walked gracefully out the door. Luke and Nancy gathered their briefcases to follow the others.

"What was that last bit with Helmut and the Bayer fellow?" he asked.

"There's always one guy in every meeting who wants his questions answered when everyone is trying to leave. It was easier in this case because Helmut had told me about Scherer, and we were ready for him. They went to the same university, though not together. Helmut will make him feel better over lunch. The labor numbers we gave him will make his slide rule come around too."

They entered the elevator. Luke pressed the button for their floor.

"You *are* impressive, you know." He smiled.

"So are you. That went better than I could have had it go, alone or with Moretti. He could handle that crowd in French, but not in English. Thanks."

"You're welcome. Are you ready to be so impressive on the court?"

She checked her watch as they stepped out on their floor.

"Our slot is in thirty minutes. See you there."

The tennis was every bit as exhilarating and intense as the day before. The summer sun in Cologne did not add to the heat load as it did in Rome. Back in her room, Nancy stretched out on the bed, drawing the air deep into her lungs. When her heartbeat settled down to normal, she sat up, pleased not to feel as stiff as the day before. She lay back to enjoy the well-being.

The telephone woke her up. The alarm clock on the nightstand read 4:30 p.m.

"Any plans between now and the cocktail party?" Luke asked. "Sightseeing? Shopping? Whatever?"

"How about all three?" He laughed.

"Especially lots of whatever. You know Cologne already, so I'll do my sightseeing on another trip. But I want to pick up a few things for my niece and my sister." It was the first time that he had ever mentioned relatives.

"Meet you in the lobby in thirty minutes."

A half hour later, Luke grinned when Nancy stepped off the elevator.

"Did someone put out an order for the Uniform of the Day?" He wore a light blue polo and khakis with comfortable boat shoes; she a light blue blouse and a tan skirt.

"I would change, but I don't have anything else."

"I'm the one with a list. I should get a different shirt."

They walked into the sunshine and turned right toward the upscale shopping district near the hotel.

"What are you looking for?"

"For one thing, my sister collects those small sterling silver souvenir spoons. I try to buy her one in each city I visit. Elly is fourteen going on forty, and I haven't a clue what a teenager would like."

"I can help with both of those. Maybe we can buy you some new pants too."

Nancy could not remember a day so relaxed since Joe was little. They found the spoons first because she knew those stores. After checking dozens of windows, they settled on a teddy bear in lederhosen for the niece, as well as a record by the Beatles.

"The Beatles in German?"

"They became famous in Hamburg before becoming the sensation they are now. I'm sure Elly knows that, but she probably doesn't have the record."

"You sure about this?"

"Positive. She'll be the envy of her friends."

They had Black Forest cake at a tea house and walked by the Rhine River. Nancy took him to the Cathedral, which she had visited often, and which left him speechless. The shadows were long when they returned to the hotel.

"That was fun, Luke." They put their keys into their doors.

"I feel like I've been on a date. Thanks."

"Thank you. Now, the reception."

"Want to go in together?"

"Not for a social event like this. I don't want our people or Bayer thinking we're an item."

"See you there, then. I'm glad they all speak English."

She smiled and let herself into her room.

As she had hoped, she spotted Luke already at the reception when she came in. He was standing with Klaus Durst and his wife. *Maryse?* Nancy thought. *French.* Luke lifted his glass at her but turned back to the couple without missing a beat. Nancy sought out Count von Kracken, who stood close to the door.

"Nancy, how good to see you. May I present my wife, Leonora?"

The countess stood easily as tall as her husband, with broad shoulders, but otherwise slender, like a swimmer. She had a firm, confident handshake.

"Countess, an honor."

"Leonora, please, Doctor Lockhart." An English accent.

"Nancy, then. Delighted to meet you. Watching Otto this morning, I expected that you would be an interesting woman."

"Oh, in what way?" She looked with mock suspicion at her spouse.

"Purely professional. I think we shared an awareness of meeting dynamics."

"Right you are, Nancy." von Kracken smiled and arched an eyebrow. "Rather conspiratorial of us, wouldn't you say?"

"Indeed." Nancy took a glass of prosecco from the tray passing by, with a smile of thanks to the waiter.

They clinked glasses. Leonora considered the two of them.

"Otto does like to people-watch," she said. "He has long been a student of human beings. I never understood why he ended up in the pharmaceuticals business."

"I started as a physician. The ultimate people-studying career."

"I agree," said Nancy. "I learned more about working with people in medical school than in business school." Catching sight of Helmut and Maria Gottleib coming in the door, she waved them over and did the introductions. The conversation shifted to German. Nancy remembered from the research file that Leonora's maiden name was Coburg. It came out that most of her cousins were German.

Excusing herself, she moved among the guests, meeting each of the Bayer representatives with a quick efficiency that being single made possible. She saw Luke circling the party, too, and making a point of casually introducing Smithson couples to Bayer couples. *He's a natural*, she thought.

After about an hour, the count stood and tapped a spoon on his glass. The room went still.

"No speech tonight," he said, to noises of feigned disappointment. "I want to thank you all for coming, and for being who you are. I have never seen such a compatible group in a business setting. Whatever happens tomorrow morning, I hope we stay in touch as friends." He lifted his flute of yellow wine. "To friendship."

The assembly raised their glasses and repeated the toast with gusto.

Nancy had slipped behind him. She touched his elbow gently and stood forward.

"And I would like to thank Count von Kracken and the Bayer team for your hospitality and this warm event. To lasting friendship." The crowd answered her toast even more enthusiastically. That being a signal that leaving was permitted, couples began to find each other to go to dinner or home.

Nancy saw the Gottleibs and von Krackens, the Schmidts and the Scherers, and the Dursts and the production manager (who was a bachelor) leave as three groups. As a single woman, she was not obliged to invite anyone to join her, so she could slip out before someone caught her. Almost.

"Going to dinner alone, Frau Doktor? I hope not."

Luke stood behind her in the hall, his athletic frame silhouetted by the lights of the room behind him. *Damn, he's so hot*, she thought.

"Didn't you get a dinner offer?"

"I did, but I told them I had an outside engagement and was deeply sorry."

"You didn't!"

"I did, and I do."

"Might I know who this 'outside engagement' is?"

"Yes, you know her." He smiled, took her arm, and they headed for the door.

He had the doorman hail a cab and ordered the hack to take them to a restaurant that Nancy recognized.

"You *have* done your research."

"A reliable recommendation was easy to obtain in that crowd. I collected a half dozen for future trips. But this one is from Sandro, whose judgment in all things gastronomic I trust."

"You do know he's a sommelier, don't you?" When the president of Smithson Italia invited you to dinner, it would be a night to remember.

"I know. Sometimes, I'm amazed by the different things we all did before we got into this business."

"I think the kitchens of every Michelin-rated restaurant in Rome have his picture on the wall."

Over grilled fish and a fine Moselle, Nancy assessed the success of the reception.

"You were brilliant tonight, matching all those couples up. So smooth, I don't think anyone noticed but me."

"Because you were doing the same thing. I read the files in Rome, but it wasn't hard to pick out who would get along with whom."

"Easy for you, but the rest of us need to work at it. You size up people very quickly – and accurately, I might add."

"Thanks for the compliment. I don't know what it is. A sixth sense?"

"It's a gift, and one of the reasons I wanted you here for these meetings." She sipped her wine. "I envy you sometimes."

"Well, there is the downside."

"Oh?"

He looked at her for a while, his face a little darker and sadder.

"One of the things I like about you is that you've never asked me why I never married."

"None of my business."

"Interested?"

"In marriage?" Nancy grinned.

"No, silly!" Luke's face lit back up. "In the answer."

"No, but if it has something to do with your gift, then yes."

"The usual line is that I never met the right woman." Luke took a sip of his wine. "Meeting women isn't the problem. Seeing through them is."

"Perhaps you judge them too harshly."

"I don't think that I judge them at all. I genuinely like the people I meet, women included. But I have a problem with phonies or people who want to use other people."

"Let me guess. The women want you for something else, not you."

"Something like that. I'm a catch, not a person."

"Is it really so sad?"

"I *have* met a few wonderful women I could fall in love with."

"Let me guess again. They're all married."

"Except for the lesbian and the one who became a nun."

"You're kidding!" She laughed.

"No. Really. They were smart, honest, fun, and interesting. Everything I like in a woman. It just wasn't meant to be."

They shared lighthearted conversation after that, mostly about Joe, and Luke's niece, Elly.

"You're very fond of her, aren't you?"

"She's probably closer to me than anyone in the family. My sister is a nurse. When I lived in New York, Elly would come to my house after school when Bea worked the afternoon shift. She's a fun kid, maybe because I'm her uncle, not her father."

"Bea's a single mother, I take it."

"Yes, Jim was collateral damage in a gang drive-by shooting on the Upper East Side. He was bringing home pizza for supper."

"I'm sorry."

"Me too. Elly was seven. Too young to understand, but old enough to remember."

"Same age as Joe when his father died."

Luke nodded. They sat in silence for a while.

"Dessert?" he asked.

"I'm full, thanks."

He signaled for the bill. On the way back, Nancy thought about his gift.

"So, what will you do when you find an unmarried woman who isn't after your money or your career prospects?"

"Depends on what she wants. It's not about me."

The cab pulled up to the hotel. Outside their rooms, they paused. They each reached for the other's hand at the same time.

"Thank you," they both said together. And laughed. Then they stood there, each knowing what the other wanted, unable to speak. Finally, Nancy took her hand back.

"The door's unlocked. Come on over...."

# 23. Rome, Friday

THE NEXT MORNING, Sandra called as Joe washed the coffee maker and his dishes.

"Need a ride?" he asked, trying not to sound too hopeful.

"I would love one, but Claudia – remember her from Mr. Wolcowski's office? – just called to tell me that an embassy car's coming for both of us."

"I'll see you at the office then."

"Next strike, I'll schedule a Vespa ride in advance!" He imagined her smile over the line.

"You do that. Bye."

"Bye."

Joe put down the handset with a sigh. He wrote out a note for Angela that he expected to be late again. His mother would be back tomorrow, and his routine would go back to normal: no late nights translating. Maybe he could take Sandra on a date.

He gathered up his backpack and walked down to the garage. The sun blinded him as it rose in the cloudless sky. The city gave off the fresh, clean smell and feel that follows a storm. He took the side streets parallel to the Viale delle Medaglie d'Oro, just to be different. He also decided to park on Via Liguria on the back side of the embassy annex building, rather than out front. He locked the scooter and started walking toward the Via Veneto.

Joe sensed something. He started to turn around, but both his arms locked up behind his back and his feet came off the ground. Whoever lifted him moved to the curb, as a dark blue car screeched to a halt in front of them. A new Fiat 1900, but the engine sounded heavier. A man jumped around him and opened the back door. Joe's head involuntarily jerked down as the one holding him pushed him into the back seat while the other held the door.

Joe reached for the left door as one man slid in behind him. The door opened and filled with the bulk of the other man, who swung into Joe's face as the car burned rubber and took off. He sat on Joe's hand, pinning him to the seat. It smelled of plastic and perfumed cleaner.

The car went too fast to be going through the downtown streets. Joe guessed that they were taking the Viale del Muro Torto west to something smooth-flowing, like the Lungotevere by the river or the Via Flaminia.

Joe tried to twist and get up, but the thug on the left punched him hard from above and pushed his head into the seat cushion. After a second try, Joe took the hint and looked out the window from where he was. He saw the tops of trees, tall fountains, and buildings. His head ached from the twisted position. His back throbbed between his shoulder blades.

His pinned hand went to sleep. He knew when they crossed the Tiber because open sky filled the window. Then they went through a tunnel, which had to be the Porta Cavalleggeri south of Saint Peter's. Soon they were climbing the Janiculum Hill., with its unique park-like setting and pine trees. The statue of Garibaldi went by after the road leveled off. They would head out of town on the Via Aurelia Antica.

The high walls of exclusive villas, Pontifical Colleges, and private schools confirmed his guess. This was Rome's first highway, which carried Julius Caesar's armies to Pisa on their way to Gaul. At this point, Joe did not care. He had lost all feeling in his left forearm. His shoulder and neck ached from not being able to move.

The car slowed and turned into a villa. Joe recognized the carved lions' heads on the gateposts. Betty Walker's old house. The Walkers had moved back to the United States a year earlier when her father received a surprise reassignment. As the car rolled slowly down the driveway to the stately entrance, Joe wondered who lived here now.

No one, it turned out. There was a "for sale" sign on the door. The thugs jerked him from the car. Someone pinned him to the ground, face down, and almost tore his arms out pulling them behind his back. Joe tensed up hard from the pain and made fists while the thugs wrapped rope around his wrists and legs. Joe struggled until one of them punched him in the back of the ribs.

"Live one, this fish," said the one kneeling on his back.

"*Stronz'americano*," said the other one. Shit American. "I'd like to finish him off and get out of here."

"The general told us not to hurt this idiot," said the driver. "Even where you hit him might get us in trouble."

"Shit, I'd give him worse."

"His backpack is in the front. Don't forget it."

Joe did not recognize their accent, but they were neither locals nor Southerners.

"Let's get him inside," said the driver. Pain shot through Joe's shoulders as one thug knelt on the backs of Joe's knees and yanked back on the bound wrists. The driver and the other man grabbed Joe under the armpits and picked him up as the first thug stood back. Joe had never been unable to move himself before, and that bothered him more than the pain. The driver traded places with the first thug and went back to the car for the backpack.

The two thugs dragged Joe into the house, never really letting him stand. The dust on the furniture told Joe that the owners had not rented it since Betty and her family had moved away.

They dropped him on the couch. The one who talked about finishing Joe off pulled back his jacket and pointed to a large pistol in a shoulder holster, then pointed at Joe and smiled. Two missing teeth complemented the scar on his cheek from whatever brawl.

Joe sat still. This kind of fear was new to him. His left forearm hurt worse than his shoulders, and his fingers tingled. *At least the blood is moving again*, he thought. As the Fiat crunched the gravel on its way out, he got his first good look at his assailants.

The nasty one was about Joe's height, but heavy-set. Not fat, but Joe understood why his arm went to sleep under that sturdy bulk. His round face included a two-day beard. The other one was as thin as his partner was hefty, with a five-o'clock shadow. Both men moved quickly and stayed alert, but the thin one's movements were jerkier. They sported small, thick mustaches.

"I'm going to check out the kitchen," said the thin one.

"Right. You're hungry again," said his partner. "Good luck. The house is empty, you know."

"You okay with this one?"

"Sure, what's he know?" They watched Joe while they talked. Joe tried not to move and stared back. He had learned that any movement caused them to react. For some reason, this felt like the bus rides Joe took when he was small. He would sit and listen with a blank expression while older kids would talk about him. Joe considered that these two might not know that he understood Italian. For the first time since being captured, he enjoyed a slight sensation of control. The thin one grunted and walked toward the kitchen.

The heavy one sat in a leather-covered wooden chair across the room. He pulled the *Gazzetta dello Sport* from his jacket and folded it open to the racing pages. As he read, he rocked, and the chair squeaked, rhythmically. He paid no attention to Joe's backpack, which leaned against the end of the couch on the floor.

Once Joe shifted slightly. He noticed how the man's attention switched to him from the racing pages. Clearly, he was not going to be able to work his way free or do anything clever while they were here. He settled in to wait, listening to the creaking chair. It sounded like a sailboat rocking at anchor. Joe imagined the slapping of water against the hull to fill in the picture.

He heard the Fiat returning. The thin man came back from the kitchen, and the driver walked in. The driver was younger than the other two, slender, athletic, and clean-shaven.

"I called him. He'll be here in twenty minutes, and we'd better not be."

"Okay, let's go." The big one stuffed the newspaper in his pocket. He walked over behind Joe to check his bindings. Joe tensed his hands again, tightening up the ropes.

"This one's not going anywhere."

The door slammed so hard as they left that Joe winced. In the silence, a piece of plaster over the front door fell to the floor. The trees and tall walls gently muffled the sounds of the traffic on the Via Aurelia Antica and the noise of the great city below the hill on which the villa stood.

Time raced in his mind as Joe worked to loosen the knots. He forced himself to relax his wrists as he tried to squeeze his hands free.

Finally, the ropes came off his hands. He worked feverishly to free his ankles, the panic rising as he struggled to undo the knot. He stopped to breathe long and deep to regain his composure. At last, he found the end of the rope and began to liberate his legs. The excitement rushed to his head as the blood flowed to his freed feet.

Gravel crunched in the driveway. Panic again. He grit his teeth and thought. He hoped that his kidnappers did not know the house and yard as well as he did. He grabbed his bag and headed away from the front door, down to the basement. He closed the door silently. At the foot of the stairs, he put his pack on and tightened the straps while his eyes adjusted.

In the dim light, he crept among the equipment and wheelbarrows to the small door leading out to the garden. Moving quietly and deliberately, he reached the edge of the house and crouched behind a bush that hid him from the parking area.

A navy-blue Lancia sat there, one of the souped-up, bulletproof versions used by high-ranking carabinieri officers. The white license plate – EI-004 – confirmed it as an official army car. The driver was a slender man in civilian clothes, standing erect by the rear passenger door. Two men came out of the house, one tall with gray hair, the other had short red hair and looked about forty years old.

A chill ran through Joe's chest. He recognized the older one from the magazine articles he had translated: General Ettore Arcibaldo, the retired Commander of the Carabinieri Corps.

"*È scappato!*" He escaped! Rage contorted the general's face. He pointed to the driver. "Quick, Santini, you search the grounds. Rossi is searching the house. Sangemini, call for backup, maybe Leonardi if he is nearby."

"Yes, sir!" said the redhead. He got in the car and picked up the radio. The driver trotted up to the main gate and began scanning the fruit orchard in a systematic search of the yard.

*So, there are four of them,* thought Joe. Carefully, he eased away from the scene. The landscape terracing concealed him as he bent over on his way to the brush-covered hole in the wall that he had used when Betty still lived here.

Thinking of Betty, he patted the wallet in his back pocket. *She left so suddenly. We almost got that far.* The condom was still there, from the packet that Nancy had given him when he started shaving. He slapped himself mentally and focused on parting the bushes noiselessly.

Outside the walls of the villa, he walked through the neighbor's olive grove down the steep hillside to the alleys that led from the Janiculum Hill to the river. A half hour later, he was sitting on the number 60 bus, headed downtown.

# 24. Hunted

JOE COULD NOT GO HOME if the carabinieri were on the lookout for him. It was time to check in with Agent Redwood and to stay off the streets. He got off the bus at Piazza Barberini, two long blocks from the American embassy.

The bus was warm enough, but the heat really hit him as he crossed the piazza. It reflected off the white marble of the buildings around the square and the water of the massive Triton fountain in the center. It rose off the black asphalt and the windows of cars parked around the fountain. This was only July. By mid-August, everyone who did not flee the city for the annual Ferragosto vacation was going to melt.

Joe slowed down when he reached the welcome shade of the tree-lined Via Veneto. He stopped when he rounded the gentle bend climbing the hill and spotted the carabinieri outside the embassy and the annex. Of course, carabinieri, as well as police, usually patrolled the streets around major embassies. *Are there more carabinieri than usual?* he wondered. *Doesn't matter.* He ducked into the narrow streets behind the annex, where he knew there was a payphone out of sight of the Via Veneto.

On the Via Lombardia, he turned to cross the street, which made him look behind him. The stranger that had followed him on the Vespa the week before was turning onto the Via Lombardia from the Via Veneto. He was moving slowly, scanning both sides of the street. Joe tried to hide by jumping back behind the corner.

Joe heard the Vespa motor speed up, hard. He ran back down the street, heart and legs pumping, seeking an escape. Before the Vespa made it to the corner, Joe turned into an apartment building. He ran past the portiere's station (*empty*, he noted gratefully) and up the first flight of stairs. A window at the end of each floor looked over the street. He peered cautiously out to see the Vespa rider. He also counted four entrances on each side of the street like the one he had used.

The stranger rode to the end of the block, turned and rode back. He seemed to be trying to decide whether to commit himself to checking one of the apartment buildings. At the corner of the Via Porta Pinciana, he dismounted at the payphone and made a call. His eyes never left the street, even as he dialed. After a short, animated conversation, he stood outside the booth, scanning the street.

Joe and the stranger remained like this for about two minutes. Then the other mounted his Vespa and drove down the Via Lombardia toward the Via Veneto.

Joe had to pee. Badly. He could not remember where the nearest *vespasiano* was, now that the city was removing most of them. The Emperor Vespasian had installed the pissoirs throughout Rome in the first century, which cut down on the urine-soaking of walls and improved public health in the crowded city.

Joe remembered the new public restrooms on the Pincian Hill, not far from the Pincian Gate at the top of the Via Veneto. He wondered if he could use the restroom at Jerry's Bar and Grill or one of the cafés on the Via Veneto without being spotted.

He walked downstairs and back onto the street, heading away from the corner where he had last seen the stranger on the Vespa. From the Via Ludovisi, Joe crossed the Via Veneto and went into the Excelsior Hotel from the Via Boncompagni side. The lobby was almost empty, and no one paid any attention to him. He used a stall in case someone walked into the men's room.

As he came out of the restroom, a pair of carabinieri entered the lobby. Joe turned away and headed down the hall. He took a service door that led back to the Via Boncompagni and was soon walking to the Via Lombardia payphone.

He approached the Via Lombardia carefully, scanning it from the edge of the building. Crossing the street quickly, he stopped outside the booth to dig Doug Redwood's phone number from his pack. He dialed while holding the token over the slot, in case the line were busy. It was. He scanned the street as he stepped out of the booth. A dark-blue Lancia with army plates was easing down the street, almost exactly as the Vespa had done only a half hour before. Joe stuffed the backpack behind the phone booth and ducked behind a parked Mercedes.

Four men were in the Lancia. Looking through the glass of the Mercedes, Joe recognized General Arcibaldo's erect form in the front passenger seat. Joe dropped down as the car passed.

He eased up after what felt like an eternity. The Lancia was waiting at the corner, though there was no traffic. Joe realized that the driver was alone just as someone grabbed his arms and pushed him to the ground. The two men from the back seat of the Lancia pulled him up and carried him into the car. The general was already getting back in. The car headed down the Via Francesco Crispi toward the Pincian Hill.

Joe's sides hurt, squeezed by the men on either side of him. The General spoke without looking back.

"*Lo zaino, dov'è?*" Where is the backpack?

Joe kept silent. The man on his right drove a fist into his ribs. Joe gasped and held back tears.

"Don't play stupid with me," the general said in English. "I know who you are and what you translated for Mr. Arland."

The driver stopped the Lancia for a tour bus unloading at the Spanish Steps. He drummed his fingers on the steering wheel, while forty middle-aged German tourists crossed the street, pointing and clicking their cameras in every direction. The general lowered the sun visor to hide his face. The two thugs gripped Joe harder, while they smiled at the tourists.

When the crowd passed, a man on a Vespa sped up from behind and zipped around the Lancia. The driver swore and gunned the accelerator, tires squealing as the high-powered sedan flew out of the piazza.

"*Lascialo!*" barked the general. Leave him be. Suddenly the Vespa slid and fell. The Lancia driver slammed on the brakes. The car skidded and side-swiped a big tour bus coming in the other direction. The windshield exploded into the car over Joe's head. The sound of tearing metal hurt his ears. Pinned between the two thugs, Joe felt the car spin and stop as it crashed broadside into the stone wall to the right. The horn stuck.

Joe opened his eyes. The thug on his left was falling out of the opening where the door had been. All four men were unconscious.

Joe climbed out and ran back toward the Spanish Steps, ignoring the pain in his side. He was vaguely aware of shouting behind him as he bounded down the stairs two at a time. He took a sharp right across the Piazza di Spagna and ran at least two blocks north on Via del Babuino before he slowed to see if he was being followed. The pain eased as he caught his breath. He would be a sight when the bruises started showing.

Joe was alone in a sea of tourists, shoppers, and businessmen. He saw a Vigna Clara-bound bus slowing at the stop ahead and ran to catch it. Vigna Clara was where the Redwoods lived. If the phone was busy, someone was home.

On the bus, he noticed the other passengers staring at him. He put his hand to his face, and it came back bloody. *The glass*, he thought. Only then was he aware of the burning from the tiny cuts on his face and scalp.

He used his handkerchief to wipe some of the blood. It was already clotting. A housewife pulled a roll of paper towels and a bottle of mineral water from her shopping bag and came over to sit next to him.

"It doesn't hurt, signora," Joe said. Her face relaxed.

"Oh, I thought you were a foreigner," she said, "I'm going to clean you up. Sit still. You're a mess."

An old man with a veteran's pin on his lapel and a cane leaned toward him.

"Bunch of little scratches," he said. "Were you in an accident?"

"Shattered window," Joe said. "Not serious, but like the signora here said, messy. I'm going home now."

Everyone seemed satisfied that he would be okay and went back to their other concerns. He offered to pay the housewife for the paper towels and the water. She insisted that he drink the rest of it. She got off at the Villa Giulia, halfway to the end of the line.

With time to think, he considered the Vespa and the way it fell. A deliberate tailspin! Joe had practiced them for hours. He tried to remember the Vespa driver, but everything had happened so fast that he could not recall the details.

Leaving the scene of an accident was the least of his problems. As soon as the carabinieri arrived, they would recognize the general and hush the whole thing up. No one would ever know about him or the crash.

But every military policeman in a black uniform would be looking for Jason Joseph Lockhart, Jr., *americano,* eighteen years old, 1.75 meters tall, sandy hair, hazel eyes. If he did not get some protection soon, there would be nowhere to hide.

The bus reached the end of the line, not far from the Redwoods' apartment building. Though the scabs pulled on his face, Joe felt much better. He went to the front of the bus to step off and froze.

Carabinieri and police with sub-machine guns patrolled all four corners of the square. Most of the residents of this sterile development outside the city were expatriates working in the larger embassies or for multinational companies. There was often a police car cruising around, but nothing like this.

*Now where do I go?* He could not go home. The carabinieri would stake that out right away. He checked his watch. It was only five o'clock. Angela was not expecting him and would not be back until Monday. No one would miss him. He could not make it to the Redwood house or the houses of any of his classmates in the area.

Joe decided he was safest right where he was.

"*Ho dimenticato qualcosa.*" I forgot something. He paid the driver for another ticket. Soon the bus was on its way back toward downtown. This gave Joe time to think of a different destination.

He got off behind the Navy Ministry building, across the river from the Prati neighborhood. He knew that the police only manned the front gate. He headed away from the ministry to cross the river. Soon, he was walking the familiar streets off the Viale Mazzini until he reached Via della Giuliana.

Joe walked to the café across the street from Sandra's apartment building. He bought a handful of telephone tokens. He put them on the shelf in front of the phone and got out the slip of paper that Sandra had given him.

No answer at Sandra's apartment, so he called the FBI office. A recorded message told him that the office was closed until Monday.

He called the Redwood home. The phone was busy.

The maid at the first minister's residence answered and explained that the family had gone to Capri for the weekend.

Nothing to do but wait. He bought a caffé latte and a doughnut. He went next door and purchased a *ciriola* bread roll and a bottle of mineral water. He picked up a newspaper and a magazine at the news kiosk.

Joe watched Sandra's building until the portiere left his post for a break or an errand. Then he walked inside and up the steps to where he had a view of the entrance, but out of sight of the portiere.

The building had one of the new elevators that did not take coins or tokens, so no one used the stairs. Joe settled in for a long wait.

He finished the bread, half the water, and the whole newspaper as the sun went down. The portiere turned on the hall lights from the ground floor while Joe hid on the landing above. The old man closed his little guard shack, stepped outside, and pulled the big portone shut behind him. Joe stood and ran up and down the first set of stairs a couple of times to wake up his legs. He could not go out now without a key.

It was almost nine o'clock when he heard the big door open, and the familiar blond ponytail backed in. Sandra carried full shopping bags in both arms. Joe took the stairs two at a time, to wait for her at her apartment.

Sandra froze as she stepped off the elevator. She let go of the bags and quickly caught them.

"Oh my God, Joe! What happened to you?"

"Two run-ins with General Arcibaldo's men. It looks a lot worse than it is." He walked up and took the bags from her. "I met the *generale* too. They were all unconscious when I left them."

"What did you do to them?" She opened the door and motioned him in. "Tell me about it while I clean those cuts up better."

It was a small apartment. A single long hall led from the door to a window at the end of the building. Two bedrooms faced each other, and a combination living and dining room lay across from the kitchen. He sat on a kitchen stool while she put a few things in the refrigerator and went to the bathroom for a first aid kit.

As she fussed over his head and hands, he concentrated on recounting the events of the day. He wanted to stop and breathe in her scent. He was looking at her neck and imagining her skin against his.

"And then?" she asked. He snapped to, embarrassed that he had stopped talking.

"I caught the bus to Vigna Clara. I figured my house would be staked out, but who would guess that I would go to Doug's house? At least until they figure out who my friends are."

"Good thinking. Why didn't you go to the Redwoods?"

"At the end of the line, the whole neighborhood was crawling with police and carabinieri. I couldn't get off the bus without being spotted, so I came back toward town, and walked here from the navy building."

"Did you call Agent Redwood?"

"I tried, but the line was busy. The Stocowski's went to Capri, and your office was closed. I figured that you were on your way home. At least I hoped so." He winced as she discovered a sliver of glass in his scalp that the lady on the bus had missed.

"Sorry!" She used tweezers to pull out the splinter. "Just today, the Ministry of the Interior ordered increased security for all neighborhoods with important foreigners. This thing is coming to a head."

"Vigna Clara would qualify. Good thing you live in the low-rent district, or I would have nowhere to go."

She laughed. It was a light laugh that filled him with pleasure. He chuckled too.

"Well, Agent Redwood should be home by now. That will get Vittoria off the phone."

"It's their maid on the phone?"

Sandra rolled her eyes. "She talks to her sister for hours when no one's home. At least we know she's okay, and no one else is there. Drove me nuts until I learned that a busy signal for more than five minutes meant that the Redwoods were out.

"I'll call him. Take those bloody clothes off, so we can run them through the wash." Joe dropped his jaw. She laughed again. "Keep the underwear on, silly. I have four brothers. Unless your shorts are pink, I've seen it all."

While she dialed from the phone in the hall, Joe peeled off his sports shirt and jeans. With the summer weather, he had not worn a suit and tie. He blushed when she returned.

"Did you get through?" He eased behind the kitchen table. She grinned knowingly.

"Uh-huh. He said that the safest place for you now is right here. No one follows secretaries. He'll pick you up here in the morning."

"You don't mind?"

"Of course not! In the middle of this whole mess, we have an evening together without having to go through the dating protocol. I think this is great."

Joe grinned. "Me too."

"Can you do laundry?"

"Naturally. Angela cooks and cleans, but I do the laundry."

"Good. The machine's over there, and the detergent is on the shelf. You wash your clothes, and I'll put the rest of the shopping away. Then we can think about supper."

Joe went over to the closet-like space that served as a laundry area. The clothes hamper was full.

"Mind if I run yours, too? One shirt and a pair of jeans is not a load."

"Okay. Thanks."

Joe found some stain remover near the detergent and pretreated the bloodstains on his clothes. He sorted the hamper and started a hot water wash, so his stuff would be done first.

"About supper. I could take us out."

"No way. Strict orders from the Federal Bureau of Investigation. You're not to step outside until Agent Redwood gets here in the morning."

"Makes sense, I guess."

"Besides, I want to wow you with my culinary skills."

"What do your four brothers say about that?" He grinned. She faked a pout and mock-threatened him with a large spoon.

"Can I trust you with a knife?"

"The *generale* can't, but you can."

"You'll find makings for a salad in the crisper. Make yourself useful."

Joe gave her a salute. He took the knife she handed him, and a cutting board from the counter. He located lettuce, tomatoes, fennel, cucumber, radishes, and some aged pecorino. Setting himself up near the washing machine, he went to work.

It was a companionable experience, the two of them talking about their families as they cut, stirred, and tested. Sandra had grown up in the Midwest on a farm. Her father became a farmer after a career as an army musician. Her mother was the art teacher in the local high school. There was always painting and music in the house. One brother became a navy musician, another joined the marines. The two younger ones were still at home. Number three son wanted to take over the farm someday.

"I saw the instruments in whatever you call the second bedroom. Do you play them all?"

"Some better than others, but yes. Viola is my first instrument. After voice."

"So why art history instead of art or music?"

"I love the stories behind the art and the music."

She turned the flame down under the *ragù* to let it simmer. Joe put the two salads on the table in the next room. The washing machine buzzed. He went over and moved the load to the dryer, then loaded a cold-water wash with her clothes.

Sandra stopped stirring the ragù and eyed at him with a sad look.

"What?" he asked. He glanced down, to be sure his underpants still covered everything. She laughed.

"I'm sorry. I didn't mean to embarrass you. I was wondering – well." She paused, looking embarrassed herself. "About your father. I know there's just you and your mother."

Joe shrugged. "No problem talking about it. Dad died when I was seven."

"How did he die?"

"There never was a diagnosis. He got sick suddenly and wasted away in about six months."

"That sounds terrible. I'm sorry for you."

"Don't be." He reached out and brushed her cheek with the back of his hand. "I can talk about it."

"Okay." She brightened up. "So now you've heard about my family. Tell me, what's it like living with a famous mom?"

"Pretty normal, I think. She's not famous at home, just Mom."

"From what I hear, she's an incredibly strong character. Is she scary or anything?"

"Well, she's tough, but also fair. She calls me the man of the house, which means I share the load around the house, but she also respects my opinion."

"That's unusual, trust me. You're lucky."

"I know. But she's also a doctor. Drives me nuts how she psyches me out all the time."

"I think all parents psych out their kids, not only doctors."

She spread spices on the two beef *filetti* that he had beaten out and put them in a skillet. Joe took the laundry out of the dryer. He put his own clothes back on, folded hers, then loaded the dryer with the cold-water load. He went to the pasta boiling on the back burner. Taking a fork, he speared a seashell-shaped piece and tasted it.

"Al dente," he announced. Sandra killed the flame while he carried the pot to the sink and poured its contents into the colander. While he tossed the pasta to remove the last of the water, she turned the flames off under the *friarielle* greens, the meat, and the ragù.

"This is wonderful!" she turned around to smile at him. "I've never had anyone help with dinner here before. We have a feast!"

Joe grinned. He loved seeing her so excited about something as simple as making a meal. He could not imagine having to live alone for months on end, cooking for one.

"This calls for candlelight," she said. She pointed to a drawer. Joe opened it and removed a box of white candles, the plain paraffin ones every family kept handy for power outages. Sandra reached into the back of a cabinet and pulled out a tarnished brass candelabra. It looked like a menorah, but it only had four candle holders.

They ate their *conchiglie al ragù* silently. It was well after ten, and neither had eaten much all day. But they both kept looking up, catching each other's gaze and smiling as they shoveled in another bite of the spicy dish. Sandra liked her sauces with lots of heat, which he appreciated. Nancy liked spicy food, but not as hot as Joe did.

During the meat course with the greens and salad, conversation resumed.

"Figured out whether you're going back to GW yet?"

"Oh, I think I'll go back in the fall. The question is, what will I major in?"

"You can't take art history, accounting, *and* international relations?"

"No," she said, "wish I could."

"Why the accounting?"

"That's something the FBI wants. They need more agents with accounting backgrounds because so much of their investigative work involves financial crimes. Even the crimes that aren't financial per se involve following the money to find a motive."

"Makes sense. So, you plan to stay with the bureau?"

"I think so. I mean, I've only seen the office here in Rome. Agent Redwood is a very special Special Agent. I may not have a good picture. How about you? I figure you're going to college. Any idea where?"

"Still working on that. I'm leaning toward the Naval Academy, Harvard, or Johns Hopkins."

"Annapolis, Ivy League, and med school. Is that what I hear?"

"Yes. I'd like to go into the navy, so if I don't go to Annapolis, I'll try for NROTC at one of the others."

"Those are hard to get into."

"So everyone tells me, but I don't see the problem." He pointed his fork at her. "GW is competitive too."

Sandra shrugged. They ate in silence for a while.

Joe felt her foot running up and down his calf.

"Feeling more at ease with your clothes on?" She raised one eyebrow.

"Yes, but I don't intend to sleep in them." She faked a shocked expression. They laughed.

"For dessert, I have ice cream. 'If I knew you were coming, I would have baked a cake,' as they say."

"I'm fine. How about you?"

"I'm full. Coffee?"

"Sure. I'll start the dishes while you make it. Okay?"

"Wow! You do laundry *and* dishes?" She rose and gathered her place setting. Joe stood too.

"Yup. I'm completely housebroken too."

She put down her dishes and leaned over to kiss him. "I may not want to turn you over to my boss in the morning." Joe returned the kiss. They separated slowly and picked up their dishes.

Joe found dish-washing detergent under the sink and ran the water. Sandra reached into the cupboard for a six-cup stovetop coffee maker and a vacuum-packed brick of espresso coffee.

"Do you mind espresso?" she asked.

"It's normal in our house. But I thought everyone at the embassy had American coffee makers."

"I started out as a student on the economy, remember. No access to the commissary below the embassy back then."

"That explains the local shopping you came in with."

"I prefer the food at the Trionfale market to the frozen and canned stuff at the commissary. The produce is fresh, like what I grew up on, and I don't have to lug it up the Via Veneto to the trolley."

The second load in the dryer finished. Joe pulled the laundry out and began folding it. Sandra ran over to join him, then stopped and grinned.

"You *are* well-trained." She laughed as she started folding with him. "This isn't even your laundry."

"Nothing new here. I fold my mom's too."

The coffee was ready when Sandra came back from stashing her laundry in her bedroom. They took the hot, dark brew out to the living room and sat on the sofa.

"No TV?"

"No TV. Darned things are too expensive, considering that the programs go off the air only a couple of hours after I get home. I listen to the radio. Just music. I still can't follow Italian at normal speed."

They finished their coffee together, their cups going down like a synchronized swimming routine. They turned to face each other.

The kisses were hot and passionate. No tasks awaited them. They slipped their hands under each other's shirts, as they reveled in the sensation of their hair and skin sliding together.

They left the dirty cups on the coffee table and walked back to the bedroom arm in arm.

"I'll fold that neatly, so you look good tomorrow," she said as she pulled his shirt over his head....

# 25. Cologne, Friday

FRIDAY MORNING, Nancy woke up facing the sun coming around the drapes. She kept her eyes closed and was instantly aware of the hard, muscular body behind her. She luxuriated in the feel of Luke's lungs slowly expanding and contracting against her back. She had been surprised at how smooth his skin was. His body hair was fine and soft. She liked it. She controlled her breathing, hoping not to wake him.

"Mm. You're not sleeping, are you?" Luke murmured almost inaudibly.

"Mm. Neither are you."

"Mm. Can you see the clock? I don't want to move."

"Mm. Seven o'clock"

"Mm. Do you want breakfast?"

"Mm. Maybe later. You?"

"Mm. Later." He moved his hand from her hip to her breast and nuzzled the back of her neck....

ଓଧଓଧଓଧ

On her way to the elevator, Nancy tried to focus on the coming meeting with Bayer. Luke had still been shaving when she had closed the door between their rooms. She had smiled to see him rumple the sheets and covers on his bed when he returned to his room. She hated to let go of this blissful feeling.

She had just ordered breakfast when Luke walked into the coffee shop. His tie today also set off his skin tones. Hard to believe he was as clueless as he seemed, but she figured that the clerks in the stores he frequented knew their business.

"Good morning, boss." She arched her brows and did a wide eye roll. He sat as the waiter approached. He ordered the continental breakfast without looking at the menu.

"Do you always order what I eat?"

"Continental breakfast too? No, a total coincidence, believe me."

"Okay." They paused while the server set down their coffee and brioches.

Luke opened his mouth to say something, then stopped. Nancy caught the hesitation.

"About this morning, what's the worst that we can expect?" she asked.

"I would say that Slide-rule Scherer gets cold feet, and they come in prepared to argue or turn us down."

"That serious?"

"No, but it's the worst I can think of."

A bell boy approached the table. "Excuse me, Frau Doktor, a phone call for you."

Nancy rose and went to the telephone on the counter near the cash register.

"Nancy Lockhart"

"Ah, signora, buon giorno."

"Buon giorno, Maria Grazia. Is everything okay?"

"Here in the office, yes, but I thought you should know that Bayer has scheduled a press conference for 1300 today. About their new generic line. They did not specifically mention the production RFP."

"Still a surprise."

"I thought it would be. Have you finished already?"

"No. The Bayer response comes this morning. They seem to have made up their minds."

"Maybe it is not about the contract."

"Maybe. Anyway, thanks for the warning. Dottor Arland and I will discuss it before we go in."

"*In bocca al lupo, signora.*" Good luck.

"Grazie. I'll call after the meeting. See you Monday."

Luke's face mirrored her concern when she returned. She briefed him on the news. They discussed various positions to take, depending on how the Bayer team approached them this morning. Anything about the new plant was off the table. They prepared to discuss public negotiations in progress and options that they had contracted, which they could turn into brick-and-mortar facilities faster than anyone else. They would focus on their competition's recruiting problems; Smithson Italia could hire qualified technicians faster than masons could put up walls.

Neither mentioned the night before.

Breakfast done, they went to the conference room. Nancy deliberately tarried in the ladies' room so that they could enter separately. As before, everyone was standing around when she walked in. She need not have worried about the slide rule. Conversation stopped as they all turned toward her.

253

"Ah, Doktor Lockhart, guten Tag." Count von Kracken beamed.

"Guten Tag, meine Herren. Shall we start?" She thought the scene looked a little silly as if she were the queen, but it was effective. This should be a good day.

In fact, it took less than an hour for Bayer to brief their response. The Bayer group confirmed that they would award the contract to Smithson. They had scheduled a press conference to announce it.

"Can you prepare the formal proposal this morning instead of this afternoon?" the count asked.

"Certainly," said Nancy. Helmut was up and heading for the phone bank in the hall.

"Excellent! It seems that we have a deal." He shook her hand, and the two groups walk past each other around the table, shaking hands, and punching shoulders. *Like the end of a World Cup match*, Nancy thought.

The count drew her aside and motioned for Luke to join them.

"The press conference is scheduled for 1300 hours today. Could you both be there?"

"If you like," Nancy said. "It's your show. We don't want to communicate anything that the press would misreport."

"Which they may do anyway," said the Bayer COO with an eye roll. "I think that both companies should be there. Television is changing the way we make these announcements, and my marketing people tell me that we need to remember the visual impact."

"Our PR people say the same thing. We'll be there."

"We still have the dinner tonight."

"All the more to celebrate. Bayer headquarters at twelve thirty?"

"Yes, if that is convenient."

"See you there."

They shook hands again. Luke and Nancy joined the flow leaving for their offices.

"Wow! That went much better than I expected." He pressed the button for the elevator.

"I think so too. Would you call the Schmidts to let them know that we're still on for two? I'll call Rome."

"You got it." He gave her a casual salute and a smile. They let themselves into their respective suites.

The meeting had been so short that their rooms still weren't made up. Nancy put her briefcase down and pulled the fallen bedclothes back up over the bed. She got a glass of water from the bar and sat at the desk to call the office.

Sandro Moretti had just gotten back from his coffee break. He would make the announcement at the staff meeting but warn everyone to keep it confidential until the news came out in the afternoon.

At home, Angela answered.

"The signorino went out early this morning. He left a note that he would be late getting back. I will leave food for the weekend as usual."

"Thank you, Angela. See you Monday."

She dialed Luke's room.

"You could knock on the door now," he said. She heard the smile on the line. She walked over and opened her door. She tested his doorknob. Unlocked.

"You might not be decent." She stuck her head in the door. He was sitting on the desk in his shirtsleeves, a bottle of mineral water next to him, still on the phone. He grinned and slid off the desk, returning the handset to its cradle.

"I can be decent too."

"But that wouldn't be as much fun." They laughed. "We have a couple of hours before we need to be at the Bayer building. Want to do some more sightseeing?"

"Sure. Let's close the doors before housekeeping walks in." Nancy returned and traded her heels for a pair of low pumps. She checked her makeup and her purse then went out into the hall. Luke was just coming out. The chambermaid rounded the corner as they stood at the elevator. They greeted her as the doors opened.

"What can follow the cathedral?" he asked as they stepped out into a brilliant summer morning.

"Do you like art?"

"Yes. All kinds."

"Let's go to the Wallraf-Richartz-Museum. It's the oldest in the city, and it has a wonderful collection. Lots of little jewels, rather than loads by a few artists."

"Let's do it."

They spent a relaxed hour in the museum. The collection surprised Luke. It was indeed a tour de force of some of the best representatives of European art from the Middle Ages to contemporary. Luke's face turned somber as he read the history of the museum on their way out.

"So much destruction. I didn't realize how much damage the Nazis had done, even before we bombed everything."

Nancy took his hand and squeezed. They stood briefly. Luke brightened after a moment.

"It feels almost unfair being able to enjoy this museum with someone like you. Thanks for suggesting it."

"You're welcome. Let's get back, but first, a quick lunch at the café across the square. We have a press conference and tennis ahead."

From the café, they walked briskly back to the hotel. After stopping briefly in their rooms, they took a taxi to the Bayer complex east of town near the Königsforst.

The press conference proved to be a different media event, as Count von Kracken had predicted. The usual chairs had been set out for the reporters. The count made his prepared announcement from the lectern on the podium, then invited questions.

Standing behind the speaker, Nancy counted as many photographers and cameramen as reporters. The surprised reporters jumped to their feet when von Kracken finished, each trying to ask their questions before the others. He took control of the crowd and began pointing.

Meanwhile, the photographers and cameramen zoomed in on the count's distinguished face, but even more on her and Luke. They did not speak, just moved around, filming the scene.

Luke nudged her imperceptibly. "You have a question," he whispered. "He asked if you have a statement." She looked down front to the large reporter staring at her with his pad poised.

She smiled what she hoped was a good camera smile and asked him, "*Im Deutsch oder Englisch, mein Herr?*" That drew applause from the reporters and a few of the photographers.

The reporter bowed, smiling broadly, "As you prefer, madam, George Schmidt, *Wall Street Journal*."

"English, then." She looked over the crowd, which went silent as she gathered her thoughts. "I think that this is more than a simple business contract we have here today. It represents another milestone on the road of European collaboration and movement toward the integrated economy that the signers of the Treaty of Rome envisioned ten years ago. Smithson Italia is proud to be part of that and to be part of this partnership to bring affordable generic medicines to millions of people worldwide. Thank you."

All the while, the cameramen clustered around her. She bowed slightly to them, then backed up, turning her head to the count, who was beaming from the podium.

"That's all, gentlemen. Thank you for coming."

With that, he turned and led the party off the stage as the reporters continued to shout for attention.

Von Kracken had to go to a board meeting, but he ordered a company car to take them back to the hotel.

"Thanks for the nudge," she said as they crossed the *Süd Brücke*, the South Bridge over the Rhine River. "I think I spaced out looking at all those cameras."

"No problem. I don't think anyone noticed. You were a hit with the German one-liner. What was that?"

"I asked him 'in German or English, sir.' Just buying time."

"Well, it worked. Did you feel like the cameras were all over us?"

"Yes. I think it has something to do with the 'visual message' that Otto was talking about. They like handsome people on the screen."

"Hmm. A new era, I think."

"You're ready for it. It'll be interesting to see if any of this makes the evening news."

The two hours with Hans and Rikki Schmidt challenged all four players. The German couple had played together for years, and it showed. But Luke and Nancy concentrated and soon learned to read each other without trying. Nancy felt the same rush she remembered from matches with Jason by her side, but it was not a memory that distracted her.

The games ended tied. They had to vacate the court for the next reservation.

"That was more fun than I expected," said Rikki as they gathered their gear and walked to the lobby. Tall, slender, and classically athletic, she was clearly the superior player of the pair. "I hope that you will please be our guests next time you come to Köln – together or alone."

"Speaking for myself, I accept," said Nancy.

"Me, too," Luke added. "I hope to come back here often and soon."

After agreeing that there wasn't time for a post-game drink, they shook hands. The Schmidts walked toward their car; the two Americans turned to the elevators.

"So much for Hans getting an earful from his wife about playing us."

"Why?"

"I remember her. She was Ulrike Bessemer back then. West German champion. The nickname Rikki didn't mean anything to me."

"You knew her?"

"No. We never played each other, but we studied film clips of the German pros."

"Well, I know how Hans feels. Two champions and two schmucks. What a workout."

Nancy punched his shoulder as the elevator doors opened. "You were no schmuck. You were smoking out there."

"Is that why my whole body is burning?"

"You don't feel good?" Nancy was still high on endorphins.

"I feel great. Doesn't mean that I don't feel the stretch it took."

They paused at their doors. Luke arched his eyebrows.

"Cocktails before dinner at seven. Don't you want a siesta?"

"Up to you. The door's still unlocked."

They went into their rooms. Nancy went to the liaison door and opened it. He was walking toward the door himself.

"You weren't kidding."

"My shower or yours?" He grinned. Desire ran all over her sweaty body.

"Let's set the alarm, in case we do take a nap." She stepped into his room….

ଔଓଔଓଔ

The wrap-up dinner started in the hotel bar, where a wing had been roped off for the group. *The alcohol is not what makes this party seem so merry*, Nancy thought as she walked toward the crowd. *These people genuinely like each other.* Otto von Kracken detached himself from the couple he was talking to and came over to her. He bowed, kissed her hand, and asked her to join them. Besides his wife Leonora, there was the CEO of Bayer, a tall, blond man with broad shoulders, and his hair parted almost in the middle.

"Kurt Hansen, delighted to meet you, Doktor Lockhart." He bowed and kissed her hand.

"Nancy, please,"

"Kurt, then. This is my wife, Mathilde." Nancy shook hands with the rosy-cheeked woman, who could have been cast as the fairy godmother in a Cinderella movie.

"Call me Matty. It is a name that I save for my American friends."

A few moments later, Luke appeared, nodded to Nancy, and paused to chat with Hans and Rikki Schmidt, who happened to be by the door. Nancy caught his eye and waved him over to meet Kurt and Matty.

There was not as much circulating tonight because the groups of friends had sought each other out. They made their way to the dining room amid much laughing and storytelling. By the end of the evening, some couples made plans to go clubbing together. Others extended invitations for ski trips and house visits during the coming winter. Nancy sat between Otto and Kurt, Luke between the two wives. From what she saw, he was charming them effectively.

After the cordials had been served, von Kracken made a thirty-second speech, followed by equally short remarks by Nancy and Kurt, not long enough to stop the flow of the conversation. The noise level went back up, but everyone was free to leave. When about half the room had emptied, the Bayer managers both excused themselves for the evening, with much thanking all around and best wishes for a mutually beneficial relationship.

Luke came around the table.

"Let's say goodbye to Hans and Rikki before they leave." They intercepted the couple, who had risen and started to the door.

"Thank you for everything, including the great match today," Luke said as he shook hands.

Hans put his hand on Luke's upper arm. "Remember to come see us."

"I would not mind a rematch," said Rikki. "I don't get that level of play often."

"Because I am such a klutz," said Hans with a smile.

She punched him playfully. "You are not a klutz, but we don't find such a challenge in doubles here." She studied Nancy's face. "It did not come to me yesterday, but I know you from somewhere – and in a tennis outfit."

"Guilty as charged. I was Nancy Ardwood."

"Ah yes! I saw the movies of you. Very fast!"

"I only remembered the movies of you after we played this afternoon. Bessemer, right?"

"Ja. So, you were the secret weapon today."

"Hardly. I only started playing again this spring, after many years." She looked at Luke. "He got me back on the court."

"No. Joe did that. I just happened to help."

"Joe is your son, no?" asked Rikki. Nancy nodded.

"He wanted to learn."

"Bring him, too, sometime. He would be welcome."

"Thank you." They shook hands again and walked out together. The Schmidts went out to their car. Nancy and Luke stopped in the lobby to talk to the general manager, who was on hand to greet the VIP's in the group as they left.

"We've had a wonderful stay, Hans," Nancy told him. "Thank you for the arrangements. We could not have done so well without you and your staff."

"I am a happy man, then, Doctor Lockhart. Tomorrow, we will have a car ready at nine o'clock to take you to the airport."

"Thanks, Hans. Would you send the invoice to Rome, as usual? I don't think that I charged any personal items this time. Luke?"

"I made some phone calls."

"Telephone calls are complimentary, Doctor Arland."

"Thank you, then no, I did not charge any personal items, either."

They shook hands with Mr. Ulsdorf and watched him move to the next party leaving.

"Too tired for a nightcap?"

Nancy looked around. "I think I'd like to have that nightcap upstairs myself."

"Okay." They took the elevator up to their rooms. Inside, both liaison doors were unlocked....

# 26. Saturday

THE NUMBER 8 TROLLEY CLANGED ITS BELL as it stopped outside. Something was different. Joe's room on the Monte Mario was at the back of the building, where he could not hear the street. He opened his eyes, suddenly aware of and delighted by Sandra's smooth skin neatly fitting into every bend in his own body. The predawn light leaked through the slats of the shutters.

Joe lay there, breathing as gently and evenly as possible. He did not want this moment to end, nor did he want to wake this wonderful person next to him.

"You're not asleep, are you?" she said without moving.

"No, I'm just loving this moment."

"Me too." They lay there for a few moments.

"What time is your boss coming for me?"

"I think about eight. Shall we have breakfast or something before he comes?"

"Mm. How about something first." Joe nuzzled the back of her neck and pressed closer.

The phone rang.

Sandra grabbed her nightshirt on her way down the hall. When she came back, He was sitting on the bed, with the sheet over his lap. The alarm clock read six o'clock.

"That was Agent Redwood. Things are moving, and they need you. He's on his way here."

Joe leaped from the bed. They hastily donned their clothes. While he washed his face and ran a comb through his hair, she grabbed some cookies and an apple and put them in a bag for him.

"He said to go down to the *portone* and hold it open. As soon as the police car pulls up, run out and jump in the back. He'll get out to let you in."

"What about you?"

"A car's on its way for Claudia and me again. We have to staff the offices this weekend. Go, now."

They embraced and kissed, and she stepped back. He went out the door, adrenaline pumping and breathing with passion, a mixture that he had never experienced. He was not sure it was good for him, but he decided to revel in it as he took the stairs two at a time. He did not even think of the elevator.

He had been watching out the door for about a minute when he saw the blue flashing light come speeding around the corner from the Piazzale Clodio.

"A *pantera*!" he said aloud to himself. The Ferrari 250 GTE 2+2 purred eerily, considering the speed with which it approached. It came to a silent stop so fast that Joe expected burning rubber. Only a leaping panther, such a dark red that it was almost invisible, interrupted the gleaming black finish. He had never been inside a Ferrari, much less one of the police-equipped ones. Every police department in the world envied the cars. Criminals used to outrunning their police hated them. The Italian police hired retired professional race car drivers to pilot the powerful machines.

The passenger door opened, and Redwood leaped out. He pointed to the back seat. Joe ran out and jumped in. The FBI agent flipped into the front seat and closed the door in a single motion. The car silently accelerated to open highway speed in less than a block. The driver was a grim-faced man with chiseled features and short, graying hair. He did not acknowledge them, but his eyes moved constantly as his face pointed forward.

"Sorry about the early call. The government is racing to stop the generale and his people before this turns into a civil war between the carabinieri and the *polizia*."

"Sandra didn't tell me you would have a Ferrari pantera, sir." Joe could not keep the awe out of his voice. Redwood smiled.

"The *Squadra Volante* lends me this for special work. I've only ridden in one twice myself."

"*Andiamo all'ambasciata?*" the driver asked. Are we going to the embassy?

"Can you lead us back to your backpack?" Redwood asked Joe.

"If it's still there, yes."

Twenty minutes later, the car idled down the Via Lombardia. Agent Redwood ran to retrieve Joe's bag from behind the phone booth and jumped back in the Ferrari. The FBI man scanned the papers as the Ferrari carried them down the Via Veneto and up the Via Bissolati.

"This does it," he said. "If we can move fast enough, we can nail them."

The Ferrari moved quickly through the traffic, occasionally aided by traffic police waving them through. But with only one blue light and no siren, it still took time. "Sirens are for chases and emergency calls," Redwood explained.

They stopped near the locker at the Termini train station, where a plainclothes policeman met them. He took Joe's locker key and retrieved the rest of Joe's copies while he waited in the car.

The radio crackled, and the driver took a message down. He handed it to the American policeman. The FBI man nodded and motioned to the plainclothesman to follow them. Joe watched the agent go to another pantera. The cars rolled and the sirens started even before they closed the doors.

"It's happening, Joe. We caught the general trying to reach a military plane at Ciampino. He slipped out of the hospital almost as soon as he came to."

Joe was only half listening. He was glued to the window as the morning traffic flew past him in a blur. His mouth was dry, and his heart was pumping. The driver slalomed around the parked taxis and the fountain of the Piazza della Repubblica and accelerated down the middle of the straight Via Nazionale in the oncoming lane. In less than ninety seconds, he ran four stoplights and climbed two Roman Hills. Joe twisted to see behind. The other pantera was right there.

The cars turned into the Quirinale, the Presidential Palace, between two *corazzieri* Presidential Guards. The cloudless sky reflected off their armor and horsehair-topped helmets. The pantera glided past the inner courtyard where Joe and Nancy had walked to attend a concert in the Pauline Chapel. A liveried servant opened the door of the car, and a *corazziere* officer led them up a wide grand marble staircase to a grand hallway. At the end of the hall was a tall set of double doors, guarded by corazzieri who were expecting them.

They stepped into a large room, filled with men Joe recognized from the evening news. One group stood around a table covered with maps of Rome, Italy, and Western Europe. Another group was poring over the Arland documents. At various times the men ordered one or another of their assistants to run for file folders or answer questions. The American investigator joined them.

Joe took a seat in an armchair in a corner, happy to be ignored, and feeling safe. He tried to hide his awe and be as inconspicuous as possible.

"Joe, would you come here?" Mr. Redwood's voice startled him. Embarrassed, Joe got up and approached the table.

"Joe, these gentlemen would like to meet you." He introduced the president, the prime minister, the ministers of interior and defense, and an admiral from the intelligence service.

"You have rendered a great service to our country, Mr. Lockhart," said the president in English. "Until this afternoon, we were hurtling toward the disintegration of democracy and a certain civil war. You have saved us from both."

"Thank you, Your Excellency," Joe answered in Italian, looking at his feet and back up at the president. "I just translated some stuff." The men laughed.

"Modest, too," said the minister of defense. Joe remembered that this man had kept the job for the last four governments under three prime ministers, setting a record for political survival in the Italian Republic.

"Mr. Lockhart," said the admiral, "we have a question about two abbreviations in these two documents: BR here and – here it is – B-M. We saw those codes in other places too."

"BR stands for *Brigate Rosse*, sir." The Red Brigades. Joe pointed to a line on the page. "Here is its code word in this letter. This other letter explains that it is a new group organizing somewhere in the North."

"And B-M?"

"I'm not sure, sir. There isn't much about it, but it's in Germany. I think the letters stand for two names because the code word for B-M is two words, *Antonio e Cleopatra*. Just once, Cleopatra was used alone, as if it were a person."

"Remarkable," said the admiral. "Our people in Germany can follow that lead. Thank you very much." Joe took that to be a dismissal. He looked at Agent Redwood, but the FBI man was talking intently to the president. Joe started back to the armchair.

"*Un momento, giovanotto,*" the president called out. One moment, young man. Joe turned around.

"I am sorry, Excellency. I thought the admiral was dismissing me. I was just going back to the chair to wait."

The president cut him off with a wave. "Relax, young man. It seems you've been wounded. Are you all right?"

"Really, I'm fine, Excellency. A lot of small cuts from glass. It looks worse than it is."

The president considered Joe's wounds. "I know what this youngster's problem is. He's hungry." He turned to the others standing there. "Am I right?"

"Well, Excellency, I did collect him at dawn," said Redwood. "I don't think he expected me so early."

The president snapped his fingers, but the corazziere was already moving toward Joe. "Please take him down to your legendary army mess and see him properly fortified."

"*Certo, Eccellenza.*" Certainly, Excellency.

"And notify his mother. Wait, maybe Mr. Redwood or the FBI should do it."

"Excuse me, Excellency," Joe said, "but she's not here. She should be returning this afternoon." The president seemed surprised.

"She is at a business meeting in Cologne this week, Excellency, with Doctor Arland," Agent Redwood explained. He looked at Joe. "They are under surveillance."

"Shouldn't the agents reveal themselves now?" Joe's tone revealed his surprise and some annoyance.

The FBI representative caught Joe's expression. "We're satisfied that she is not involved in any of this. Doctor Arland called the FBI in New York to report his suspicions about what he thought were coded messages in the material he was sending to New York. We're still checking out his story, so we have not yet assured ourselves that he is an unwitting participant in all this. My counterpart in Bonn has gone to Cologne to brief Doctor Lockhart away from him."

The interior minister added, "we need to be discreet, and not tip off Doctor Arland as long as he is still a person of interest."

"Bring her here if they return before we finish making the arrests." The president gestured to the interior minister and the FBI agent. "You two can figure out how to proceed, but she should know where her son is as soon as possible."

The president turned to Joe. "Thank you, Mr. Lockhart. We will save our questions. Follow Lieutenant del Piave here. Have some breakfast. We'll see you later."

"Thank you, Excellency." Joe nodded and turned to follow the corazziere officer.

They walked down the hall at a brisk pace. The corazziere stood at least six feet five. His easy amble required a serious stride for Joe. He caught up as they made their way downstairs to the garrison area of the palace complex. Army personnel were walking in all directions, looking purposeful. Now and again, they would pass a pair of sergeants standing by a doorway chatting. The enlisted men would stop and give the officer a sharp salute.

"Lieutenant del Piave," Joe said, in Italian. "Any relation to the Cavaliere Giuseppe del Piave?"

"My father. You know him?"

"Yes. I translated a book for him."

"So, you are the young translator he was so excited about."

Joe blushed. "I didn't know he was excited."

"Very much." He slowed and turned to smile at Joe. "You should have heard him carrying on at family dinner when he brought the book home. He beat my brothers and me over the head about how your Italian was better than our English, and shame on us." He winked. "All in good humor, of course, but clearly you impressed him."

Joe's stomach growled. He could smell fresh baking. Del Piave led him through a crowded, noisy mess room where men were having breakfast. All wore uniforms, mostly army. Some were carabinieri. Some were corazzieri relaxing in their dress uniforms just coming off duty. Specially carved posts held their helmets. No one paid attention to the lieutenant and the civilian. In the mess, enlisted men could ignore an officer just walking through.

Del Piave opened the swinging door to a small dining room off the back. Inside, officers ate the same breakfast as the troops, in relative quiet. He motioned Joe to a table and hung his helmet on a post.

"Are you having breakfast too?"

"I was about to come down here when you arrived. I had already turned over to my relief when I overheard the conversation about your hunger."

They went up to the buffet and helped themselves to pastries and caffè latte. Del Piave also had some muesli and yogurt. The teenager and the giant both filled their trays.

"Excuse me. I don't want to offend, but aren't the corazzieri also carabinieri?"

"Yes, but we are a unique regiment of carabinieri. In fact, we are the oldest military unit in the country."

"How old?"

"Thirteenth century. The first royal guards were archers. The corazzieri have been called that since the fourteenth century. Always the king's personal guard, to protect him in battle mainly. Of course, with the Republic, our mission became to protect the president."

Joe nodded. His mouth was full.

"I always admired the carabinieri," he said after swallowing. "That is why this whole thing surprises me."

Del Piave raised his finger to his lips. "Please do not speak of what goes on upstairs outside the room. What you are seeing there is highly confidential." He checked around to be sure that no one sat close enough to hear.

"Oh, sorry. No one told me."

"No problem. I am glad that I could be here to catch you before something got out."

They ate in silence. A messman came to clear the table, and they stood. Del Piave collected his helmet.

"I am off duty, but I will walk you back to the command room." Again, Joe struggled to match his stride.

At the door, they were greeted by another corazziere, who saluted del Piave and escorted Joe into the room.

"Ah, Joe! I'm glad you're back." Agent Redwood waved him over. As Joe approached, the policeman handed him one of the latest letters. "Did you ever see this name before?"

Joe read the letter. Someone had circled the name "James Fountain" in purple. "No, sir. I would have noticed because purple isn't usually used for people, just places, events, and organizations."

"We noticed that too. We think this is the leader. We had our suspicions, but this clinches it."

"An American?"

"No, Joe. An Italian from the north, Giacomo della Fontana. The security services have been watching him along with members of a neofascist cell that he has several friends in. He's a local politician in the MSI." The Italian Social Movement was the right-wing political party closest to the neofascists.

"Why has his name only come up now?"

"No idea, but your – or, rather, Arland's – stash of correspondence is a gold mine for us. Everyone here can read the originals, and we can compare them to other data coming in."

"So, Mr. Arland is involved?"

"No. We just confirmed that with the FBI in New York and offices in the different places originating the documents. Apparently, he was funneling duplicates of documents for the information of the people in New York who were helping to finance the coup. It was a clever setup: the conspirators bought enough stock in Smithson to get on the 'major investor list' then started using the Rome office, through Arland, to keep informed. We still don't know how information goes the other way or which shareholders are involved. Arland couldn't have had any idea. He knew none of the players, and none of them knew him."

"He did mention at the beginning that everyone else had read the material he gave me, that it was from the files. That is why it surprised me that lately nothing has been less than a few weeks old."

The commander of the State Police waved at the FBI agent. Redwood excused himself and went around the table. As Joe headed toward a chair against the wall, a naval officer approached him.

"Mr. Lockhart, I am Commander Mario Perla." He shook hands with Joe. "I work in SIFAR, the Military Intelligence Service."

"Pleased to meet you, sir. How can I help?" Joe recognized the copies of his translation work.

"This may be a bit tedious, but I would like to sit down with you and record the exact chronological order of the translations."

"I think that they're all dated, sir."

"Yes, but we would like to be sure of two things: one, the order in which you received the Italian letters, and two, to make sure that the attachments – those magazine articles and such – are attached to the correct letters in this pile."

"Yes, sir, I can do that." They walked over to one of the small tables near the catering area. Joe went over each of the "jobs" with Perla. The naval officer took notes on an A4-sized note pad.

Shortly after noon, Commander Perla finally stacked the papers together and gathered his notes. He shook Joe's hand and walked over to the other corner of the room, where an army officer and a civilian waited. The trio began comparing notes, occasionally walking over to one or more of the senior officers around the map table to answer questions or provide new information.

"That was a useful session." Joe started as Agent Redwood came up from behind him.

"Sorry, sir, you caught me in a daze." Joe got up.

"Sit down, Joe. Would you like a cup of coffee or something?"

"Coffee would be nice, sir. Thanks."

Redwood returned with two cups of espresso and sat across from Joe. "How sure are you about Luke Arland's ability in Italian?"

"Well, I'm not an expert, but he tries very hard. He still can't follow a conversation at normal speed."

"Normal Italian speed or normal American speed?"

"Normal Italian, sir," Joe said with a chuckle. "People who get to know him learn to slow down. My mother or I interpret at other times."

"Can he read it?"

"That's coming slowly, too, as far as I can tell. Mom said that even by Christmas, he couldn't read anything more complicated than a menu. Until about a month ago, if he didn't keep the business letters in their files, he couldn't get them back together because they all looked the same to him. I had to be careful to keep the source documents and the target translations together when I delivered them."

"What happened a month ago?"

"He started asking me about various lines in the letters and guessing them right more often than not. Like I said, he was trying hard."

"That jives with our background checks. There doesn't seem to be anywhere that he could have learned fluent Italian in his past. That's a relief. Now we don't have to arrest him at the airport."

Joe sat up. "Are they back?"

"No, but they're in the air. We couldn't get your mother aside before they left because our man never could catch her without Arland. I'll pick them up after lunch."

"Can I come?"

"You'd better not, Joe. We're only starting the first round of arrests. Until we have certain players in custody, we don't want you out there. We think that they don't know what we have here, so they're still looking for you and your papers."

"Any idea how long I'll be here?"

"You'll probably go home tonight, assuming we get the right people off the street by then." Agent Redwood checked his watch. "What do you say we have some lunch?"

They got up and walked toward the door to the hallway that led to the army garrison mess hall.

"Where will you take my mother and Mr. Arland?"

"I'll bring her straight here. We don't think that she'll be safe until you are."

"And Mr. Arland?"

"He'll be our guest, but you won't see him at first. We'll be doing in-depth interviews, so we can sort out how these people used him."

As they left the command center, the conversation switched to the prospects for the school basketball team. Doug Redwood would be team captain for his senior year. The FBI agent walked him back after lunch and turned him over to the corazziere at the door.

"You're a big help in there, Joe. I'll see you soon with your mother."

"Thank you, sir. See you later."

He stepped inside. The multiservice team that had been poring over the translations stood back from their table. Commander Perla waved him over.

# 27. Flying Home

THE SUN COMING AROUND THE DRAPES woke Nancy again on Saturday morning. She lay there, reveling in the feel of Luke behind her.

"Alarm in less than one minute," he whispered. He reached over her and hit the button on the clock before it could go off. She rolled over and kissed him fiercely on the mouth, lying on top of him.

"Now *that* will wake me up!" They clung to each other for a moment, then slid off opposite sides of the bed.

"We should eat a full breakfast this morning," he said as Nancy went to her room and tore back the bedsheets.

"I get airsick, remember."

"We won't be in the air until late in the morning, and you'll be able to control your nausea better if you're not also empty."

"Okay, as long as you hold my hand like you did on the way here."

"But, of course, milady."

She closed the door.

Forty-five minutes later, they sat in the coffee shop, eating their steak and eggs. The bell captain had sent a porter for their luggage.

At nine thirty, the hotel limousine stopped in front of the international terminal at the airport. Luke held the door for Nancy while the driver got their suitcases.

"I can get out of the car by myself, you know."

"But then I'd have to carry the luggage." She gave him a playful punch as they approached the counter. Ten minutes later, they joined the other passengers at the gate. The Cologne airport did not share space with the Luftwaffe, so the terminal effectively dampened the noise of the civilian aircraft outside. After waiting another fifteen minutes, the passengers filed out to the waiting Lufthansa jet.

As soon as they sat, Nancy took Luke's airsickness bag and put it in the pouch in front of her.

"Oh, woman of little faith." He put his hand over hers. "You'll be fine."

"First, I'll be prepared, then I'll be fine."

The flight attendant went through the safety briefing as the aircraft taxied to its position on the runway. She finished just as the pilot called for the cabin crew to prepare for takeoff.

Nancy took Luke's hand and leaned back in the chair.

"Don't press so hard. Let the acceleration push you back. No more pressure than that."

She stared at him in disbelief. "You're kidding."

"Come on. Try it. I'm still holding your hand. You can close your eyes if you want. Pretend you're flying the plane yourself."

Nancy took some deep, slow breaths as the engines revved up for the bolt down the runway. When the brakes came off, she made her legs relax. She looked at

Luke. He had turned his head toward her. He smiled warmly. She smiled back, then forced herself not to tense as the g-forces continued to pin her to the seat. She closed her eyes, but she opened them immediately. She preferred to look at him.

The pressure came off as the jet leveled in flight.

"We can't be at altitude already." She relaxed her grip.

"Time flies when you're having fun."

"Wise guy."

"Really. By forcing yourself to relax, you focused on your own body, not on the aircraft or the acceleration."

"Did you just make that up?"

"Kind of. At least that's how I explain it. It works, doesn't it?"

"Yes. Thanks."

"You're welcome." He squeezed her hand but left his resting easily over hers.

"What happens if we hit another storm, like my flight back from London last month?"

"I have some ideas, but this will be a smooth trip."

"What makes you so sure?"

"I called the airport weather office from the room. No thunderheads or verticals today, even over the Alps."

"Amazing. You were able to talk to them?"

"I was a pilot. Aviation English is my only fluent foreign language." They laughed.

The cabin crew came through with the snacks and drinks. They both had orange juice.

As she opened her little tray of German rye bread, cheese, and fruit, Nancy said, "Luke, in Rome we go back to normal. Agreed?"

"I know. You don't do office romance." He smiled, but his eyes betrayed his feelings.

"Besides, I'm the mother of a very observant teenager."

"Although he's probably cheering for you in this regard."

"Why do you say that?"

"Because I think he'd like to see you happy, as would I."

Nancy pondered his statement for a while. She cut and ate her apple with the steel knife and fork but did not peel it. She knew about the nutrients in the peel. Luke cut his in half but picked up each half with his fingers.

He had touched a deep issue for her. She had avoided involvement ever since Jason died. Luke was the first man to break through the walls she had built. Joe had rightly called her on the way she used her work as a shield.

She turned her head. He was still looking at her.

"What would a teenager know about my happiness?"

"He's your closest relative. He loves you more than anyone on earth. As you said, he's extremely observant. He's also a young man now."

"He's still my son. I can't just bring you into our life."

"I'm already there every other weekend on the tennis court."

"True," she admitted.

He swiveled to face her better. He gave a quick look to the nearby seats, to make sure that the conversation was still private.

"Let me ask you this. Has he asked about going on a date yet?"

"He goes to Il Klub sometimes."

"That's with his gang. Right?"

"Yes."

"Not the same thing as a date."

"So?"

"So why not? He'll be a senior next year. Did he take anyone to the junior prom?"

"Now that you mention it, no, he didn't."

"Why"

"Because Betty Walker, the girl he would have taken, went back to the States."

"When did she leave?"

"Last summer. Her father was reassigned suddenly."

"Last summer? Don't you think a handsome guy like him could find a date for the prom in the next nine months? How big a deal is the prom to young girls nowadays?"

"Still pretty big, I gather. What's your point?"

"The point is, how does he ask his single mother about dating when she never dates? Maybe he hasn't figured it out yet." Luke squeezed her hand quickly to punctuate his comment. Nancy sighed.

"Good point. I think I missed some signals there."

"He is comfortable talking to you about almost anything, from what I see."

"You're right. Sometimes I don't appreciate his maturity. I keep seeing the little boy I miss."

"Normal for a mother, I would say."

"So, any ideas, Doctor Arland?"

"A couple. For starters, let's not do anything."

"What?"

"Like you said, back to normal – at first. We still meet for tennis, maybe picking it up to every week. I enjoy our three-way matches."

"What about after the 'at first'?"

"Go out to dinner once in a while. Date again. There must be men who want to take you out. I'd line up for the chance if you'd let me."

"You're already more than a date."

"Granted. But remember what I said about my problem with so many women. I don't have that problem with you. I could spend all night just talking or dancing with you. I'd even get you home by curfew."

Nancy laughed. "There's a strange thought."

"I think he would welcome the sight of his mother having a life outside the office. It might make him feel free to date too. You're both single. It's a different relationship than most young men have with their mothers."

Nancy was silent as they let the flight attendant collect their snack trays and drink cups. The image of Joe staying up late and meeting her in his bathrobe as she tried to sneak in after curfew made her laugh again.

"Thanks, Luke. I didn't expect to use your people skills on my personal life, but I'm glad for it. You're a real friend."

"Thank you. I want to be your friend in any way you need." The look in their eyes as they stared at each other said so much more.

The lights flickered in the overhead panels. "The captain has turned on the seat belt sign. Please return to your seats."

"So soon?" Nancy felt the plane turn gently in its landing pattern.

"Time flies when you're having fun." He took her hand. "Now, don't lean back so hard."

"Is this another Luftwaffe bomber pilot? It seems smoother than usual."

"Might even be the same guy. The flying style feels the same to me."

"I should get his name and book my flights when he's on."

Nancy looked past him to the window. She had never dared do that during a landing. She squeezed his hand hard when trees and fences zipped by. As before, she was not sure just when they touched down.

"Backing engines – now!"

She held on to his hand and let the deceleration pull her sideways over him. Face to face, she almost kissed him.

"That was fun." She giggled. Luke seemed as pleased as a teacher watching a struggling child get it right.

"We'll make a jet-setter out of you yet."

When they came out of the terminal with their suitcases, Adriano was waiting. He relieved them of their bags and went to the company car to load them. A pair of four-door Alfa Romeo *pantere* flanked the car, their doors open, engines idling, drivers inside. One car had a police major and a large corporal standing by it; the other had a *commissario* and Agent Redwood next to it.

Nancy and Luke stopped on the curb. So did most of the passengers behind them. A family struggled to rein in their young boy trying to run to the Squadra Volante chase cars.

"Hello, Jim. What brings you to Ciampino?" she asked.

"You do, actually. If you'll please come with us, we'll explain on the way." He held the door to the pantera. "Hello, Luke, we're here for you too. Major Giannini will brief you in the car."

"What's this all about?" she asked. Luke closed his mouth, having been about to ask the same thing.

"Let's not discuss it out here. You're not in trouble, but the matter is confidential and very urgent."

Nancy and Luke got into their respective cars. As soon as the doors closed, the pantere moved swiftly out of the parking lot, lights flashing. Nancy saw the other passengers standing in stunned silence.

"That was quite a scene back there. Where are we going?"

"The Quirinale. Sorry, but I could hardly announce it in front of a crowd, could I?"

"The President's Palace. Why?"

"Because Joe is there."

"Joe? My God, is he okay?"

"Yes, he's fine. In fact, he's something of a hero."

"Explain, please." She tried to control her anger.

"Do you know anything about me besides the fact that I'm Doug's father?"

"You work in the embassy annex, which means you're government, but not Foreign Service."

"Right." He pulled out his credential pack. "FBI."

"What's this got to do with Joe?" The trees on the Via Tuscolana flew by faster than they had during the landing of the Lufthansa flight.

"I'm getting there, please. You knew about Joe's translating letters and files for Luke, right?"

"He told me about a couple of letters back around Christmas."

"It turned out to be more than that. He's been turning around an unbelievable amount of material. Luke told him everyone else had read it. He didn't want it known how poor his reading ability was."

"He could have asked me." A feeling of betrayal by the two most important men in her world crushed her heart.

"According to Joe, Luke said he couldn't. He said you already work harder than anyone else in the office, and from what Joe thought, he was particularly reluctant to ask you."

"I'm supposed to be supervising Joe. What the hell was this material?"

"Luke has to forward paperwork to the major investors in New York, right?"

"Yes. It comes in every week from our offices throughout Italy."

"He couldn't read it. He forwarded it with his regular reports. Everyone else in the office had seen it, he thought."

"He thought? What's going on here?"

"The material contained coded messages. We'll show you when we get to the Quirinale. Joe noticed a system of color-coded circles linking words in the letters with items in the enclosures. It turns out that some of your major investors are financing a right-wing coup, which is being dismantled as we speak. When Joe read that a coup was scheduled for August seventh, he came to my office, and we've taken it from there."

"You mean Luke is a spy?" The anger rose again. She resolutely pushed it down.

"No. As best we can tell, he didn't know about the coded markings. They weren't in the English translations, so he only caught them last week, when he started to try to read more of the Italian himself to improve his skill. He called our New York office from Cologne because our Special Agent in Charge there is a friend of his. Our man in New York told him to continue as normal so as not to tip our hand. The SAC called me, but we already knew, thanks to Joe. We checked him out while you were in Cologne. He was an unwitting participant. The conspirators never expected him to notice the coded circles. They used him as a channel specifically because he couldn't read Italian."

"So, Luke isn't under arrest."

"Nope. We're taking him to the Quirinale too. We need to keep all three of you off the streets while the government arrests the leaders and reassigns the units involved."

"Why? What have Joe and I done?"

"It's not what you've done. It's what Joe knows. By extension, you're in danger, too, and so is Luke."

"How dangerous?"

"Very. Now that you know he's safe, can I tell you what's been happening to Joe?"

Nancy nodded. Her heart pounded.

"Yesterday, he was abducted twice and escaped both times. He made his way to my secretary's apartment. We had set up three places he could go to after-hours if he needed us. She called me, and I picked him up and brought him here. We've had a crisis command center working in the Quirinale since yesterday."

"Abducted? By whom? Is he hurt?" She struggled to keep control.

"Some highly placed retired and active carabinieri officers directing the coup. He's okay, really. Some bruises from one of the thugs in the first snatch, and some glass cuts when the kidnap vehicle sideswiped a bus. The men holding him down were knocked unconscious. Joe got out and ran."

Nancy sat back, too stunned for words. The pantere switched to sirens and lights because of the traffic. They flew around the Coliseum and down the Viale dei Fori Imperiali.

She sat in silence as they sped up the Via Nazionale and into the gates of the Quirinale.

They pulled up inside. "How long will we be here?"

"Probably until tonight."

"And our luggage?"

"Your driver is bringing it. We'll see you home when you'll be safe."

A liveried footman held the door for her. She saw the second pantera stop at a different door, farther down. Luke looked back at her and shrugged as he accompanied the police major into the building.

A corazziere lieutenant met them. "This way, dottoressa, if you please." Agent Redwood fell in behind her. The lieutenant led them up the grand staircase and down the hallway. Nancy breathed as slowly and deliberately as the stair-climbing and the corazziere's stride would allow. She alternated between wanting to kill Luke, worry about Joe, spank her son, and run screaming from the place. She was boiling under her best acting face.

She had never been in this part of the Presidential Palace. The Pauline Chapel, the venue for classical concerts, was an impressive exhibition of Renaissance architecture and art. It did not surprise her that the rest of the complex was just as grand.

Enlisted men, officers, and civilians were coming and going through the doors at the end of the hall. Two corazzieri stationed at the door checked the ID of people they did not recognize.

The lieutenant said, "Dottoressa Lockhart" to them, then held the door for her.

She entered a vast room with an enormous hardwood table in the center, covered with maps. She recognized the president, the prime minister, and some of the Cabinet. At other tables, men engaged in various activities that she could not make out.

The room went silent as the men turned toward her. She regretted not having had a look in a mirror before coming here.

Joe stepped out from a group around a far table.

"Hi, Mom."

They walked toward each other, both wanting to run, but aware of the crowd around them. Like a part in a surreal play.

The president started applauding. The clapping was taken up by the rest of the room. Nancy and Joe hugged about halfway across the room. She gave up fighting the tears. Joe was safe. She did not even mind the scratches.

When the applause ended, she looked up. The president stood there with the prime minister.

"Dottoressa Lockhart, I hope that you are proud of your son. He saved our democracy from its greatest threat since Fascism. We are all grateful to him – and to you."

"Grazie, Eccellenza." This was not a speech-making moment.

"And let me apologize for not notifying you sooner. It proved harder to do in Cologne than we expected. All this came up since Wednesday, you see."

"Accepted. I'm just glad that he's okay."

"For that, you must thank Agent Redwood and your son himself. He is a remarkably tough man to capture." He extended his hand.

Nancy considered the men staring at her after she shook the president's hand. She faced the FBI agent. "Jim, do you think we could find a corner, so you can finish explaining all this to me?"

The president interrupted, in English. "We can do better than that. Lieutenant del Piave, would you please show the Americans to the guest suite? They should have some privacy now."

"This way, please." The corazziere led them to a door in another corner of the room, then down a short hall to an apartment. He held the door for them.

"Laura will come shortly to see if you need anything."

"Thank you, Lieutenant," Nancy said as del Piave closed the door behind them.

# 28. Denouement

JOE SCANNED THE APARTMENT: a sitting room, a bedroom, and a dining room. The furniture fit perfectly with the Renaissance art on the walls. They made themselves comfortable in the sitting room as a slender, thirty-something blonde attendant came in and asked if they would like coffee, something else, or perhaps lunch. They all asked for coffee, and Redwood suggested a *tagliere*, a cutting board of meat and cheese. Nancy had not eaten lunch.

After Laura left, Nancy eyed Joe and the FBI agent and asked, "Who is going to clear this up?" She spoke pianissimo, like an opera singer: clearly audible to everyone in the room, but also conveying the hushed nature of the music. Whenever Joe heard that voice, he trembled and wanted to become invisible.

"Mom, I'm sorry." She held up a hand.

"We'll deal with 'sorry' later. Now, I want to understand what's going on."

Agent Redwood put a hand on Joe's arm to calm him.

"Nancy, I won't try to defend Joe or Luke about translating company correspondence, but your son has behaved in an exemplary manner, with a wisdom and intelligence far beyond his years. When he tries to explain it, please hear him out."

"Okay, but I'm wearing three hats here: scared mother, furious company executive, and somewhat bewildered bystander. Joe, do you think you could take me through this from the beginning?"

Joe recounted the story, starting with Luke's approaching him at the Alfa Romeo dealership before Christmas. They paused while Laura rolled in a serving cart with three wooden cutting boards laden with cold cuts and an assortment of cheeses, a thermal carafe of espresso, bottles of mineral water, and a tray of pastries.

"Please ring if you would like anything else at all." She pointed to the pull cord by the fireplace.

They thanked her, and she withdrew. Redwood served the coffee and placed a tagliere in front of Nancy.

Joe continued his tale. It was the first time he had ever talked so long to his mother without her stopping him with either a question or a comment. Shadows billowed across her face, but not a muscle moved.

When he got to the part where he went to the FBI office, Nancy looked at the agent. He nodded and motioned Joe to continue.

He took her through the adventures of the last four days (omitting the part about sleeping with Sandra), until the moment Nancy walked into the command room.

He sat back. For more than a full minute, no one spoke. Joe tried to read his mother, but he couldn't. That scared him more than anything.

"Mom, any questions?"

She continued to look at him.

"You say you think this Vespa driver put his scooter down on purpose, causing the crash?"

"Yes, I think so. I practiced the same maneuver myself, so I could do an emergency put-down. The guy saved my life, but I don't know who he is."

"I can clear that up," said Agent Redwood. "He's a motorcycle officer with the *Polizia Stradale*. As soon as Joe came to us, I asked for protective surveillance on him, and they put their best man on it. We didn't expect Joe to be so good at spotting the tail and eluding him. Have you seen him drive his scooter?"

"Yes. He's given me rides often enough." She did not take her gaze from her son.

"We can arrange for you to meet him, Joe."

"I would like to thank him, sir."

Nancy still looked at him with a stern expression.

"Why spend the night in the secretary's apartment? Couldn't you go anywhere else?"

"Let me answer that, too," said the FBI agent. "As Joe explained, he had strict instructions to go to only three people if he was in danger: me, my secretary or the first minister, Steve Wolcowski. He came to me first but wisely turned around when he noticed all the carabinieri at Vigna Clara. The Wolcowski's were out of town. My secretary called me as soon as he showed up, and I asked her to put him up for the night. Her house would not be a target for surveillance by the conspirators, but your apartment, my place, and Wolcowski's certainly would. We couldn't risk having him on the street trying to get to us."

"Are all the carabinieri involved in this?"

"No, not all, and it's not just carabinieri. Thanks to Joe's work, we're rounding up the leaders. Soon, we'll know which units were compromised. Until then, Joe was smart to get off the streets and stay out of sight."

"Did she have a nice place?" Nancy smiled at her son. Joe let his shoulders relax. The amount of tension draining from them surprised him.

"Small, but two bedrooms and a washer and dryer, so I could wash my bloody clothes. Plus, she had just been shopping, so there was something to eat for dinner."

"I wondered why your clothes were clean. Your face and head are a mess."

There was a knock at the door. Lieutenant del Piave came in.

"The police interrogating Doctor Arland would like Agent Redwood to join them if he could spare some time."

The FBI agent rose. "This is a good time to step out, anyway. I am sure that you two have things you want to talk about without me." He went to the door.

"We meant what we said about calling Laura if you need anything at all, or to send a message." The lieutenant tilted his head toward the call button. "And there are toiletries in the bathroom if you need them."

"Grazie, Ercole," Joe said. The corazziere winked and closed the door.

"Ercole?" Nancy arched her eyebrows.

"Lieutenant del Piave is Pino del Piave's son. I told him I knew his father. It came out that Dad holds me over his sons' heads in a funny way when he wants to pick on them about their English."

"But his English is excellent."

"Yes, it is. I've been a running joke in the family since the cavaliere brought the book home to dinner one night."

She reached over and squeezed his hand. "I'm glad you're okay now. Why couldn't you call me or Maria Grazia?"

"I couldn't call anyone, Mom. It all started happening too fast. I was running for my life all day yesterday."

"Couldn't someone here have called?"

"The president himself ordered them to tell you as soon I showed up, but they hadn't finished checking on Mr. Arland. They told the FBI man in Cologne to get you aside without him, but he could never catch you alone before you got on the plane."

"So, Luke was the problem?"

"In a way, yes. They only confirmed that he wasn't involved while you were in the air. That's what Mr. Redwood told me before lunch."

Nancy was silent for a while, a faraway look in her eyes, which Joe had never seen.

"Our rooms were next to each other, and all the meetings were in the hotel. The FBI man had a problem."

Joe stood. "Want some more coffee, Mom?"

"Sure. And one of those bottles of water, if you don't mind." She finished the last two pieces of cheese on the cutting board.

When Joe sat, she drank some water, then fixed him with the stern gaze that made him squirm.

"About working for Luke behind my back." Pianissimo again, with the consonants cutting sharply.

"I'm sorry, Mom. It was the worst time in my life, and I just couldn't figure out how to get out of it."

"It was company correspondence."

"He's a company VP."

"But I'm your supervisor at the company, not just your mother."

"Right." Joe hung his head.

"That was your out, do you see?"

"I should have reported it to my supervisor."

"Yes. And Luke shouldn't have used company employees for personal business."

"I never saw it that way."

"I can tell. One of those things you'll learn when you start working on your own. It's why we have security training and confidentiality rules. He's more to blame because he should know better."

"Are you going to fire him?" Nancy laughed, which made him uneasy.

"Oh, Joe." She shook her head. "As I keep reminding him, he doesn't work for me. We both work for Sandro Moretti, the president. On Monday, Luke and I will explain it to him. We may need to change some of our company procedures."

"I guess you'll fire me, though."

"Maybe. Let that hang over your head until Monday night. Normally you'd be out in a flash for this, but there *is* the fact that no one on the board, including Moretti, wants me to become the board's confidential translator again."

Another knock.

"*Permesso?*" May I come in? Luke's sandy head appeared. Both Lockharts jumped up.

Joe could tell from his mother's smile that she was delighted to see the man who had caused the whole mess.

"Luke! No handcuffs? Are you free now?"

"Yes." Stepping into the room, he gave Joe a two-handed handshake. "Am I ever glad to see you! I hear you had quite an adventure while your mother and I were playing tennis in Germany."

"Yes, sir. You could say that."

"Joe, if your mother doesn't mind, would you call me Luke? You're twice the man I am."

Nancy looked at him and paused. Then she nodded.

"So, what happened to you with the police?" Nancy asked.

"They grilled me about all the people and documents I'd been passing to New York. It all squared with what they knew from Joe here. I could tell them the names of all the offices that sent letters for me to forward, but they knew already from the company records. This is causing quite a stir at the office."

"I just became aware of that. You and I will need to sit down with Moretti on Monday." Nancy was not smiling.

"I may need to dust off my resume."

"I wouldn't jump to any conclusions. There are the results from Cologne too."

Joe interjected. "By the way, how was the trip? Did you get the contract?"

"Yes, we did," said Nancy. "What's better, we established some excellent relationships with the Bayer management. Luke had them eating out of his hand."

"Now wait a minute," said Luke. "They were eating out your hand. I was just the straight man."

"I'll bet you looked like a doubles team at the presentation," Joe said.

"We did," said Luke. "Then, after that, we played real doubles with one of their executives. Turns out his wife was a German champion when you-know-who was playing at Forest Hills." He cocked a finger at Nancy.

"Must have been something to see."

The sun was turning the sky red outside and bathing the pastel stucco of the buildings with a golden light. There was another knock on the door. Agent Redwood walked in.

"Are you all caught up?"

"I think we are," said Nancy. "How's the round-up going?"

"The consensus is that we have broken the coup. We can send you home."

"Great! When do we go?"

"Not so fast, Nancy. The president wants Joe back in the command room. You're both invited too. And there's some paperwork for all three of you."

"What kind of paperwork?"

"Debriefing forms. We need to give you security clearances for what you witnessed, then swear you to secrecy."

"Is that a joke, Jim?"

"No. The reason that the 'round-up', as you so aptly called it, took so long is that it was conducted with utmost discretion. We managed to haul in all the leaders and redeploy the military units involved without leaking it to the public. The whole thing is going to stay top secret for a long time."

Luke asked, "What about the fact that Joe was translating Smithson correspondence? Weren't you tracking it back?"

"We had the finance guard do that. As far as your company is concerned, the poor people who worked late on Friday were responding to another surprise audit by the Treasury."

Nancy eyed Luke. "We're still going to see Sandro Monday. About the personal translation services." Luke nodded.

"Just don't mention what happened to the documents," said Redwood, looking at Luke, "except that you read them and filed them. Okay?" Three nods.

Nancy said, "Do you mind if I take a minute to freshen up?"

"Not at all. All three of you can use the facilities while I check on the cars and the meeting in the command center. I think it'll be in about twenty minutes." He let himself out.

Lieutenant del Piave appeared seventeen minutes later to escort them back to the large room. The maps had been cleared off the table, and staff was stowing papers in carrying cases. Bottles of champagne lined the coffee counter. Army messmen passed out flutes of the bubbly yellow liquid.

When they entered the room, another round of applause went up. The president stepped forward and motioned to Joe. He walked over, aware that he was blushing hotly.

"Signor Lockhart, when we leave here, we are all going to act like nothing ever happened. So, before we go, I wanted everyone here to have a chance to toast you and to thank you for the work you did exposing this attempt to bring down our country." He lifted a flute of champagne. "*Viva il traduttore!*" Long live the translator!

"Viva il traduttore!" went up in unison from four-dozen healthy voices. Joe looked around: everyone was smiling, including Nancy and Luke.

"Thank you, Excellency. And thank you all, especially those involved in watching over me. Someone saved my life by causing a car crash, which is a strange thought. Thank you."

The applause was not so loud this time because so many held champagne flutes.

While various officers and government officials came up to shake Joe's hand, Agent Redwood opened a file case and took out some forms for Luke, Nancy, and Joe to sign.

"Read it carefully, Joe," said Nancy, glancing at her form. "There are some serious penalties here if you let it out."

"I read it this morning before they typed in the personal information."

Nancy opened her mouth, then closed it. She turned her attention to her form and signed it. Luke had already returned his.

"Can I talk about this to you in your office?" Joe asked Agent Redwood.

"When it's just you, me, and my secretary. Let's not make a habit of it."

Lieutenant del Piave came up to them.

"The cars are ready with your luggage."

"Good. Let's go home." Nancy motioned for him to lead.

After a final handshake with the president and the Cabinet ministers on the way out, the Americans left the room for the last time.

In the courtyard, two black limousines waited. Luke and Agent Redwood got in one, and Joe and Nancy took the other.

An hour later, they sat at the kitchen table, eating the reheated lasagna that Angela had made the day before. Nancy was in her stocking feet. She had thrown her jacket on her bed.

They ate in companionable silence. Each had brought something to read to the table, but each kept looking up from the unturned pages of their books to catch the other staring at them.

"What?"

"Nothing, I guess. Just wondering how you became such a man under my nose."

"But you've been calling me the man of the house for years."

"But this week, I started seeing you as more than my little boy for the first time. And feeling it too."

"Well, for a mom, you're pretty cool to have around. I'm glad you're back."

# 29. Later

"HAND ME THE SCISSORS, would you please?" Nancy said, pointing to the other end of the coffee table.

Joe picked up the scissors and passed them to her. She snipped the bright gold ribbon and placed Angela's Christmas present on the floor near her chair. Outside, a cold rain beat hard against the windows. With the heavy curtains drawn, the room felt warm and cozy. Carols floated through the house from the phonograph in the corner.

Joe was wrapping Matchbox toys for Angela's nephews. Her sister and brother-in-law with their two little ones were still living with the Ceccarellis.

"Want some more hot chocolate?" Nancy asked.

"Sure. Any more panettone?"

"Plenty. I'll bring some." The soft cake was a favorite for both, which they could only find around Christmas. Fortunately, the Easter *colombe*, in the shape of a dove, seemed to be made from a similar recipe, so they could satisfy their craving twice a year.

Nancy returned from the kitchen with the leftover panettone and a Spode teapot. She sliced off a piece and put it on the plate near Joe. He reached for the pot and poured hot chocolate for them both.

Nancy began sizing paper around a Raggedy Ann doll.

"You know what, Mom?"

"What?"

"This Christmas feels weird."

"In what way?"

"Because it's like all our other Christmases."

"That's weird?"

"Yes. This time last year, I had barely met Sandra, and you hadn't dated anyone or played tennis in years. And you still smoked. The only thing different tonight is that you don't smoke."

"And both of us are playing tennis now. I get what you mean. I wish Luke were still around. He was good for me – and you, too, I think."

"Why did he really go back to New York? I can't help thinking he was fired or 'kicked upstairs,' as they say."

"Looks that way, but no, there was no fallout from the Arcibaldo affair. They want him to work his magic on some deals in Canada and Latin America. It made sense to return to New York. He actually isn't there much."

"You saw him in London and Basel, didn't you?"

"Uh-huh." She gave him a wink. "I trash him on the court every time, but he doesn't go down easily."

Joe smiled. "I read in the *Herald Tribune* that those four investors in New York pleaded guilty. Did Luke have something to do with that?"

"In a way. When Arcibaldo was arrested, the investors made a big mistake. They sold their Smithson shares all at once. It came up at Luke's first staff meeting.

He guessed the real reason for a sell-off by four major investors when the market was otherwise quiet. He called his friend Bob Worthman at the FBI. In less than a month, they traced the money being sent to Italy and issued indictments. The case was airtight against them."

"I thought the coup affair was still secret."

"Yes, but they violated American and Italian currency laws."

"Makes me think about how the government finally caught Al Capone on tax evasion after all the murders and extortion."

"It does, doesn't it?"

Joe finished wrapping the pile of little trucks and cars and reached for the books on the table. Angela's children were getting ready for university, and they had a reading list of English literature.

Nancy finished the doll. She picked up one of the books.

"Is this one for Mario?"

"Adriana, his sister."

Nancy moved the pink ribbon closer and used the same paper as she had used for the doll.

"How's tennis with Aldo?"

"Great. If I hadn't met Luke, I might never have found out that Aldo plays."

"Too bad the school doesn't have a tennis team. You two would be varsity lettermen."

Joe shrugged. "Maybe next year."

"Speaking of next year, first semester is over. What's the latest on your college search? We've talked about more places than I can remember."

"I'm down to the Naval Academy, Harvard, or Columbia."

Nancy arched her eyebrows. "Just three now?"

"Georgetown, maybe."

"While you're looking at all-boys' schools, did you consider UVa?" The University of Virginia.

"No. Why?"

"People talk about a public Ivy League: schools like UVa, Michigan, and Berkeley are all state universities, but well-endowed, with world-class faculties. They're classic universities, where you can major in almost anything."

"Anything else?"

"Charlottesville is a very pretty place."

"Not far from Richmond, if I remember my geography. You're still planning to go back, right?"

"Not immediately, but it'd be a logical step from here after you leave."

"If I want to be near home, I could go to George Washington." He wiggled his eyebrows.

"Do I detect a romantic angle there?"

"Just kidding, Mom. Although Sandra would only be two years ahead of me, having missed last year."

"You really like her, don't you?" Nancy held her place, folding the wrapping paper.

Joe sighed. "More than like. It was wonderful being able to date her normally last summer after I wasn't working nights translating for Luke or getting kidnapped."

"She'll always be the first one, something like that?"

"Something like that."

"Have you heard from her lately?"

"A letter in her Christmas card. She added accounting for a double major, and she got into a pilot recruiting program at Quantico. She can train part-time before she graduates and work summers. It will cut her training pipeline in half after graduation."

"She wants to be an FBI agent after all?"

"Yes. Having a service jacket already with a SAC Commendation made a big impression when she applied."

"A lot of guys there. Not so many gals."

"Yeah." He ignored the inference. "She's the only woman in the new training program, even though the Bureau is supposed to be opening up."

"Your social life this fall doesn't seem to suffer. Are you still seeing Priscilla – or is it Penny?"

"You're picking on me." Joe grinned. "It's both of them, and you know it!"

"My point exactly." She smiled.

"My turn. You've been out more since Luke left too. How's the handsome tennis pro at the Cavalieri Hilton?"

"I'm afraid my dates aren't as interesting as yours, Son. The tennis pros aren't much older than you, and the others have egos the size of their bank accounts. I see what Luke meant now."

"How's that?"

"We see through phonies. It's why we click. Neither of us wants or needs anything from the other." She got up to turn over the stack of records, which had finished playing. As she turned back, the lights went out.

"Damn! I should still be smoking. I'd have a lighter." She went to the window and pulled back the curtains. The rain had stopped.

"No problem." Joe flicked his lighter on. She reached to the shelf above her desk and brought a candlestick to the table.

"Are you still lighting cigarettes? You stopped doing that for me last spring."

"No. I carry the lighter out of habit, and to be prepared for blackouts." They laughed.

"Kind of Christmas-y, doing this by candlelight." The lights flickered on and off, then stayed on. They left the candle on the table and closed the curtains.

"So, no one special?" Joe asked.

"Nope. But I'll always be glad that Luke – and you – got me out of my shell. No one will ever replace your father, but there's a life out there, and it's not so bad." She chose another book.

Joe put one book down and took a drink of hot chocolate. It was not staying hot.

"I always wondered what happened to the general. I think he was the only one who got arrested in Italy."

"Jim Redwood told me he would be tried for misappropriation of government property. Using all those cars and planes after he retired. It'll take ages to go through the court system, and he probably won't serve any time, but his political career is through, and he could lose his army pension."

"Is that serious?"

"For most high-ranking people, it would be a disaster, but his powerful friends and many sympathizers will paint him as a hero to the cause. I'm glad that you'll be away from here for the next few years, at least."

"But you'll be here."

"My promise was only to let you finish high school. I could be right on your heels."

Joe put the wrapped book down and picked up the last one.

"Do you want me to go to UVa?"

"I have no opinion. I only mentioned it because I've visited the school often. The tennis team won the Nationals in 1952 and often places in the top ten. If I had been a boy, I'd have gone to UVa for that."

"How do they play mixed doubles?"

"They don't, but the girls watch them play and stay for the parties."

Joe thought about what he remembered of Charlottesville. Not much, except a Palladian-looking building with miles of white marble stairs out front.

"I only remember a brick building with white columns. It looked like the Pantheon."

"The Rotunda. Used to be the library. Now I think it's the administration building."

"Mr. Quadroni in Guidance probably has a catalog or can get one."

"A reference or two wouldn't hurt. May I ask your grandfather if he can get a list of alumni living in Italy? We might know someone."

"Okay. Thanks."

They finished the last two presents just as the last record ended. The sun was out now, but the shadows were long.

"How about a walk to the Parco della Vittoria?" Nancy suggested. "I feel like looking at the city at sunset."

"Sure. Can we get some hot chocolate on the way back?"

A moderate westerly breeze whipped their coats as they stood at the railing below the Vatican Observatory. Bathed in the golden light of the weak winter sun, Rome seemed to give off more light than the orange globe slowly sinking over the Janiculum Hill to their right. The air was fresh from the rains that had only stopped an hour earlier. The wind carried the pungent smell of pine up from the woods below them. Beyond the city, the clouds over the plain leading to the Alban Hills glowed in reds and golds with crystal-blue holes, reflecting the low beams shining from the west.

They waited until the sun sank out of sight, and the last red cloud dimmed to gray then disappeared. The moon peeked over the Apennines to their left. Joe knew that Venus was hiding in the clouds above the moon.

"Thanks, Mom."

"What for?"

"For everything. For bringing me here. For making this my home."

"You're welcome, Son."

The breeze picked up. Nancy wrapped her coat around herself tightly as they turned around. She slipped her arm into Joe's as they walked back to the lights of the Piazzale Medaglie d'Oro.

**the end**

# Author's Note

In addition to the usual reminders that all the characters are fictional and any resemblance to real persons is coincidental, I must point out that *Lockhart* is not an historical novel. It is the fruit of my imagination and my experiences growing up as a young translator in Rome.

About that time, Italy was rocked by extremist violence from the right and the left, not to mention the anarchists who hated both sides. The rise of various violent criminal organizations exacerbated the political situation and confused the issue. By the 1970s, these bloody years had acquired the moniker *gli anni di piombo*, the Years of Lead. I deliberately set the time of the story at a different point.

After I wrote the story, the *Piano Solo* papers about the attempted coup d'état were declassified. To my surprise, my tale had captured many aspects of the real coup attempt. I went back and changed characters and times, lest you be misled into thinking that I was reporting on actual events.

Unlike Nancy, my mother was far from being a well-off executive in a multinational company, but she did make it possible for me to attend Notre Dame International

School during the time in question. And, yes, I did buy myself a Vespa 50 with my after-school earnings, after riding my bicycle in all kinds of weather for seven years.

Look for more adventures with Sandra and Joe. If you enjoyed this, please pass the word or write a review.

Grazie. Thanks.

JT Hine.

Made in the USA
Middletown, DE
19 September 2023